BEYOND
the
BLUE

a novel by

ANDREA
MACPHERSON

RANDOM HOUSE CANADA

Random House Canada and colophon are trademarks

www.randomhouse.ca

LIBRARY AND ARCHIVES CANADA CATALOGUING IN PUBLICATION

MacPherson, Andrea, 1976–
Beyond the blue / Andrea MacPherson.

ISBN: 978-0-679-31422-6

I. Title.
PS8575.P465B49 2007   C813'.6   C2006-903003-0

Quotation from the Dundee Heritage Trust, Verdant Works,
used by permission.

Every effort has been made to contact copyright holders; in the event
of an omission or error, please notify the publisher.

Design by Kelly Hill

Printed and bound in the United States of America

10 9 8 7 6 5 4 3 2 1

for my grandmother, May Rowbottom

1927–2006

from her wee lassie

To a Scot, the past clings like sand to wet feet,
and is carried about as a burden.
The many ghosts are always a part of them, inescapable.

GEDDES MACGREGOR

BOOK ONE

After

AGAINST A CLEAR BLUE IT FALLS, a seamless white trajectory to the water below. Cutting the sky, leaving it split into memory: before and after.

If you were not looking closely, you might think it was a bird blinded by the morning sun; a crisp bedsheet; a child's kite lost to the greed of the wind. It seems to be suspended in the air, cupped gently on its path to the Firth of Tay.

A sudden disaster of white and weight. A scream across the sky.

It falls and falls, then disappears into the Tay.

Before the Time of Birds

"Dundee was known as a *woman's town* or *she town* due to the dominance of women in the labour market. In the jute mills, women outnumbered men by three to one. A unique breed of women evolved from the hardship of life in the mills and the responsibility of being the main provider for the family. Dundee women gained the freedom to act in ways which often ignored convention. They were *overdressed, loud, bold-eyed girls* and the sight of a woman being *roarin' fou* or drunk as a man was commonplace. Despite the hardships, many former mill girls recall their working days with fondness."

—FROM DUNDEE HERITAGE TRUST, VERDANT WORKS

A LIGHT SO SHIFTING, so grey and wavering, they might be figments. Their figures are dark, shadowy in the morning light. A steady stream of the dim bodies come up Caldrum Street, past Murphy's restaurant on the corner and the tenements toward the Bowbridge Jute Works entrance; some may speak to one another, but most are quiet, still reminiscing about the warmth of their beds. Morag might see them from the window of the tenement flat if she was inclined to look in the moments before she leaves.

It is early morning in the early spring of 1918. Imogen and Caro are still asleep. Wallis has lit the stove and makes strong tea. Women walk by the tenements, their shoes loud on cobblestones, their coats like the long tail of a kite. As if they are all one, indistinguishable and vague.

The four women live at 96 Caldrum Street, behind the chimney stacks, the blocks of stone and brick, the huge expanses of mills. Close to the heady nature of Hilltown, close enough that they must continually pass the Hilltown clock that never keeps time. A few blocks from Clepington Church, where they have always gone to worship. The women cluster in a city populated by mills and their thick smoke, pubs where the remaining men drink away their wages, churches and boats rolling into harbour heavy with jute or whales. Dundee.

The four women in the small tenement flat on Caldrum Street are no different than the other women in the town: women left abandoned, forgotten, freed. They keep their anger and secrets close as bone. The scent of tea and smoke fills their lungs and infiltrates their dreams. To dream of smokestacks, to wake with the scent of ash in your hair.

Morag and Wallis walk across Caldrum Street and into the grounds of the Bowbridge Jute Works. Always, there is the camel with its hump, its downward gaze, its hard eyes: the suggestion of something exotic as they all slip into the dullness, the boiled-down necessity and daily cruelty of the Works.

This morning, Morag walks under the high arch with the large, gloomy camel and sags just a little. Another reminder for her that there is only this town, only the plethora of mills and smoke and women learning disappointment. Morag steels herself to another long day with the incessant noise, the looms that need constant tending, the sight of children working through the complicated territory of exhaustion.

Wallis says, "Another day."

Morag looks at her youngest daughter with a mix of recognition and shallow guilt. Wallis walking with her under the arch, into the fumes and danger of the Works. Morag feels she has failed; she never wished this fate on her children, but now, here Wallis is, stoic as ever, walking in her black boots into the grounds of the Bowbridge Works.

Morag and Wallis part ways quickly once they enter the grounds; Wallis turns toward the carding room, and Morag disappears into the weaving warehouse, where she will tend her two looms for the next fourteen hours. Wallis, however, will have a more difficult day; she will be bent over a carding machine where she will pull the loose fibre until the jute is an even colour. Morag imagines Wallis watching the jute fade in her hands until it is paler, even, than dreams.

Morag turns before she enters the warehouse and looks for Wallis, her dark coat in a sea of dark coats and long skirts. She sees her, finally, as she hesitates next to the lacklustre beige stone of the Works; she watches her daughter cross the threshold into the carding room, taking one sure step into the building.

Wallis pulls at the thick, dull jute, lets it fall into the large barrels. The rollers revolve at various speeds, fleecing the jute with metal pins before it is condensed into the fibre they call *silver*. Silver, as if there might be something beautiful, something breathtaking about it all. Instead, there is this: women crammed into small, close rooms; heat, dust and fumes of grease and oil; noisy machinery that makes ears ache and heads throb with the constant whir and din.

Wallis looks down the row of girls at their carding machines, each surrounded by barrels quickly filling with the silver; she has learned enough about them in her years at the Works to feel that she knows each of them as she might know a friend, a sister. Lottie Duncan with her three small children and absent husband; Elsie McRae with her hard, difficult mother and her ailing grandmother; Jean Grant, another young Union member; Mae Abernathy with her lost fiancée, her unending, unflinching hope. Wallis does not need to be clairvoyant to know how all their lives will end. They will stay, work, and find themselves slowly, painfully dying from bronchitis, pneumonia or some other respiratory disease. She holds a hand to her chest, as if she might be able to feel the rumblings of disease there. Mill fever.

God help me.

Wallis tugs at the jute and lets it fall through her fingers. The jute might be something else, something kind and lovely, if she were only able to shut herself off to the carding room, the gossip between the women around her, the whine of the machines.

"Been to any dances, Wallis?" Mae asks over the din. She is a few years older than Wallis and pretty with dark hair and light eyes. She smiles.

8

"No."

"Caro hasn't dragged you out?"

"Not lately. But I'm sure she will." Caro is always begging Wallis, always suggesting that Morag trusts them more when they go out together. Usually, though, it is Caro who dances and Wallis who stands at the side, watching her sister spin in the arms of another man left behind by the War. She has watched these men, their broken, ruined limbs—an arm that will no longer bend, a leg that is permanently stiff, stilted, or, worse, a man who has been bombed and blasted into silence—and felt a slow, sad sinking. Wallis says, "Any word from Peter?"

Mae's eyes well up, and Wallis immediately regrets the question. Mae says, "No," in a voice barely audible.

Wallis closes her eyes to the broken-apart look of Mae's face; she knows that look, knows the pained feeling behind her pale eyes. She is about to say, "I'm so sorry, Mae," when there is a crack, a loud, hard sound in the air around them. The chatter of the women stops just as suddenly. Wallis is absolutely still and silent for a moment, before she hears the cry. The long, anguished cry of someone in unbearable pain.

Mae breathes, "Good God."

Wallis does not look down the row of women in the direction of the cry. She does not see Elsie caught in the carding machine. She will not know how to explain it later, but she does not want to see her tangled body—a body that she will later be told had been bent, broken, trapped by the rollers—and the possibility of her own future. Such accidents are possible, probable, and Wallis does not want to commit the scene to memory.

Wallis takes a step backward, away from the other women who are rushing forward, burdened with their unfortunate curiosity. She is paralyzed with fear at the possibility of the sight of Elsie; Elsie's eyes, her body wrenched into the machine, and the sheen of her dark, polished boots. Wallis counts the buttons on her own boots—*one, two, three*—and gets to six before the men rush in, mumbling and cursing as they try to pull Elsie free.

"Stand back, stand back." The biggest man, Joe McGivern, warns all the women away. His stomach will be straining against his shirt, pushing into the air between them. A button pulling, and Wallis becomes transfixed by the prospect of it: the pucker, the pull, the possibility of a tear.

"Dammit, get them out of here." It is one of the managers—perhaps Fergus or Paisley in the quick flash of the moment, the confusion of bodies, Wallis can never be sure—holding his hand up against his mouth. There is a rush of movement, the crush of women's bodies to one another, and the dull, washed-out sound of Elsie's cries. Wallis and the other women in the carding room are herded out, pulled away from the pulse of the machines and into the courtyard.

Jean breathes, "Lord help us all."

Lottie asks, "Will she be all right?"

"Sure she will," Mae says. "They'll get her out."

Wallis does not speak but, instead, looks up to the blue sky and the camel that hangs between the warehouses. She does not want to answer Lottie, to tell her that she knows—without having looked at Elsie, without seeing her eyes, the taut fear that must have been there—that Elsie would not be all right. That Elsie was damaged, had been torn apart and forgotten by the machines, as so many of the women had been before.

How many is that now? Does anyone remember them all?

Wallis looks around to the women standing in the courtyard with her, hoping that the sky will remain the clear stretch of blue while they wait—coatless—close to one another. She wonders how many of them will give themselves over to the same fate. In ten years, how many of them will still be here, perhaps even standing in the air of a crisp day, while another woman is pulled free from angry machinery.

Later, Wallis steps into the courtyard again, but the sky has darkened, relinquishing the faint light of day for the navy of evening. It's cold for a spring night; Wallis pulls the collar of her coat tighter. She moves from one foot to the other—her foot aching from the tight edge of her boot—as she waits for Morag. She knows Morag will ask her about Elsie, will wonder what she saw, what the carding room sounded like in the moments just after the accident. Death is not unusual in the mills. A girl loses her hand while spinning. A man is caught by a belt and revolved around the shafts three times. Women go deaf. Children are hit, boxed in the ears, dangled out windows three storeys up when they fall asleep at their machines. But, still, there is that thick stab for Wallis each time an accident occurs; another reminder of their own slim trajectories in the mill.

Wallis is stamping her aching foot when Morag appears, rushing across the courtyard in her long dark skirt.

"What happened to Elsie McRae?"

"You must have heard."

"She was caught. Did they get her out?" Morag seems desperate for information. Her eyes are bright, wide.

"Yes," Wallis says.

Morag sighs. "Thank God the girl is all right."

Wallis and Morag start across the courtyard, toward the arch with the camel and out into Caldrum Street. Just a few steps across the street and they will enter their tenement building, climb the three storeys to their flat. Look out the window and see the Works, always.

Wallis says, "She died."

Morag stops in the middle of Caldrum. She grasps Wallis's arm. "She died?"

"Yes. The injuries were too severe. She died after they pulled her out."

Morag looks up to the darkening sky and then back to Wallis. New shadows come across her face, cutting her features in two. One eye. Another. The curve of lip. "The poor thing." Morag takes Wallis's arm to cross the street and they walk up the stairs to their floor. The hallway is deserted, quiet, as they push their door open.

"Another girl was killed at the Works." Imogen stands in the centre of the room, as if she has been waiting for them. Desperate for the gossip, the macabre details of death.

"Imo," Morag says harshly. The room becomes still. Quiet for horror.

Caro sits by the window, her thin legs curled up under her. She says, "Was another girl killed?"

Wallis nods. "Elsie McRae. She got caught in a carding

machine. She died when they pulled her out." Wallis looks away from her sister and back to Imogen. She is still in her school uniform—Wallis remembers the obligatory itch of wool against bare legs—and Imogen tugs at her skirt anxiously. Next year she will be finished with school, expected to work, perhaps at the same machine that cradled Elsie McRae. Wallis desperately wants to keep her from this fate; she would like her to continue with her schooling, to have something more than the ragged hands of a mill worker.

"Were you there?" Imogen asks. She wants all the messy details, Wallis can see it in the light on her face. For Imogen, there is always a story, always a discovery; lies and truth mingle and sway.

"They kept it quiet in case it frightened the others. They took her out as quickly as they could."

"Did you see it?" Imogen asks.

"Don't be morbid." Morag's voice is hard, sharp. She prefers death to be distanced, clean, quiet. Wallis thinks that, perhaps, Morag does not want to remember her own mother's death. Nor Brigid's.

There's always Brigid.

"Elsie McRae was only a wee bit older than Imo. Just sixteen," Caro says from her spot by the window. Wallis removes her coat and crosses the room to her chair, the faded tapestry chair that used to be their father, James's, before he went to the War and disappeared. There are marks from bodies, buttocks and thighs, the long expanse of forearms from elbow to wrist, in that chair. Ghostly imprints. Wallis settles into them.

"And not much of a face on her," Caro says.

"Caro." Morag's voice is spiked like fences.

Caro turns away and looks out the window. Small windows in the parlour open to the closes, the alleyways and courtyards between the tenements. Long lines of clothes flap in the wind, tethered to pulleys from kitchen windows, turning damp in the incessant rain. Women hang out their windows, hoping for someone to talk to. The flats are all the same, interchangeable: greys and browns and faded reds that might once have been shocking, the scents of meat boiling, potatoes cooking, women giving up. Before the War, it had been different; men had marred the tenements with their harsh voices and their bulk. There had been loud fights, dishes smashed, women shoved halfway out the windows after their husbands returned, empty-pocketed, from pubs. Sometimes there had even been joy: the bright orange explosion of it, engagements, new babies, marriages mended. Then, everything hadn't been so desperate, so intimate in the flats. Wallis knows they all miss the presence of men, their strange smells and slanted smiles.

Of course, some men are still in Dundee; those too old, too young, unfit for war. Men who have been returned from the fighting, broken and still breaking. They wander the city like ghosts, or something more forgotten than that.

⟳

When the flat is dark and the girls are all asleep in the small bedroom, Morag lies in her slim cot in the kitchen alcove and looks at her hands. They are rough and hardened, scarred from the uncompromising jute; she touches the calluses and thinks she has been given more than her share of disappointment. She holds it tight like unused breath: a place where memories of her mother and sister and all her wasted years are stored.

Morag is not sure when she first learned disappointment, but knows it had something to do with Brigid's terrible, beautiful face, when Morag looked in the mirror and saw her own plainness. There is something stark and unforgiving about Morag. She has always understood the fickle nature of beauty.

She has lived across the street from the Bowbridge Works for twenty years, since her daughters were born, walking across Caldrum Street and under the sloped eyes of the carved camel of the Works gate into the expanse of the mill grounds. The damned camel to give the impression of something fresh, something other than another day of weaving. The sound of the bell, the *bummer,* in the morning is like a hand on Morag's cheek, reminding her of the day ahead. Morag looks at her own hands again and imagines what they might look like had they belonged to someone else, someone who knew a different kind of life, someone who had managed to keep it all whole.

If her mother had not died. If Brigid had not worn that gauzy nightgown, had not been so desperate, so torn in two. *Brigid.*

Every day, Morag moves quickly between the two looms she tends, with her sister's name still loose in her mind, as if she might use it tomorrow to call out to her across the tenement courtyards, just when Morag might see her walking up Caldrum. Brigid something like the sight of an eclipse, just as startling and bright. Morag cannot remember a day when Brigid was not in her thoughts, appearing over the quivering sounds of the mill, the endless din of the rooms, the impossibility of escaping it.

Morag stretches her fingers to relieve their ache. They are gnarled, marked with evidence of years of hard use: first in her father's house, then in her own tenement flat, then in the Works. Her hands carry the memory of bleach and new peas and baby skin and stiff laundry. *What these hands have known.* The old grey folds of a dying man's body. Thick salt and the shock of the waters of the Tay. Rope unravelling between her fingers. Morag puts her hands under the blankets and, in doing so, imagines she puts all her secrets away.

Imogen tries to make herself small in the bustle of Victoria Road, angling herself away from the women—always it is women now, in their felt hats and hands clasped over their pocketbooks—pressing past her. Imogen has spent her whole life surrounded by women—first her mother, then her aunt and cousins—and is tired of their unhappiness. Imogen wants to be thoughtless, cavalier. She wishes she had been able to fight in the War, to cross the Channel to France and Germany, maybe even Africa. She wants everything outside this flat, the ocean on her face, sun on her back, lovers, strange rooted vegetables. She imagines that Wallis must want it too, that she must go there when she gets that odd, distant look.

Wallis can make her face so blank and doughy and vacant, as if she forgets about herself for a while and travels to some other place. Imogen is sure that other place would be nothing like their flat: a tight bedroom, a parlour crowded with photos and chairs and knick-knacks and a tiny galley kitchen with a bed in the curtained alcove. Imogen knows they are fortunate to have a toilet in the flat; most flats share a toilet on the landing, or on the external stairwell. Imogen has never known any different; the flat she shared with her parents, Oliver and Brigid, was airy, roomy, full of small, good things.

Full of ghosts.

Some days, Imogen believes that she is a sort of ghost; she is that pale, that delicate and temporary. She thinks that, perhaps, she might be able to turn herself invisible; in this way, she imagines, she could let herself into the locked rooms of other people's lives. She wills herself to be invisible when she follows Wallis down the streets of Dundee; she must follow her because, otherwise, Wallis would never let her into the secret parts of her life. Already, Imogen has followed Wallis to her Union meetings, to the shoemaker on Hilltown, to the harbour where she looked out across the even, blue water. Wallis is both complacent and shrouded in mystery.

Today, Imogen has followed Wallis down to Victoria Road, where she slipped into the bank with the thick door quickly shutting behind her. Imogen imagined the *swoosh* of the door, the small push of wind that would have lifted the hem of Wallis's skirt. Imogen stood farther down Victoria Road, where she could watch for Wallis in peace. She waited as others went in and out of the bank, all looking terribly efficient and pleased with themselves, wondering what had prompted Wallis's new, frequent excursions to the bank. Imogen imagined Wallis saving for something extravagant and secret: a strand of real pearls to wear to church, a pair of calfskin boots. When Wallis finally came out, she walked farther down the street toward the red brick of the *Courier* building, and Imogen immediately thought of Oliver. His fingers stained and dark from the ink. She had happily followed Wallis through the haze of the day, meandering through Dundee, waiting for something dramatic, something interesting and mysterious to occur. There had been nothing. Only the grey of the day and the city, even the grey of Wallis's skirt.

Later, Imogen thinks she'll keep following Wallis wherever she goes, disappear for a moment with her somewhere into the fading, aching orange.

Caro wears a smart black hat as she leaves the post office and walks alone up Dens Road in the early-evening wind. As she turns onto Isla Street, she can hear them though they are still blocks away: loud, cackling laughter and the tight pitch of excited voices. When she passes Clepington Church and turns onto Main Street, the voices get louder. She hates how common it all seems, how desperate the women are for anything to fill the few free hours of their days, leaning out the windows of their flats, gossiping across the close to other women, their voices carrying down neighbouring streets. It weighs on her, the possibility that her life will be nothing more than this, that everything has been laid out before her like a smooth cement path. Caro walks through the close quickly, avoiding their eyes and their bodies pressed up against the windowsills.

"Hullo, Caro!"

"Ah, Caro's on her way."

She raises a hand to them. Other times she ignores them completely, keeping her hands tucked tight in her pockets. Caro absently touches her black hat. Long, loping wash lines hang between the windows of these old, untended tenements. They have lived in the flat all her life; she has seen women come and go from the flats around them, their dark shoes loud on the hallway's bare floors. And she has heard the low rattling in their throats at night, consumption and mill fever and diphtheria, echoing through the small tenements. Everything seemed to pass so quickly between the cracked windows: joy, grief, laughter and sickness.

Caro does not intend to become like her mother, married to a useless man and later left alone with two children in a claustrophobic city that is full of smoke and steel and sweat. Caro walks up the three flights to the flat, determined that she will get out, somehow; she doesn't know how yet, but she is sure it will have something to do with a man. Everything always comes back to men.

"Back from the post office, are you?" Morag is holding a cup of tea, sitting on the small chesterfield, when Caro comes in. Caro unbuttons her coat in the heat of the room.

She was pleased to get the position at Maryfield Post Office, because she hated the thought of working at Bowbridge with Morag and Wallis. She didn't want callused hands and coughing fits and the dour expressions they came home with. Instead, Caro comes home having handled letters and cables and announcements. Births, deaths, marriages, doomed romances. Women in the tenements are wary of her, worried that she has special knowledge of their children and their sisters and their husbands. Mostly, their husbands, who stare at Caro with the eyes of predatory animals. There is always the hot flush of recognition from a man; she knows how they see her: smooth, dark hair; a creamy cheek; waist small enough for a handspan. Men who might want to be near her, to touch her maybe, to keep her like a possession. And Caro might let some man do this, but not just any man. She's seen other girls become desperate about men; she pities and berates them at the same time, amazed by their foolishness. Like Lucy Bell, who got all teary-eyed and listless when her boyfriend left her for another girl, a more beautiful girl, and her letters were returned to the post office. These things, Caro thinks, are bound to happen. It's the temperament of men.

Caro moves across the flat to sit by the window. "Desperate women, heavy letters," Caro says. She holds her hand up to rub at a smudge, to make the view clear. Bowbridge Works. The spire of Clepington Church. The pub, where Morag might stop to have a whisky. If Caro could see farther, she would see the Tay or, better, Broughty Ferry.

"Mmm," Morag mumbles. "It's all desperation now."

If Caro imagines her life, it is full of the walled houses among the Ferry's tall, graceful trees, the private washrooms, each room heated in the winter, a car to drive all the way to Edinburgh if she liked. She imagines this life free of her family; as if extricating herself from them might make Caro's life easier. She would not want to see Wallis's face, stunned and silent when mounds of clotted cream or Dundee cake were passed around. Wallis, who would move through the house leaving sticky fingerprints on everything she saw:

fine paintings, heavy woollen blankets, Waterford crystal sparkling at a windowsill. The thought of it turns Caro tense, stiff. Sometimes, she thinks she is a tight ball of nerves and control, pulsing like mad. She wonders if she might explode from all the pressure, an ugly red mess on Morag's floor. No doubt Wallis would mop it up, quickly, so that they might forget about it and soldier on.

Caro looks down to Caldrum below, hoping for anything other than the stones, the smoke, the stream of women from the Works. Dark skirts moving across the street. Small, quick feet on the cobblestone. The town has been stripped of men, left barren and rocky as an abandoned mine. The only men left here now have weepy eyes, flattened limbs, or lovely, lush houses in the Ferry.

Before the War, the men went mad for Caro, everywhere the girls went. Dances, pubs on Saturday nights, even Murraygate on a busy afternoon, men stopped to watch Caro pass or smiled shamelessly at her. Their intentions simmered just below the surface. She kept crimson lipstick in her pocket and applied it in a small gold mirror, patting her lips together and saying, "There." At the dances, Caro was spun around the floor until she was slightly dizzy, either from dancing or the sips from hidden flasks. Her throat burned sinfully and brought a smile to her lips. She could still taste the thick, amber alcohol mingled with the waxiness on her lips. Wallis sat at one of the tables, looking bored and ashy under the smoky air and dim lights. Most nights, Caro forgot about Wallis until it was time to leave and some man was trying to steer her out into the crisp night air. Then, she was glad for Wallis in her cardigans and simple dresses. They would leave with their arms linked together, Wallis greedy for details.

"How close did he hold you? Did he try to kiss you? Did you let him? Tell me."

Caro was vague, shrugging her slim shoulders and cocking up one thin eyebrow. Some nights they giggled like children, until their stomachs ached and they had to lean against a door frame for support. Those moments were rare, bright patches between them. They transported Caro back to childhood, when there was still the possibility of normalcy for them all. She was just Caro then, her face tight and shining in the moonlight as her sister held her elbow.

Caro is restless in the flat. She stretches, leans against the window and then says, "I need some air. I'll be back."

She walks down Hilltown, through Murraygate and on until the Firth of Tay gleams cold and silver in front of her. The new Tay Bridge—people still call it new despite its being built thirty years ago—stands sleek and straight above the water. She pulls her coat tight against the cold, adjusts her hat; it might start to rain and she has forgotten an umbrella. She walks parallel to the Tay, mindful of the grey sky.

From here, Caro thinks she could slip onto a boat and go anywhere. She could disappear and become someone else: forget Wallis's huge, plaintive eyes, Morag's disapproval, Imogen's frailty.

A tramcar comes behind her, wheels loud and metallic on the tracks. She watches the smooth arc of it as it passes by on the curved road. A half-moon and then it's gone, leaving a lone automobile behind it.

Caro always notices the people who drive cars: they are the people she wants to become. No more walking in the rain, no more crowded stench of tramcars. The pure, spoiled luxury of pedals beneath your feet, wheels whirring.

It's Desmond Lindsay, the man who owns the Bowbridge Works. She can tell by the shining black automobile and his peppered hair behind the windshield. She doesn't need to see his face to know him. For a moment she thinks he is slowing down, he will perhaps stop to offer her a ride. Caro pauses, smiles.

No. He is simply cautious in the new rain, afraid of veering out of control. Perhaps afraid, mostly, of crashing into the girl who just stands at the side of the road, staring.

At seven, Imogen spent most of her time with her fingers in her ears. Plain refusal. Maddening to anyone around her, especially Morag, who longed to reach across the table and tug her slim hands from the air. *There. Listen now.* Morag would not have allowed this sort of behaviour from Caro or Wallis, but there was something so torn about Imogen that Morag relented. Imogen a reminder of Morag when she lost her own mother. Morag as a small, staring four-year-old, waiting for the train car to resurface. Morag recognized the pained eyes and the tendency to bend and whimper at the slightest disruption.

Morag watched Imogen and thought she could see the fracture in her: *this break here, this is Brigid's death.* Morag knows the fissure has been tentatively sutured only because Imogen does not remember. If she remembered, she would be split and raw and left to the elements.

Morag believes it is the kind thing to do, to allow Imogen a gentle reprieve from it all. This is the only way, really, to keep her from breaking apart again, quick and thrilling, to the bone. To let her forget.

If only we could all forget. If only I could forget.

The day after Brigid's death, Imogen woke early and came out of the bedroom. Her face was creased from the pillow. She stood still and stared at Morag's silent body in the alcove bed beside James. Morag looked back at her. Imogen's eyes were dull. Blank.

"Where's my mum?"

Morag stared. "Your mum?"

"Where is she?"

Morag sat up, careful not to wake James. "She's gone, dear."

"With my dad?"

"No. Gone."

Imogen rubbed her eyes. Squinted. "She's left me?"

Morag said gently, "Don't you remember, Imo?"

Imogen shook her head. Waited for Morag. She was so small.

"There was an accident, Imo." Then, "Your mother has gone to be with God. You don't remember?"

Imogen said, "No."

Morag thought it the generosity of the mind, the way Imogen's memory was turned into corridors, then into rooms, then into doors with locks. Her mother's death was shut away and locked and forgotten.

Every day Morag worries that one of these doors will be unlocked, swing open with the horrible sound of an unoiled hinge, and everything will spill out. It is only a matter of time before Imogen lets herself remember.

Silent Deaths

AFTER ELSIE'S DEATH AT THE WORKS, Morag dreams about the bridge, the lightning, the shrieking wind, the collapse. The way the centre of the bridge snapped, then crumbled into the Tay below. She dreams about hands pressed up to the glass, desperate to escape the compartment of the train. She sees the o shapes of their mouths, the way their eyes began to go mad. Yet, she never dreams of her mother's face like that; in her dreams, her mother is not on the train but at home in the flat, her hands tired from sewing all day, small circles on her fingers from the thimbles. Morag dreams her mother alive.

The bridge had only been open a year; though she was only four then, Morag insists she remembers the celebration, the first lumbering train to cross it. The bridge seemed impossible to her; all that concrete and steel held up in the air like a gift to God. She loved the clacking sound of the train running over the tracks, the possibility of hovering over water. She had watched from her mother's arms as that first train eased its way onto the rail bridge; they had clapped as the train became smaller, moving steadily toward Edinburgh. Morag remembers the lavender scent of her mother's hair, the heavy wool of her dress, the heat of her body so close.

Morag holds on to these memories as if they were lifeboats; as if she were the one drowning.

⁓

In the photo, his hair is neat, combed to one side with a part that shows the white of his scalp. Wallis has looked at the photo so many times that she even knows the spot where he was careless and the part jags to the left, into his thick brown hair. There is a small worn corner of the photo where Wallis's thumb has held it, obliterating Paddy's elbow.

The photo does not belong to Wallis. It belonged to Mrs. Hennessey, who kept it in a black photo album in her parlour. One afternoon when Wallis was seven, she silently opened the album, freed the photo from its corners and tucked it into her dress pocket. Later, she put the photo under the mattress with the stolen rosary. Slept for the next twelve years with Paddy's face and Rosemary's rosary beneath her.

Now, Wallis holds the photo to her face and breathes in, expecting the lingering odour of gas.

⁓

No one wants to work the carding machine Elsie McRae's body was pulled from. Wallis says that people stand idly by and stare at it; Morag knows that soon there will be rumours of hauntings, sightings, but Morag dismisses superstition. Instead, she wonders what they did with the jute from her machine. It would have been stained red with her blood.

Desmond Lindsay visits on the pretense of sorrow over Elsie McRae's death, but really, he is there to make certain everything is running smoothly. Even he can't afford to close the Works for a full day just for a carding girl. Morag imagines he will say how sorry he is, what a tragedy it was, all the while not even knowing who the girl was. She wasn't pretty enough to be one of the girls Mr. Lindsay remembered.

Everyone knows about Desmond Lindsay, though some of the girls pretend not to. Those girls smile up at him with coy, lowered eyes and admire his wide smile. Desmond Lindsay loses interest in these girls quickly. He leaves them crying, plaintive, ashamed. Morag has heard that he has children by such girls, girls who suddenly disappear to Glasgow, Edinburgh, places where they are less likely to be noticed. Places where they can wear a gold band and people might believe their husbands are heroes at war.

Mr. Lindsay comes into the weaving warehouse flanked by two managers. The men are talking to him, pointing out repairs and improvements. But Desmond Lindsay is busy looking at the backs of young girls at the looms, seeking out that tender spot where their hair touches their necks, that hollow begging for a thumb or lips.

He is stiff and straight, crisp in pressed trousers, a fitted jacket and tie. His shoes click on the floor. His strides are long, smooth, despite the fact that he is relatively short. Desmond Lindsay is one of the richest men in Dundee. "Good morning," he says, flashing some of the prettier girls a smile. They blush and mutter, "Morn."

There is sudden, muted excitement. The girls feign concentration on their looms, stand with hips cocked to the side. These girls, Morag thinks, are ridiculous.

Morag is thankful when Desmond Lindsay passes her wordlessly, moving quickly past her looms. Once, before she had been weathered down to transparency and essentials from daily toils in his mill, Desmond Lindsay might have paused to notice her thick, brown hair and smooth skin. She touches her cheek, now, and feels only the pull of age and weariness.

Morag turns her attention back to her looms, to the continual sound of them, as Desmond Lindsay exits the weaving warehouse. She pities the girls around her. These women would all carry Desmond Lindsay with them as if marked by his fingertips, the pungent smell of his wealth.

To wake from a dream, so full and weighted by it that you might think it has reshaped your morning, this day, your life. This is how Imogen wakes after dreaming of Brigid. She opens her eyes to the small room and believes, for a moment, that she is in the flat on Park Avenue, that the last seven years have dissolved like candy in her mouth. She does not want to turn her head, afraid that even the slightest movement—the slightest acknowledgment of a day spread out before her—will break the crystalline texture of her dream.

Close your eyes. Go back to sleep. Drift back into her.

Imogen had been dreaming about her mother, about her mother's white gloves and her face as she stood with Imogen at the harbour. There had been sun—a sun too high, too hot and yellow, to belong in Dundee—but the harbour had been

Dundee's. Imogen and Brigid had walked there. They had stood, watching boats pull in and out, Brigid insisting that if they only stood there long enough, if they had enough patience, they might see Oliver's face on a deck.

In the dream, though, as in truth, there had been no Oliver; no tanned and weathered face, hardened from long hours working the masts, breathing in the sea. There had only been Brigid and Imogen, standing with their toes at the edge of the dock, staring at the sea.

Water, water everywhere.

The wind comes whistling against the window, and Imogen turns her head to it. It is not the window of Park Avenue, but the window of Caldrum Street. Outside, lines of wash flap in the wind. Smudged, grey windows look back at her from across the close. The dream slips away from her and, with it, any memory of her mother's face.

She stretches and tugs herself up from the bed. Caro and Wallis are sleeping still; it must be early. There is no noise from the parlour, so Morag must have already left for the mill. She stands at the window and looks out to the cool, grey morning. Imogen touches the small table and picks up the picture of Brigid. Not quite a smile, not quite looking at the camera; Brigid in profile, her gloved hands. Imogen touches the line of Brigid's golden hair, traces the suggestion of her spine. She stares at Brigid's face—tries to hold the image very still and quiet—and then squeezes her eyes shut. Tests herself. The image of Brigid's face wavers, then disappears.

"Imo?"

She snaps her eyes open.

Caro is awake, lying on her side and staring at Imogen.
"You're awake."

"Yes." Imogen puts the photo down, turns to smile wanly at Caro. "I can't keep her face in my mind."

"Imo."

"It's like I never really looked at her at all. When I close my eyes, I can't see her clearly."

Caro rises from bed and comes across the room to stand beside Imogen. She picks up the photo of Brigid and sighs. "You look just like her."

"I do?"

"Imo, look in a mirror." There is an edge of exasperation in Caro's voice.

"How do I look like her?" Imogen cannot resist asking; she watches the purse of Caro's mouth. "Caro, how?"

"You are both fragile. One little bird and another." Caro turns away from Imogen and looks out the window. She sighs. "Rain again."

Imogen follows Caro's gaze. Imogen puts her hand up to the pane. It's cold and her palm is damp when she takes it away. She says, "Oh, I wish there was sun."

Caro smiles. "I wish we were somewhere else."

"In the sun."

The two of them stand together, staring out the window at the stone courtyard, at the low, pale blue sky, at the clouds that promise rain until everything beneath them is sodden with it. Small birds fly between the tenement windows, dotting the sky with their black and dark-blue bodies. Imogen leans her head against Caro's shoulder and thinks, Look, little birds like the rain.

—

Every second weekend Morag washes the steps between the second and third floors. She scrubs, dunking her hand back into the soapy water before moving to the next step. She and Bessie Lyon share the duty, alternating weekends. There were uncertain moments kneeling on the stairs beside Bessie when they moved into the building twenty years ago. Bessie's small hands brushing up against Morag's, the thankful moment when Morag realized that she might have a friend across the hall in Bessie. That she would not be left alone with James. Morag on her hands and knees, smiling as she scrubbed the dull, worn stairs.

Morag doesn't mind it, really, because she likes the look of it once it's done: cleaner, cared for. She has time to think while sloughing away the grime of people's feet. Morag has precious little time to herself, so scrubbing the stairs becomes a meditation for her. She is scrubbing and thinking when Caro steps swiftly over her. A quick word, and then only the thoughtless back of her, Caro's small waist in her coat as she moves away. Morag supposes that is her fault; whatever Caro has become, Morag made her. Or allowed her to be. Morag scrubs harder.

She has been dreaming about James. If not dreaming, then thinking. Morag can't tell which any more. She has begun to crave him in an unexpected way—perhaps not *him*, exactly, but his body is the only she has ever known. Its heat at night. The insistent probing of his hands. The stubble of his chin at her neck, leaving a red rawness. These things she once pushed away now come back to her with want.

Shameful, she thinks. Shameful, but present nonetheless. This sudden greed for a man has shocked her into ambivalence. What can she do, really, but remember what it was once like to be beneath the bulk of a man? A dead husband, lungs filling with jute, two grown daughters and a cast-off niece. She cannot imagine another man pressing himself into the weight of all that. It is all so far away from what she once imagined, so far from her father's dream of long, flat fields of green, lush vegetable gardens, before her hands learned the intimacies of jute and rope.

"Morning, Morag." Bessie Lyon comes up behind her as Morag coughs. She holds her hand to her face to push it back. It seems now all she does is cough—cough until there are white spots behind her eyes, until her chest feels raw. Bessie looks down at her quizzically, her face tightened into concern.

Morag swallows and smiles up at Bessie, whose arms are full of grocery sacks, a slab of margarine wrapped in parchment and a loaf of white bread peeking over. She is taken back to years ago, first seeing Bessie's face, when Morag was heavy and pregnant with Caro; Bessie was older and wiser with a three-year-old son running about the flat. Bessie crying, "Angus! Angus!" infiltrated Morag's dreams so that she woke feeling tired from the boy. She watched Angus Lyon grow into a handsome young man, the kind of man she wished for her daughters. Now, Bessie is alone; Ian Lyon is still at war and Angus is buried in the cemetery out on Arbroath Road. Killed in battle at twenty-four.

"It's fine out today—you should have left that for tomorrow night. Rain by then, I'm sure."

"Aye." Morag is trying to forget about her desire for James, or any man like him, but she keeps remembering the red patches on her knees, much like the ones she will have now. Savage rooting.

Bessie leans against the hallway wall and sighs. "I miss him every day," she says to Morag.

Morag looks up to her. She imagines that Bessie spends every day missing her son, imagining his voice, his feet on the stairs. Bessie's heart breaking and shattering over again.

"Oh, Bessie." Morag gets up and puts her arms around Bessie, who sags and cries against her shoulder. Morag's worries seem trivial now; she has been worrying about Caro and Wallis since they were born, since before then even. She worries that all her hopes, her late nights praying and wishing and bargaining, will have been worthless. The girls are grown now, elusive and secretive and full of furtive glances, and Morag can't help but worry that they will choose as badly as she had or, worse yet, as Brigid did. Choices are dangerous, shifting things.

Before Angus Lyon's death, Morag had hoped that Caro or Wallis would marry him; she had often wished that they lived somewhere like India, with its arranged marriages. Morag has seen some of the girls who come to Dundee with the jute ships, dark and shy and coy, and she thinks that this solution would suit her daughters quite well. She would choose better for her daughters than she had for herself. She has learned so much since the day she stood before the minister in a plain frock, stained at the edges, looking up at James, this hardened man she was tethering her life to. She thinks that now she could spot a man who might have a problem with the drink, or who might be mean or tight with his wife. What if she had known all this so many years ago? What if she had wished for something more? But Morag is not one for wishes. Wishes are for children and fools.

Bessie shudders a little against her, her chest rising. Morag rubs her back absently. Bessie is what many of the women left in Dundee have become, remembering dead sons. First Angus, now Ian with his withering lungs at the front. Husbands. Brothers. Morag looks down to the floor and sighs a little. Realizes she'll never get it truly clean, she'll never get it all out.

Caro persuades the girls to go to the Ferry for the day. It's no use protesting or arguing with her; once Caro has made up her mind, she is as stubborn as a sinking ship. Wallis wearies at the thought of spending the day wandering about the prosperity of the Ferry. It would be more bearable, even, if they could take a walk along the pier and watch the sky waver through shades of blue. Stand inside a church and listen to hymns as the sun sets. Instead, she will spend the day trailing behind Caro, searching for Imogen, keeping track of their basket and money and brollies. Wallis sighs at the prospect, but resigns herself to the day.

They walk down Hilltown to catch the tramcar. They sit close to one another, their bodies bumping and shifting with the tram.

"Remember the day Daddy took us to the Ferry? I'd love to be in that car today. Remember when we rolled the windows down? The wind in our hair." Imogen is smiling as she stares out the window. Imogen has always been so sensitive, Wallis thinks, so raw and splayed open.

"I remember that Oliver went off with some young girl and left us to drown," Caro says.

Imogen's smile fades from her face. She turns ashy.

"Caro." Wallis never understands Caro's sudden cruelty; Imogen stares at her with her drowning blue eyes. Imogen, who has somehow become Caro's closest friend.

Imogen shakes her head and puts her fingers in her mouth. A leftover from childhood, like soft toys or worn blankets.

"Well, what do you think he did when he left you and Brigid?" Caro laughs as she says it, as if it has never occurred to her that Imogen might not know, that she might have kept Oliver safe in her mind, locked away and innocent.

Wallis understands how Imogen thinks of Oliver—it's the same way many young girls remember missing fathers: tall and laughing, smelling like smoke. These definitions of their fathers have not changed in the years that they have been gone, and for Imogen it would be the same: Oliver hanging vibrant in her mind, certain with his inky hands and thick, jet hair. Wallis looks at Imogen and sees the brightness of her eyes, the possibility of tears.

"We're off." Caro is up in an instant, touching her hair briefly.

Wallis sees the way the men on the tram watch Caro as she passes them. The old men, the ones who have lost their teeth, wear eyeglasses thick as the bottoms of beer bottles, look up when she moves past them. Even the other men, those who have returned from the War with shattered bones and lost limbs, search Caro out. They pass a young man who cradles his right arm, an arm that would have been healthy and strong but is now stunted, ending abruptly below his elbow. He looks up with hollow, listless eyes. It's a strange, sad mix of longing and grief. Wallis moves silently, unnoticed, behind her. She wonders if this is a gift or a curse, her ability to move through crowds with ease, unencumbered, free of attention.

The rain comes down in angry pelts. A late-spring storm. Wallis opens her umbrella and Imogen scurries under. "Another day, then?"

Caro flashes Wallis a wide, insincere smile. This is the smile she uses on men, mostly, and some of the disapproving women from the kirk. "We can still go for a walk."

Caro is not usually prone to such fancies as walks in the rain. Wallis bites at her lip, feeling anxious, and follows Caro down the street.

To their left, the sea sits like a mirror, reflecting and refracting the new spring rainfall. It makes everything about the day seem shot through with silver. People dash from the pier, pack up their beach chairs, stand under striped awnings to avoid the rain. Caro holds her own umbrella in her fist and strides ahead, leading them past the shops and restaurants. They turn up a side street. Caro is far enough ahead that she must stop and wait for them.

"Come on, then," Imogen urges Wallis. Wallis has just polished her lace-up boots, so she tries to avoid the large puddles. Mud would be difficult to scrub from her tan skirt. She should have worn the darker one.

The three of them walk together at a languid pace down a residential street in the Ferry. The houses are grand here, lush and complete with flowerbeds and front walks and amber-lit windows. High stone walls to keep them private. These are the homes of the men who oppose the Unions, who want only to remain soft and sheltered. Caro slows in front of some houses to peer in at them. Just as quickly, though, she moves away again.

What is she looking for?

Wallis feels water slopping into her boots, and fears another chill. There is something sinister about this sudden journey to the Ferry. "Come on, Caro. Let's at least stop somewhere to have some lunch and dry off."

"In a minute. In a minute." Caro moves ahead and turns down Ellislea Road. The same rich houses, the same inviting windows. All this was not meant for them, Wallis is sure. They are meant to live in small flats and work for these people. Let their lungs fill, their ears weaken, their backs curve.

Imogen is busy singing a nonsense song when Caro suddenly stops. She stands stock-still in front of a pale yellow house, staring. The house is kept safe from the street by a thick stone wall; leafy bushes line the walk with flowers planted in the beds below the front windows. If you peer through the gate, you can see the heavy knocker on the front door; the front door a deep, rich shade of blue.

"This is the one," Caro says. "This is the house I will one day live in." She glances at Wallis and Imogen. "Or something like this."

Wallis sees the new desire that clouds Caro's eyes. This is what they have come for: so Caro can stand here in the rain and imagine a life she will never have. Wallis suddenly feels sorry for her. Wallis has her own dreams, dreams that will be realized. One day Caro will cross the Irish Sea to visit Wallis and will say, "Remember that day at the Ferry? What a fool I was." Caro expects so much of her life that she cannot help but be disappointed. Wallis knows better than to lay her own dreams bare before anyone.

"Come on, Caro, let's go now." Wallis touches her sister's shoulder. Caro must be freezing; she has let her umbrella droop to one side and her shoulder is soaking wet.

"I am hungry." Imogen stoops to pluck a bluebell from a bed. She tucks it behind her ear and poses with one hand behind her head for them.

"Yes, yes," Caro says. She lets herself be led back from the houses, back along the snaking path and into the abandoned seaside.

Imogen squeezes under Caro's umbrella, and they walk ahead of Wallis, looking for somewhere dry to lay out their lunch. It will be difficult now, with everyone huddling to hide from the rain.

Wallis feels peaceful as she watches her sister and cousin walk in the rain. She is content to hear the gentle pat-pat of rain on her umbrella. She is glad for the commonality of wet feet in sodden shoes. Wallis feels as though something has shifted; the promise of joy has tilted and fallen into her lap. She follows behind them, smiling.

It seems so simple to Caro; she is almost embarrassed not to have thought of it earlier. The promise of a breast. A gentle yielding of limbs. A giggle, a smile, an adoring glance. Men are impossibly simple, she thinks. Primitive and plain.

I will plant heather, she thinks later. Not those ridiculous, leafy bushes that Mary Lindsay had put all up and down the walk. And, after the day at the Ferry, Caro can imagine herself in the front window of the house, pulling back the dark, heavy drapes to look out at Ellislea Street. It would smell of tobacco smoke—of course he would smoke, perhaps in a low wingback chair—and the slightly wilting scent of cut flowers, and her own perfume. He is not so bad to look at; he might learn to be a kind man. It could be worse. She is sure he would demand little of her, sure he would be preoccupied with her youth and her beauty.

The kind of man who will not expect much from a woman, simply because she is a woman. He would not be able to imagine a use for her besides bending her body back and pushing himself in. Again.

Caro ignores the nagging thought. All she wants is to be free of Dundee, free of the sickening smoke from the jute mill, free from the helplessness, the hopelessness of it all.

Caro will be the woman who plants heather down the walk of the Lindsay house, the woman who stands in her garden shoes staring at the small purple buds, the way the colour makes the day seem brighter, the sky more blue. Yes, she will stand out on the front walk, pleased with all that she has accomplished: a husband, a house in the Ferry, and this straight, purple line of heather.

It all comes down to him. His suits and polished shoes and house on Ellislea. Desmond Lindsay.

It began as a game, fourteen-year-old Imogen following Morag or Caro or Wallis just to see if she could, but then Wallis began doing interesting things: ducking into dark closes, lurking about the gravestones in the Howff, checking over her shoulder.

Here I am.

But tiny Imogen was much quicker than her cousin. She learns more this way than she has ever managed by asking questions. She sees people as they really are, unaware of other eyes on them. Wallis bites her lower lip when she is anxious. If Imogen looks closely enough she can see the red impression of Wallis's front teeth, the right one off-centre because it is crooked and pointed. These small marks give Wallis away every time.

This afternoon, Imogen has followed Wallis from the flat lazily down Hilltown, Imogen glancing at leather boots and bolts of patterned fabric and fish heads so that Wallis would not notice her. The impossible things they put in shop windows. Rabbit legs. Scraps of delicate lace. Imogen almost loses Wallis while she is gazing at the photographer's shop. Fine women with starched collars and coloured lips only worn for special occasions. The smile was always the same. Slight. Uncertain. Imagine being unable to tell if they were at a funeral or wedding.

Imogen looks back up to the busy street and the throngs of strangers, heads in hats. Wallis will surely do something delicious and regrettable now that Imogen has been so careless. Imogen peers, finally finds Wallis's soft grey hat and moves ahead, closer.

Wallis carries an umbrella with her, and it bumps against

her thigh. It's not raining quite yet, but the sky is full and docile with held moisture. It's the black umbrella with a long handle, the one Wallis usually takes to church. Small details like this are not lost on Imogen. This means Wallis must be going somewhere important.

Imogen has watched Wallis change since she began following her. She looks lovely; just look at her rosy cheek when she turns to watch a car sailing around the bend. And her mouth, usually so straight and set, now seems to be pressing back a smile. Slight, so that you'd have to be watching to notice. That's Wallis's gift, Imogen thinks, that she can be slight and quick, moving in circles unnoticed.

Wallis stops suddenly, and Imogen bumps into an old man. She moves quickly to keep out of Wallis's sight. In the buzz of Commercial Street, with the McManus Galleries and the red *Courier* building, Wallis has stopped, as if she means to be noticed. Wallis will not turn around and notice her: Wallis is busy looking for someone else.

Look left, look right; bite, bite. Wallis is a mass of repetition, her foot in its sturdy boot tapping slightly. She bites her lip again.

They wait—together but still separate—for close on fifteen minutes. Wallis with her black umbrella just across the street at the corner, while Imogen waits with her hand on the lamppost, willing herself to be small and invisible. Imogen scans the face of everyone who passes by, assuming she'll know who Wallis waits for when she sees them.

Rain begins to fall and Wallis has to put her umbrella up. It is heaving with the weight of the rain when her smile starts in earnest. She's looking ahead, barely aware of the pedestrians around her, when she crosses the street. She's looking up, as if there could be something there in the sky.

Imogen has been a fool. Wallis was not waiting for someone, but something: a sign. Wallis disappears while Imogen stands wondering in the rain.

Women with small children. Women in dark, dreary frocks. Limping men newly returned from the War. People moving along the street, unaware of the girl behind the red-silled window, her quick eyes on them. Caro stands at the post office counter, looking out to the street before her.

"New suitors, Caro?" Ruth Munro works alongside Caro. Usually her acid tongue makes Caro smile, but not when it is directed at her. Caro is cautious, eyeing her with a sidelong glance.

"Not to speak of."

"No dances, then?"

"No."

"Do you girls some good to get out. Before the chance is gone."

"We're young still," Caro says and watches Ruth make a sour face. "Besides, Wallis doesn't much like going."

"She needs to go if she ever hopes to find a husband. Mind you, it's only cowards and rejects we have now."

Caro thinks Wallis would be grateful for any attention, Wallis with her great compassion, oozing like a boil. She feels a swell of regret as soon as she thinks it.

"She's not got your face, you know." Ruth is sorting letters and a warm, yeasty smell comes from her. "Is she after mooning over someone?"

"No."

"Poor, wretched thing. She'll be nursing your poor old mum while you are away with a husband and children of your own." Ruth winks. "Mark my words."

Caro has believed the same since she was old enough to understand why people cooed over her in the street. Morag thought the acknowledgment sinful, but Caro thinks beauty is something you can count on, something universally recognized. Nothing good ever came for Morag, who used up any beauty she had on James and two small children. On looms and scrubbing floors. Caro thinks her mother let herself be used up early in life, so that it might not hurt so much later; swiftly severing and avoiding the possibility of another life, happiness.

But Caro's escape will take more than beauty or skill. Nerve, she thinks, and forces herself to stand a little taller. Maybe it's nerve. Even ladies sometimes need to act like common whores to get what they want.

"It's about time you decided on a man," Ruth says with her hands full of other people's news, the white mess slipping between her fingers.

"I have." The words come too quickly, unintentionally. Caro looks at the floor.

"Go on, then. Who?" Ruth is greedy for scandal; her face has turned pink and delighted.

Caro says, "It's bad luck." She turns her attention to stacking notepaper, envelopes, stamps. She puts aside the few pieces of mail she will take home with her; there is another letter for Wallis from Rosemary Hennessey. Caro can tell by Rosemary's slanted writing and the small Irish stamp. One day this will all be a memory: the slick grime of ink, the shrill whine of Ruth's voice, Caro's wan reflection in the post office's windows. She smiles and wipes at the smudges of her fingers.

⁓

April 5, 1918

Dear Wallis,

I've met a lovely man, Joseph Devine. Imagine, a surname like Devine! He is dark and tall, and he knows Paddy, though he promises me it's not anything to do with the Citizen Army. I think I believe him. Wallis, when will you come to visit . . .

Each time Wallis opens a letter from Rosemary Hennessey, she feels the past sliding back to her, settling like a lost friend. She misses Rosemary now with the same fervour she had as a child; it seems impossible to Wallis that a dozen years have passed since she last saw Rosemary, last felt the gentle warmth of her hand.

Wallis hoards the letters as if they were sweets. She lets each letter melt into her, reading it slowly before reading it again. Savouring Rosemary's neat script, the small inclusions to her life. Wallis wishes to be there by her side, across the tumultuous Irish Sea, nestled into the Hennesseys again.

He must feel the same. I can't have wished this into being.

Wallis puts the letter aside. More than anything, she wants to stand on a boat and see Ireland before her, but she cannot bear the thought of Morag's hard disdain: *Catholics. Leaving us for Catholics.* Now, the memory of her father's

bitterness, his spite, his trampling on the slightest suggestion
of her happiness.

She closes her eyes and holds all her secrets to herself;
the picture of Paddy; Rosemary's rosary; the money she has
tucked away. She watches it grow and is torn between guilt
and fear and excitement. She never realized that the emotions could be so closely twined.

But John.

Certainly things have become more complicated with
the new arrival of John, but she cannot resist his knowledge
of saints and his eyes so like Paddy's. Wallis thinks that this
relationship is her first real selfish act.

Caro feels like a sinner when she enters Clepington Church.
She does not feel the strange love for cathedrals and spires
that Wallis does. Wallis, whose eyes become like a doe's
when they arrive, so big and so adoring.

Caro follows behind Morag and Wallis, who walk with
the certain step of those who have already been saved. Imogen
is somewhere ahead of them, floating down the centre aisle.
Caro can just see the golden glow of her hair ahead, made
brighter and almost transparent by the morning light coming
in through the windows. Caro walks through the jagged patterns of red, blue, yellow and green from the stained-glass
windows. There's Malcolm I ahead, looking as gaunt and
pious as ever from his high front window. That one Wallis
would be mad for, someone saintly and terribly delicate.

Caro looks around the congregation, sees the open,
blank faces of the members. Bessie Lyon sits up and to the
left in her dark cardigan. She raises her hand to Morag and

smiles. One son is dead, and the other remains fighting at the front. Battling through trenches and chlorine making them blind and ill.

Bessie sits next to Mrs. Griffin from across the close. Caro recognizes most of the members from the tenements, or the post office, or the Works. They all seem to have the washed-out look of women left to carry the burden of their families. There are only a handful of old men with watery eyes, or the red noses of drunks, young boys on their mothers' knees and the few young men who appear to be healthy, but must be afflicted in some way. Even Clepington—the kirk— has taken on the flowery scent of women, mixed with candle wax, heavy cleaning solutions.

Caro sees him at the front of the kirk, can tell it is him by the back of his head, the tidy part in his peppered hair. He is one of the few spared from the War by nothing other than their wealth, their importance. In his place, boys with yellowed teeth, greasy skin and short, sloping frames have been sent across the Channel to serve the King with pride. It's this power that Caro admires; as if he is immune to the degradation, the simple everyday horrors of war or a common life. Caro imagines touching him, the luxurious rub of his good linen suit beneath her fingers.

Mary Lindsay sits beside her husband, dressed in a tan frock, ever meek and respectable. Her hair is tinged with silver, pulled severely back into a tight, high bun. A coil like a fist, menacing and unkind. *His wife.* That elusive, scant word. Something ancient.

Morag moves forward into their pew, the pew they have always sat in, four from the front on the left. Imogen sits next to Caro, close enough that her leg presses up against Caro's thigh. Caro is glad for the bodies between herself and Morag; she does not want her mother's suspicious eyes on her.

Caro watches Desmond lean over and speak, briefly, to his wife. She watches his lips as they move close to her cheek. She watches him touch the back of his neck where he must be sweating, the spot just below his hairline, where skin touches the lip of his jacket.

Look at me.

Caro thinks her eyes must be burning hot holes into the side of Desmond's face. If he turns to look at her, if only he sees her shy, tender smile, everything will turn over in her palm and begin: her new life, her sudden absence from the monotony of her days, a new position. Belonging.

Imogen puts her hand on Caro's arm, her fingers light, cold and precise. The sermon is nearly over. Caro has been concentrating on Desmond through the soliloquy of Reverend McWilliam. She looks up now at the Reverend's tight, shrivelled mouth and his gentle eyes. Wonders what it would be like to sleep next to him, hear him breathe and sigh and dream of God. Imogen takes Caro's hand in her own and squeezes it gently. She smiles her strange, half-woman, half-child smile.

The smile of madmen and psychics.

Caro suddenly worries that she's been obvious, indelicate. One of those common whores who pant after men.

Caro squeezes Imogen's hand in return. She tries to forget about Desmond and concentrates on the Reverend, pretending to be devout.

Moments Before the War

MORAG CAN'T BELIEVE she was ever young enough to think that her marriage to James would last. Then, just twenty, she had been more concerned with having a flat, children, than realizing the nature of a cruel man.

A boot to the ribs.

After the wedding ceremony, Morag and James went for roast beef and then returned to his small flat. It was a shock to Morag, walking into a flat on Dens Road that was then meant to be hers. There was the closed-up smell of a bachelor's rooms, and smudged windows when Morag tried to look out to the courtyard.

"There's nothing there but stones and wash lines," James said as he came up behind her. She could feel his breath on her neck—the sharp scent of whisky there—as his arms came around her. She almost let herself relax into the gentle gesture when she realized he was unbuttoning her blouse. Small bone button through. And again.

"Come to bed," he said.

Morag stiffened. "James, it's barely dark. Let's go for a walk."

His hands became more insistent, grabbing at her breast beneath the blouse. "I said, Come to bed."

She felt him pushing up against her and was suddenly afraid of the small room, the smudged view outside, her new husband's desperation and the scent of whisky.

"You're my wife now," he said.

James, who had probably only marred his twenty-four years of celibacy with a few indiscretions with prostitutes. Morag sagged a little at this thought, and James took it as compliance. She let him pull her to the bedroom, push her into the mattress and fumble with her skirts.

Not even a tender word. Not even a kiss.

Later, Morag stood at the smudged window and rubbed it with newsprint. She rubbed and rubbed as James slept in the bedroom. She rubbed as her body ached, as her mind begged her to leave the flat, to leave James and not turn back. She rubbed and rubbed until the window was spotless and she was exhausted.

Then, miraculously, she slept.

For the first months of their marriage, Morag continued to be surprised at his voracious sexual appetite. All those years of celibacy came steadily bubbling to the surface like boiling water. James wanted to learn every part of her, an explorer charting new territory, until she was raw and sore and swollen like summer fruit. She invented excuses to keep his hands off her breasts, the roundness of her backside, and then she got pregnant.

The nine months she carried Caro were a gentle reprieve; James seemed frightened, unsure of her new body. He insisted on entering her from behind to avoid the taut, shiny skin of her belly. She could count days, sometimes full weeks, between his demands. She was glad, rested, and cooed to the baby.

Caro was difficult. Morag was in labour for eighteen hours before the midwife finally tugged Caro from her. It was messy, Morag left split open like a shucked oyster. She never complained about it, not even when she found it hard to sit, when lying in bed brought tears. A year later, Wallis was easier, less complicated, a small and docile baby.

Morag remembers afternoons when James came into the flat, his back to Morag and the babies at the fire. Winter, and Morag could not keep her body warm, even with her two girls curled tight in the crook of her arm. Winter, and outside was an unending sheet of gunmetal, a steady downpour of rain. Winter, and James had been out spending gas money on pints with his friends.

James moved past Morag, past her and the girls, and into the bedroom. Morag knew, without watching the path of his body, that he would undress and collapse onto the bed in a fitful, drunken sleep. When she moved into the bedroom, after the girls had been fed and curled into small perfect pink bundles, his body lay unfurled across the bed. She moved his arm, pushed at the hard knob of his knee.

My kidneys have known that knee.

If asked, Morag would be unable to recall all the dark, thick bruises that James had left on her body. Purple moulting into yellow. The sick aftershock of them.

Morag stared at the ceiling and folded her hands on her chest. She listened to her heart thump, to her husband's uneven breath, and she began to pray.

Please help my girls. Let them be healthy and happy. Don't give them a man like this.

Morag prayed, silently, to a God to whom she had stopped praying when her mother died. She thought she had forgotten how to pray, but found her lips moving.

I will sustain James, his mean hands and stale breath, if you look out for my girls. If you keep them safe.

James had not particularly wanted children; Morag had done it surreptitiously, hoping in the dark afterwards that it had taken. The girls were hers, hers alone. It was up to her to keep them safe, to hold them tight and dear. She would promise away her happiness just for that.

On August 4, 1914, Britain declared war on Germany. A day held still in collective memory: hands dark and smeared from papers. Then, James had not left yet, though when Morag looks back on it now she thinks that he had certainly already begun the process of leaving. His boots suddenly pointed out toward the flat's door.

Over the weeks before he left for the War, James was unusually happy, elated at the promise of imminent departure. He did not speak to Morag about dreams, but Morag thought he must see the Eiffel Tower when he closed his eyes, the beauty of a lacy building high in a clear sky. James had never seen anything beyond Arbroath. This was the treachery of the War: boys and men expected a grand adventure, travelling through Europe with other boys, and signed up willingly. Morag knew, even then, that they would not return as they left; they would return as hollow, broken young men plagued by nightmares of trenches and the faces of men as they died.

Before James left, Morag even gave in to him and let him make love to her whenever he wanted. He was rough, careless in his digging at her, and she was left sore for days after. It was all, really, that he left her with. Small, complicated acts of violence would be necessary to his survival. This memory made Morag believe James would survive the War.

They went with James to the train depot. Morag watched as he stepped onto the train, as he waved half-heartedly to them. The girls waved and hollered goodbyes, but Morag was quiet. She was silently speaking to God, to a God she could now believe in again.

For a while, Morag got letters, which Wallis read aloud. He made it sound like a holiday while they were still choking on jute. England. France. Belgium. Germany. When the letters slowed, and then stopped altogether, Morag knew what to expect: James wouldn't be back, one way or another.

Morag had been married to James for sixteen years before he joined the army and disappeared. Then two more years before they got word that he was missing in action at the battle of Neuve-Chapelle and presumed dead. He'd got himself killed. That's how Morag thinks of it now: his last, desperate act against her. He got himself killed to escape the family he'd never really wanted.

Women in the tenements came to give their condolences; Morag let them in and made countless pots of tea. They did not speak of James for long, but found comfort in the company of one another. Soon, they forgot that they meant to be consoling Morag at all and moved on to gossip, despair, laughter.

Morag, who had done her grieving for her life years ago, when she unravelled from James as surely as a pulled hem, didn't mind at all.

Caro does not miss her father. James, who was her first lesson in the cruel nature of men. Her memories of him are not like Imogen's memories of Oliver; there are no gentle moments, no tender afternoons with a father she adored. Caro remembers James's eyes turning to slits after he had been out drinking, watching her as she slunk by him in the flat. Dangerous. Mean. Or the flush of purple and blue and yellow that sometimes appeared on Morag's back, her soft, loose stomach or her thighs.

The day was greyer than usual in Dundee with all its smoke and rain and stone, and ten-year-old Caro was bored, sitting at the small, round collapsible kitchen table. She swung her feet listlessly, letting them bang against the rung of her chair to a nonsense song in her head. She imagined scuff marks she was leaving there, the long black smears of them.

James sat in the paisley chair, a pipe lit and his eyes darting between the paper and Caro. He made small, wet sounds on the pipe as Caro banged her feet louder, humming a little. Rain fell in its dreary pattern on the window. There would certainly be no sun. Caro was desperate for sun, anything but the rain.

"Stop that noise," James said. He spoke around his pipe. Caro looked at him for a moment but kept swinging her feet beneath the table. The sway of her legs. The hard answer of the chair. "And eat your porridge," James added.

Caro swung her legs. Thwap, thwap, thwap. She toyed with her spoon, moving the brown mush into little piles, but did not lift it to her mouth. She felt James's eyes, steely, from across the room.

"Eat."

She banged the rungs relentlessly, let her spoon clang noisily as she dropped it into her bowl of porridge. She looked at James, turning her steady gaze when he looked back at her. The paper was folded in his lap, a neat rectangle just there.

"I told you to eat. Stop acting like a spoiled bairn."

Thwap, thwap, thwap. Caro gazed lazily out the window and imagined the rain on her bare arm. The moment extended, then snapped like a rubber band. She heard James get up from the chair, heard the scrape of his feet on the floor as he crossed the room to stand beside her. She felt the heat of his thick body before she felt the stunned force of his hand against her cheek. A shattering thud. A brilliant clap.

She lifted her hand to her cheek to feel the heat and the immediate swelling.

"You'll mind your father." James relit his pipe and the heavy scent of tobacco lifted and settled around them. The flat was silent, save for the slow roll of the rain on the windows. Caro watched the rain and felt the burning of her cheek but could not move from her seat at the table.

She does not remember where Wallis was through all this, though she thinks Wallis must have been somewhere close, lurking. Watching the flourish of red on Caro's pale cheek. Watching Caro wipe hot, angry tears from her eyes.

—

The photo sits on the mantel, beneath smudged glass. Morag and James's wedding photo. They were married in Clepington Church, but the photo was taken later at a photographer's studio. Morag must have slipped back into the blue dress and tried to convince herself it was the same, but Wallis knows Morag and James would have had to save up for the photo, made an appointment and waited. All the joy and excitement of their wedding day—the joy that Wallis imagines must have been there, just below the surface—is absent from the photo. They are stiff, posed, their smiles uncertain. Wallis thinks they look uncomfortable, with each other or the camera's flash, she is not sure.

James looks exactly as she remembers him, though it's been four years since he left. He has a beard in the photo and Wallis remembers it as chestnut red, scratchy against her palm. How many times she has stood at the mantel and stared at that red beard. Wallis, who has become the family archivist, cataloguing the past in her mind. Details that would escape anyone else rest with her, small photographs flashing before her like lightning. James's red beard; Morag's blue dress, with the collar turned up just so; the curve of the dark wooden armchair behind Morag's back.

Before Imogen came to live with them and James left for the War, he took the girls to the Greenmarket Street Fair. Whether Morag didn't want to come or James did not ask her, Wallis can't remember. She does remember waving goodbye to her as Morag stood in the flat's doorway with an apron around her waist, the blue one with tiny yellow flowers, smeared with flour handprints. Morag waved for too long, until they were moving into the stairwell, and

Wallis held that image of her all day: Morag alone, but with her hand raised and waving like an excited child.

At the fair, Wallis and Caro went on the rides, though Wallis soon felt sick from all the spinning and looping. She held her hand to her stomach, hoping to quell the nausea, as Caro led her to the carousel.

Wallis never liked horses much, especially these queer, painted ones impaled by poles. Their eyes all seemed to follow her, to sneer at her. She wanted to ride in one of the carts instead.

"Come on," Caro said. "Pick a horse." Caro pinched her arm to make Wallis move. "I want to ride a horse." Caro pulled Wallis through the horses—white, black, brown—with their bright bits and reins, their shining mirrored patches.

"This one," Caro said finally, choosing a white horse with a bright yellow mane and a pink rein. It showed its teeth, bared in the way horses did, letting anger come through. Caro slid up onto the horse's back, her feet neatly together on one side. She looked sharply at Wallis, who stood lamely beside the horse. "Right then, choose one." Caro waved her hand at all the other horses on the carousel. It was filling up with children, young girls and lovers with simple eyes and stupid smiles. Wallis felt herself swaying in front of all the bawling horses, their gaudy, coloured bodies.

"Choose one," Caro hissed.

Wallis leaned back onto the closest horse, a dull brown one, just as the carousel music began. They all started to twirl under the summer sky. Wallis's stomach contracted, propelled by fear and repulsion and hot, dry anger at Caro for making her come on the ride at all. Mostly anger, at her own ability to be persuaded, to be jostled into submission. She closed her eyes to the tinny music, to the circular motion of the useless horses. She closed her eyes and heard her body fall more than she felt it.

The day at the fair became legendary. The day Wallis collapsed. As if she had had some sort of breakdown, as if it were more than common nausea. Wallis falling off the carousel never affected anyone much at all, but no one remembers that; instead, no one talks about the day Imogen came to live with Morag and the girls. No one speaks of that breakdown.

That's what it seems to be to Imogen, a snap in her life as surely as if it were a tree branch, a bone. The moment her life was separated: before and after. Before had been bright, colourful, full of laughter and horehound and trips to the chip shop. Before had been Brigid and Oliver, the startling beauty and transparency of them. After, so far, is a flat full of women, porridge, the musty smell of a house and lives closed up tight. Closed up like locked rooms, trunks, mouths holding secrets. Imogen thinks of herself that way: two separate girls. Imogen Before. Imogen After. She often does not recognize herself.

As Imogen walks through the courtyard that lies between the Caldrum Street tenements, she is reminded of her flat with Brigid and Oliver. There had been grass and the sound of children playing there, too. From her bedroom window, Imogen had been able to see the first bloomings of broom, promising a hazy golden-orange glow. She had stared out her bedroom window when Brigid and Oliver argued, Brigid's voice raised until it was splintered and, later, when Brigid cried all day. Imogen didn't watch for broom then, but for Oliver's lazy, loping stride coming home. She never mistook other men for Oliver; they were too dull, too expected. She could recognize her father anywhere.

Now, Imogen doesn't look for Oliver much. Although she remembers the intricacies of him, the exact shade of his eyes, the way he pushed his hair from his face and winked. It's Brigid she desperately wants to remember; Brigid's face she mistakenly sees in crowds; Brigid's voice she hears on Hilltown, lamenting the price of sweets. She might even see the curve of Brigid's ear, here, in the stonework of the cobblestoned courtyard. It is possible to see Brigid anywhere. Imogen is still surprised to feel only rock when she reaches out for her mum's lobe. So many things surprise her.

Imogen looks up and out over the steely swells of the sea, the harbour. She glances back over her shoulder, as if this might remind her of the path she must have taken from the tenements to get here. Imogen often finds herself on streets, by the Tay, or up at the high tip of the Law without meaning to go there. Anywhere that Brigid might once have been. A terrace where she once looked down to the street. A spot near the sea where she held her hand to her face in the sea mist. Imogen's feet must somehow remember where Brigid once stood. Imogen lets them take her there.

Mostly, she stands looking at the North Sea, the harbour and the structure of the new Tay Bridge, and imagines that she can see the haunting shadow of the old one, where her grandmother died. Plunged and trapped: Imogen can't think of a worse way to die. She can think of a worse manner to leave your family—with guilt and shame—but not a worse way to die.

Imogen knows the way people look at her, already, with a mix of pity and kindness, so she does not tell anyone about the things that frighten her: tight spaces; drowning; the mean look Caro gets sometimes, as swift and changing as her smiles; the way Wallis lets Morag and Caro boss her, as if she was something to be pushed over, easily as heather in a storm. No one treats Imogen like that; they treat her more like cut glass, something sharp and fragile that might break, or cut you, if you grasp it too tightly.

Boats float lazily in the harbour, swaying with the wind that comes up the east coast with a fury, the wind that Imogen thinks calls her name some nights: *Imo*. Bright white sails, high wooden spires reminiscent of ancient churches, the strong length of ships laden with raw jute from India. These boats have touched foreign waters, have carried men in turbans with hands the colour of earth. Smells and sunlight and seawater would cling to the ships like gauze, layer upon layer. They are benign now, nothing of the foreign or the fantastic left on them, but still Imogen aches at the sight of their mass, tethered to Harbour Street, always slightly pulling away from the city.

She starts the walk home, heading up from the Tay against the wind and the new night chill. It is spring, flower buds pulsing and pushing out from the new soft ground, but still Imogen wears a blouse and a cardigan and her overcoat, her skin cold and dappled with goosebumps. She has never lived anywhere but this city, never known anything but this dampness and cold, this hard climate that turns people into stone, and still she shivers.

Imo.

Her mother is there, behind her, just a step back. A whisper. A breath.

The Irish Independent

WALLIS STARTED GOING to the newsagent in Lochee for issues of the *Irish Independent;* here she found strange Gaelic words, reports of daily events occurring in Ireland, small details of county fairs. Standing on the street with her paper, preparing to read news of the fight for independence, stalled now because of the War. She is flipping past articles about farming and local entertainment, seeking out news about the new civil unrest, when she bumps into a man in the rain. The bump of his elbow unsettles her grip on her umbrella and sends pooled water onto his shoes.

"Oh, I'm sorry," Wallis says.

"No bother." The man smiles. He glances down at his shoes and then peers to see what she is reading. He says, "Are you Irish, then?"

Wallis recognizes the leftover lilt to his words. "No," she says. "I have a friend there."

He smiles, as if this might be an introduction of sorts. He says, "I'm John Leary."

Wallis blushes as she folds the paper and tucks it under her arm. She holds her hand out. "Wallis." She smiles, pleased that he has noticed her. Surprised. Wallis is not used to men noticing her. She looks up to the lovely brown of his eyes, the warmth there. Pleasant. Honest. Light flecks of something like gold. Eyes that remind her of her youth, of staring into Paddy Hennessey's face. The shock of it—Paddy Hennessey's eyes in this man's face—surprises her and floats through her and settles softly.

She calls up the face of a young boy waiting to be a man. A young boy saddened as he stood in the tenement close, staring up at a wide blue sky. A face that, now, she associates with Irish stamps, news of fighting, papers tinged with Gaelic.

"Are you on your way home, then?"

Wallis looks up at John Leary's face. He seems kind with his soft features and slight smile. She says, "Not quite yet."

"Maybe we could take a walk, then?"

It is a brave question, and Wallis is unsure how to respond. She is not used to men in damp streets asking her for walks. She looks at the ground while she considers, and then back up to his face. Paddy's eyes. She thinks it might be nice to walk through Lochee with him and listen to the patter of rain on her umbrella. She nods and he offers his arm.

Shortly after their first walk, Wallis started taking long routes everywhere she went, making sure to pass by the old gated cemetery, the Howff, just in case John was still there, keen to stare again into those gold-flecked eyes. She and John took walks, talked about his young children and Morag, his quiet faith, and later about Caro and Imogen. Wallis listened to him talk, and let him into her life slowly, steadily like rainfall. She watched him swallow it whole and was pleased. She let him take her hand. She was in awe of the size of his palm, the span of his fingers, the warmth that ran into her body just from this touch. The feeling was not love exactly, but something closer to comfort. When she looked up to his eyes, listened to the lilt of his voice, it was as if this moment could erase the years since the Hennesseys had gone, those taut years filled with James's death, Imogen's orphanage, Morag's hardness. The ache of Paddy. Wallis felt safe with John, safe within the warm reliability of him, and, because of that, she kept him a secret. As if he had been shrunken, folded up a hundred times and tucked away. A widowed Catholic man. Memories of another widowing. Another flagrant departure from the strictness of faith. Another family torn apart and left to float. She did not want her family to step into it and ruin it all.

John had only walked out of the safe womb of Lochee once his wife died. Suddenly he wandered through Cowgate and Murraygate and Dundee's city centre, where he stumbled into the Howff. Read the inscription on a headstone: six children under the age of eight, all dead. Then, he realized he could have lost so much more and never left.

John is now the custodian of the Howff, where he paces around the gated cemetery with keys in his pocket: they sound like music, those keys bouncing against his thigh. Wallis loves that she can hear him coming: a small song, a gentle limp. John keeps people out of the Howff at night, when the gates are locked and grieving is done for the day. Mostly, he says, he keeps out drunks and vagrant men, but once in a while there are couples, young unmarried lovers, who are lured by the promise of dark, tended grass and leafy trees. Wallis doesn't imagine she would ever be that brave, to lie on the grass with a man not her husband. Or at least a man not Paddy. The thought of it makes her burn red. A prickly feeling coming along her skin.

John was not called to war because of his children and his leg. He'd had polio as a child. Too poor to afford a brace, he had a permanent limp from one shorter leg. And when John's wife had died of consumption two years before, she left him with a small son and daughter. Anne and Stephen, two children with dark hair and pale eyes. His salvation from the terrors of war.

Wallis had never stepped into a Catholic church until John asked her to. She had watched Rosemary and Paddy enter the other St. Mary's on Ann Street, and wanted to follow them. Yet, she had never dared to move out of her life and into this new one with the Hennesseys. Later, when John asked her to go with him, she had agreed before she had even thought about it.

Wallis walked into St. Mary's Lochee and felt the closest thing to happiness she could imagine. The length of the centre aisle. The shallow bowl of holy water. The stations of the cross. The looming figure of Mary bathed in blue. Wallis breathed and breathed and said a small prayer of thanks.

As if to take Rosemary Hennessey with her, Wallis had tucked the rosary beneath her blouse. She ran her fingers over it, comforted by the beads' smoothness and stillness just there. She had come with John, his hand at her elbow, steering her toward the pews even though she was content to stand and let the light of the Lochee church wash over her.

Even though Dundee had a large Catholic population, Wallis would never have been courageous enough to step into a Catholic church. These strict definitions of devotion. These boundaries one did not cross. As if she could cut the city into two, take one step and immerse herself into Catholicism. The Irish converged mostly in the area of Lochee, or Little Tipperary, and worked at Cox's Mill or in the shops that lined High Street. A miniature city was created within the city; there was no need for the population of Lochee to leave the area. They had their churches—three clustered together on small Bright Street—their main street lined with shops, their tenements, their mill, their park. There was a convent and the high, imposing steeple of Cox's stack to puncture the horizon. They died of jute inhalation and mill fever just like everyone else in Dundee.

Wallis knows other, local Catholics, mostly Irish immigrants who settled in Hilltown because of its proximity to the Bowbridge Works and the docks. She has spoken to Mrs. Callahan in the butcher shop nearly every day of her life. She sits with Mrs. Shea in Maryfield Post Office when she waits for Caro. And she had, of course, nestled into the warmth of the Hennessey flat. A swift, smuggled presence. Even so, with Rosemary's rosary pinned inside her frock, she was aware of her own ignorance, of the mystic qualities she associated with their faith. It was a deep, dark well she wanted to sink into. Perfume her hands with incense and altar wax. Wear long robes of blue and braid her hair.

Now, Wallis feels herself falter just a little, sink under the beauty of St. Mary's Lochee. The glittering stained-glass windows, the massive pipe organ, the thickly polished pews. A heavy weight that comes with devotion. The beautiful, sad statue of Mary. The cool marble, the faint smile. Wallis imagines these are the things that the Hennesseys saw when they stepped into church—the same things they might see now, stepping over a threshold into a cool, cavernous cathedral. As if they might still be connected, somehow, across the sea. Wallis watches the statue through the entire sermon.

Later, she and John walk in Lochee Park, pausing under the shade of a heavy-limbed tree where he takes her hand and presses it to his lips. He might be thankful for her and this feels for Wallis, for a moment, like something close to love. A small surge of emotion, a complicated twist within her when Wallis is unsure of what she feels at all. She looks at John and thinks it would be so much easier, so much plainer and possible, if only she could love him. Love him with the same intensity she felt when she looked at the rubbed photo of Paddy. She is a fraud walking in this fragrant park with John; and a fool. She is living in the past, wishing for the smile of a child, the possibility that it all might be the same once again. The precise ache for that part in his hair, the vulnerability of scalp.

John's hand comes away from hers and under the afternoon sun rests on her left shoulder. There is a slow, gentle slipping and his hand comes to touch the curve of her breast. She is shocked at the heat of it, the surprise of intimacy. She is uncertain, finding herself in a new territory. The weight of a man's hand against her breast. She turns away a fraction. He says, "What's this?"

She shifts back. He's felt the round globes of Rosemary Hennessey's rosary beneath her blouse. The story of the Hennesseys comes out like rainfall.

Wallis says, "I don't know why I took it."

"You just needed something to hold on to."

He is so earnest that Wallis cannot tell him he is wrong. The rosary, then, had nothing to do with faith. Just a small, childish act that she believed would afford her some comfort or love. The feeling of Rosemary against her chest, the possibility that Paddy might once have touched the beads. His long scarred fingers.

Wallis says nothing, but lets John believe she is honest, uncomplicated. It is the first in a series of lies she believes to be kind.

Had it been another day, another fifteen minutes later, she would not have met John with his Hennessey eyes. She would never have walked into St. Mary's Lochee, would not have been able to feel this tangible link to the past, to small knees bending as they walked up the steps to another church. She realizes the delicate balance of her life with awe.

"Shall we go down to the Tay?" In the flat, Caro thinks they are slowly suffocating from Morag's incessant smoking and Wallis's faraway eyes.

Imogen is up in an instant, tucking her arms into a coat and her feet into her black boots. Caro follows quickly behind her, drawn into Imogen's enthusiasm.

"Back for tea?" Morag asks. She is not suspicious, not concerned because of the inclusion of Imogen. Caro relaxes. Imogen still means innocence, despite everything.

"Yes."

The sky outside is cold and grey, though it is dry still. Caro hugs her coat tighter as they round the corner from Caldrum Street onto Main Street and begin to head down Hilltown.

From the Hilltown clock all the way down the street to the base where Murraygate lies round as a monocle, the street is filled with shops below, small flats above. Windows display cuts of beef, polished black shoes, soft felt hats, bolts of fabric, tea, watches on slim chains, stacks of books, margarine wrapped in paper, canisters of flour. The doors are painted all shades of red and green and yellow and blue and black, some are chipped from wear, some are slick from a new coat. Women enter these shops and leave with their arms full, their coin purses empty.

Hilltown is a mecca for immigrants to the city, for anyone who feels they do not quite belong. After Lochee and the area around Cox's Mill, Hilltown is the most popular destination for hands holding crucifixes and rosaries, the scent of altar candles, footprints leading away from St. Mary's Forebank nestled in behind Hilltown. It's Saturday, signs and banners wave outside the shops, doors propped open by bricks. Cold Dundee air rushes in with a hush.

Imogen has stopped to look into Davies Dress Shop; her fingers fly to her mouth as she looks from a brown frock to a steely blue one with lace at the collar. "Look, Caro," she says. She is fixated on the blue one now. Caro knows Imogen is imagining her small, swift fingers sewing the dress, imagining herself in it; Imogen as something fine, something delicate and lovely.

"Yes, yes," Caro says as she takes Imogen's elbow.

"It's like the one my mum wore in that photo."

Things with Imogen always come back to Brigid. "Yes, yes, it's lovely, Imo. Come on, let's go before the rain starts."

Caro manoeuvres Imogen away from the shop's window and down the rest of Hilltown. Imogen holds Caro's hand loosely, letting her fingers slip and then recapture Caro's. This is something familiar to Caro, something simple and comforting, reassuring in its predictability: Imogen's fingers coming away, returning.

The car is parked outside of Prince's Pub, as she hoped it might be. She is thankful for routine, the almost impossible reliability of men.

Caro glances quickly at Imogen; she has not noticed Caro looking at the car, or, if she has, she acts benign. Imogen, instead, watches the road ahead, her eyes fixed on the shimmering sea.

The sea, the sea. We will be consumed by the sea.

At the base of the road, they cross the street to the side that is closest to the Tay, where the sea is still and the palest blue, as if a cold shock of silver pulsates through the waters. Imogen rushes past the low benches and toward the edge of the water, her hair coming out like a golden nest all around her.

"Are you coming?" she yells over her shoulder. Her hands search blindly in her coat pockets for coins to throw in the Tay.

I need luck now, if ever.

"In a moment, yes." Caro settles herself on the bench that looks out over the sea. Imogen gets smaller, turning to a tiny speck on the horizon, as she rushes over the stones and wet sand to the water, ready to fling in the coins and make a wish. The redemptive power of coins and wishes.

How long shall we wait? How will I know when he is finished?

Caro has miscalculated. She's been too anxious. Anxious for Desmond to take notice of her, desperate for her new life to start, a life she has imagined for herself in brilliant colour. The vibrancy of it enough to propel her forward.

"Caro!"

Caro stands and crosses her arms against the wind. She knows she must go down to the water with Imogen; she makes her feet move from their place at the base of the bench, across the stones, and to the water's edge where it laps and ebbs. The complicities of a lie.

"Make a wish." Imogen hands Caro a coin.

"Imo."

"It's true, Caro. Everyone knows that."

Imogen has always believed in these superstitions, believed in a higher power in a way that Caro envies. Coins in water, rabbit feet in pockets, salt over a bare shoulder. Caro believes in little other than her own will, her determination and force, and envies Imogen's ability to distance herself from all that, from her own responsibility. Caro closes her eyes and imagines a wish, but the only thing she can think of is Desmond and his car rushing away from the pub while they are here, preoccupied with wishes and superstitions.

"Fine, then. Here goes." Caro throws the coin into the water with only the thought of Desmond, and she wonders if this makes it a wish. "Right, then. Are we off?"

Imogen shrugs and turns back to the Tay. Perhaps she is imagining her wishes already coming true; surely she has wished for something to do with Brigid, something to do with the inevitability of the past. Caro takes her hand, tugs her slightly away from the Tay and toward the stony reality of the town. "Come on."

They move back up the way they have come, Imogen giggling and losing her footing over the stones. Suddenly Caro feels certain that they must hurry, that the small window of possibility will soon close. A quick snapping of a latch closing. They pass the bench and stop at the edge of the street.

"Caro?"

Caro waits for the low rumbling of a car coming around the bend. If only she could see, if only she knew it was the right one. She begins to step into the street, but is too late; a car rushes past without noticing them much at all. She sighs, relieved. It is not his car.

"Caro?" Imogen is impatient with her rush from the Tay and this new, sudden hesitation. She has not been allowed into Caro's mind, cannot see the scene that Caro has planned. A car, an afternoon by the sea, two girls just there.

The sound of another car comes to them, and Caro waits, pausing just long enough to see the hood of his car come around the corner. *Desmond.* She puts her foot out onto the street. This one step will change everything. "Right, then," she says as she tugs Imogen out into the street. The car is moving more quickly than necessary, coming straight toward them.

"Caro!" Imogen is breathless, trying to pull away. Caro holds Imogen's hand tighter and stops still in the middle of the road.

The driver must see the women in the street, the women he will surely crash into, mow down on this lazy Sunday afternoon. Tires squeal against the road, Imogen screams, but silence fills Caro's mind: a complete and sudden clarity, a long stretch of white right before her.

The car stops mere feet from them. There is the far-off crying of gulls and Imogen's ragged breathing, a new strange stillness, something false and forced as if they are part of a long-ago photograph. The three of them in the middle of the road. Caro with her hand at her chest. She stares at the car, can see the driver sagging behind the wheel. His knuckles would be white from the pressure, his heart racing. She is oddly calm, committed to this moment. This is something they will share, something that will insist on a new familiarity.

He opens the car door and is out of the automobile. Immaculate in his suit and coat. "Are you all right?"

Caro nods. She does not move, instead lets him come to her. He stands close enough that she can smell his particular scent: soap and cloistered clothes, his skin. It is a mix of something sweet and heavy, the dense smell of mothballs. Caro exhales slowly, evenly. Everything has been so carefully calculated, even this breath.

Desmond Lindsay stares at her, perhaps searching for signs of harm. For a long, thick moment their eyes meet, and Caro can see her future. She smiles.

"And you?" He turns to Imogen, who has two bright spots of red on her cheeks. Her narrow chest heaves with laboured breathing.

"Fine. Fine."

"I didn't see you when I came around the bend. I suppose I was going a bit too fast."

Caro smiles again. Desmond returns it and seems to ease a little; he lets his shoulders sag a bit, and his smile turns from necessary to thankful. He is glad not to have harmed them. He is not yet glad for this fateful meeting, but, Caro knows, he soon will be.

"Your car is in a compromising position," Caro says. Desmond looks back to it, abandoned in the middle of the road.

"Right. You are quite right." Desmond, though, does not move. This is what Caro had hoped for: the smallest hint that he is inclined to remain, to gaze at her, this strange woman he has almost careened into in the middle of the street.

"Can I take you somewhere? It's really the least I can do." Desmond grins, more boyish than Caro has imagined, and she is reminded of his notorious charm. He is seeing her for what she is: a beautiful young woman, smiling at him in the middle of the street.

"Perhaps. But," Caro adds, "a proper introduction would be nice."

Desmond chuckles. "Of course, of course. Where are my manners?" And then, "You seem to have made me lose my head." He bows slightly to Caro and Imogen. "Desmond Lindsay. Pleased to meet you."

"I'm Caroline and this is my cousin Imogen."

"Hullo." Imogen manages. She is relaxing a little, getting over the sudden rush of nerves and emotions and blood within her.

Desmond looks back to Caro. "Well, now that we have made one another's acquaintance, can I offer you a lift?"

Caro looks at the car, and then back to Desmond, as if she is weighing her options. Considering. "No," she says finally. "I think we will walk. We've just to go up Hilltown to Caldrum." Caro is careful to suggest where they live; she wants him to be able to find her when he decides to do so.

"Right." Desmond seems put off, perhaps embarrassed still by the near accident and now Caro's refusal of his help.

"Thank you, though," Caro says quickly. "It was very kind of you."

"Least I could do, after nearly killing you." Desmond winks. He glances at Imogen, who is staring at him in that odd way she has, penetrating and imposing.

"It was lovely to meet you," Caro says.

"Perhaps we will meet again," Desmond offers, "under better circumstances."

Caro smiles again, and takes Imogen's arm. They move across the street, with Caro feigning care now as she looks for other cars. They move up the street and ease onto Hilltown. Caro turns back, briefly, to see Desmond still standing in the middle of the road staring after her, his car prone and forgotten behind him.

Morag walks down Caldrum toward Main Street and the spire of Clepington comes into view. She keeps the spire in sight as she walks toward it, quickening her pace a little. It comforts her to see her own church; the other various religious sects make her nervous in their foreignness: clusters of Catholics with their plaster Madonnas; tiny meetings of

Muslims or Hindus or Jews; the other, unknown religions that float across to Scotland from the colonies. Whispered prayers in languages that sound more like songs, incense burned by priests and rabbis. All this makes Morag uncomfortable.

She has only ever walked into a Church of Scotland, and she never intends to do otherwise. She had woken early that morning, unsettled by another dream of her mother, with the new knowledge that she must walk to Clepington, sit in the hard pews and pray.

She coughs into her hand without slowing her pace.

She turns the corner onto Isla and crosses the street to the church. The day is melancholy, and Clepington looks a little sadder in the light. She steps through the small garden of the church and pulls open the heavy wooden doors.

Inside, it is quiet and still. Her feet echo when she steps down the slim aisle and slips into her pew. She is comforted by the familiarity of it, the sight of the stained windows ahead, the heavy scent of polishing wax always present in Clepington. She breathes the scent deeply into her lungs, and is caught again by a coughing fit. She presses her hand-kerchief to her mouth, feels the stiffness of the cotton against her lips.

Please God.

Morag straightens as her lungs settle. She sits, still and calm and content, in this moment of quiet. She knows it will not last long; the coughing has been coming more regularly, her lungs aching and raw afterwards. She stares at her hands, at the burn marks from hot grease or the tea-kettle, and feels her resolve weaken. She puts her hands in her pockets and welcomes the cool chill of the ring. Morag should not do it; she should not even think it. She had promised she would only say the words once, in that dim room so many years ago. That had been her promise, her pledge.

I have nothing else.

She folds her hands together and closes her eyes. She feels the prayer before she really thinks it, sees the words form behind her closed eyes.

Please make these aching lungs go away.

Morag feels a dark well of superstition settle into her as she thinks the words. She should not have thought them, should not have come here and asked for something else. Another prayer to be answered, when God had already listened to her once. He had taken James away, had kept them safe and whole together.

He sent James to war. He left us in peace.

It is too much, now, Morag thinks suddenly, to ask Him for something else. She presses her handkerchief back into her purse and moves quickly out of the pew. She hurries back the way she had come, across Isla Street and down Main Street. She moves up Caldrum toward the flat hoping that, somehow, God had not heard her. She climbs the steps up to their flat with the thought in the back of her head: she should not have asked for something else. The day she asked God to keep her girls safe, she had promised that that would be her last prayer. She had watched James step onto the train and thought, That's it. God has heard me, he has taken James and left us safe. Now, she has been greedy.

She steps into the flat and sees Caro and Wallis sitting at the small table, a pot of tea between them. Imogen stands at the window, but turns when she hears Morag's step.

"Look," Imogen says. "The sun is just coming out. It might be a nice day after all."

Morag exhales, feels her body sink a little with the knowledge of her act, the magnitude of her prayer.

Please ignore my prayer. Please don't think I have asked for too much. Please keep my girls safe.

On Sunday evening, they walk to Murphy's on the corner to have a proper dinner, still dressed in their Sunday clothes, ready for the heavy scent of grease and endless cups of steeping tea to greet them.

Inside Murphy's, small square tables with chairs tucked neatly beneath line the perimeter, and watercolours hang on the walls. Wretched, Caro thinks. The paintings are light pink and blue, the gradients of orange: a scene at the beach with the particular shade of pink left behind by the sun. Caro finds these paintings shameful in their obvious nature.

"Elsie McRae's funeral was today," Morag says. She lifts her eyes momentarily from her plate. She says, "Such a shame."

Wallis lifts a forkful of fish to her mouth.

Caro looks out the window as they chatter on about young Elsie and her tragic death. Caro barely hears them; she has learned long ago how to close herself off to things. She concentrates on the slick street outside, the dim light thrown from the gas lamps. It's only half-six and the streets are already dark as ink. A few cars motor by, slower than usual because of the rain. Caro wishes she were in one of those cars, moving away from it all. The smooth rumble of the streets below her.

"We should have a holiday," Caro says suddenly. She has not meant to say it; rather she was thinking it, meaning it, and it came straight out her mouth, before she could reconsider.

"A holiday? Rich, then, are we?" Morag asks.

Imogen says breathlessly, "It would be lovely, wouldn't it?" She is excited by the idea. Caro can tell by the way she sits up a little straighter, the way her cheeks suddenly flush a full rosy pink.

"Where would we find the money?" Wallis says.

Imogen slouches and they go back to speaking about the funeral, the morning's sermon, the next workday at Bowbridge. Caro looks out the window again. She taps her finger on the window, hoping that it might be enough, the quick, crisp sound it makes.

Headlights come into the diner and fade again. The car is moving even more slowly than the others, as if the driver is lost or looking for something. Caro peers out into the night, thinking perhaps she recognizes the car. A dark model, the familiar front grille. She squints until his face comes into view and she understands why he is driving so slowly, what he is looking for. Slowing his car near to where she said she lived, hoping to see the curl of her hair against a coat.

Caro holds her hand up to the glass, not really believing he will see her, but immune to logic for a moment. He has been looking for her here, at the corner of Hilltown and Caldrum, right where she told him she would be. Caro imagines the night would be different if she was able to get up from the table, smooth her skirts, and step out into the evening, breaking the yellow glow of his headlights with her legs.

"Caro." Morag's voice is hard. "Eat, for mercy's sake."

Caro puts fish in her mouth. Tastes the sea. As she chews she stares out the window, watching his car move back into the long stretch of night. He will drive home now to his house in the Ferry. Later he will slip into bed with his wife, perhaps kiss her on the cheek, or perhaps make love to her in a rough, uncharacteristic way. Caro is certain that he will still be thinking of the girl he nearly ran down in the street when he touches his hand to his wife's cool thigh.

The unfurling of blue into the room. A quick wink and shudder in the light as it tumbles—falls first across Imogen's arm and then, finally, curls around Caro's hips. She imagines the shimmer of the blue as she does the tango, her hips and legs easing across the floor, bumping against the crisp pleat of a man's trousers

"A sash then, Caro?"

Imogen stares up at her with blue saucer eyes. She holds the taffeta up, draping it over Caro's shoulder.

Caro turns, juts her hip out slightly. "Yes," she says. "With a slim skirt and a lapel." She points to the picture on Imogen's pattern. "Like that."

Imogen screws up her face, considering. "Maybe a long lapel," she says. "More like this."

Around them, scattered on the parlour floor, are Imogen's patterns, the thin, crisp crinkling papers she buys from the dressmaker's shop. Sketches of women in the newest styles: slim, calf-length skirts, high waists, thick sashes, drooping lapels, smart rows of buttons. Caro stands on the footstool in her stocking feet as Imogen drapes material around her. Caro wants a new frock—needs it, really. She feels this might make the difference; she'll no longer be just a Caldrum Street tenement girl. She imagines Desmond's face when he sees her stepping quickly up Hilltown: her smooth black boots, the brilliant shimmer of the blue taffeta under moonlight, the gloss of her coiled hair.

Imogen takes the taffeta from Caro, spins it quickly around her head and fashions it into a turban. She says, "I've come from India to steal you away." Imogen twirls with the taffeta still in her hands. "What do you think India is really like?"

"I haven't a clue."

"But imagine, Caro."

"Hot."

"Not just that."

"Full of fruit."

"Mmm hmm."

"Orange."

"Orange?"

Caro steps down from the footstool and says, "Yes, orange. If it had to be a colour, it would be orange."

"And what is Dundee?"

"Grey. Always, always grey." Caro looks out the window and is greeted by exactly that. She flops onto the sofa, throws her arm above her head. She looks like one of Titian's famous painted women, reposing on a velvet lounge.

Imogen folds up the taffeta and starts to stack the patterns. She is deliberate, precise in her movements, as if this is the way to keep herself whole. Crisp lines. Tidy layers.

When Wallis comes into the flat, Caro is still lounging on the sofa and Imogen is surrounded by sewing materials.

"An awful day," she says as she bangs rain from her umbrella. She steps out of her boots, places them neatly at the fireside. She looks down at Imogen and her patterns. She says, "Sewing?"

"I'm making Caro a frock."

"Another one?"

"Blue taffeta."

Caro feels Wallis's eyes on her before she looks up to meet her gaze.

"Blue taffeta?" Wallis repeats.

Caro nods.

"A dance?"

"No."

Wallis's eyes furrow and Caro feels as though she has been transparent, ridiculous. Blue taffeta while there is a war. The sheer, unabashed beauty of it.

"It's spring," Caro says. "Blue taffeta seemed perfect for spring." She does not dare even to think his name, as if having Desmond Lindsay on her mind might make it all clear to Wallis. Clear as windowpanes wiped clean. "Don't you want a new spring frock, Wallis?"

"I've already started her one," Imogen says absently.

Caro raises an eyebrow.

Imogen says, "Green wool serge."

Wallis touches her hair. "Yes. It will be lovely, I'm sure."

"I'm sure," Caro says.

At the end of the workday, Wallis tries to get the memory of jute from her hands in the deep washbasin. She finds small scratches, small clusters of blood, from the roughness of the jute. The soap stings as she washes her hands, watches the water as it runs down the drain until it turns clear.

Wallis collects her handbag and coat, and comes out into the clear evening. She feels the weight of the day, the heaviness of her twelve hours in the Works, slide off her and away. Her purse is full of her week's wages, and she finds the new weight of it comforting. She has already counted it and tucked part of it away. She pulls her coat tighter around her and moves quickly away from the Works and toward Hilltown.

The clock strikes the hour as she passes; it is later than she thought. She will have to hurry if she wants to get back to the flat in time for dinner. She moves down Hilltown and crosses Victoria Road. She enters the cool, chilled air of the Royal Bank of Scotland and feels a distinct calm come over her. She waits, moving from one foot to the other, and then stands at the wicket. "For deposit, please," she says.

She hands over the money she has parted from the grocery and gas meter money. It is not so much that Morag will notice, but enough that each time Wallis comes to the bank, she sees her savings rise and rise. She smiles at the numbers written on the slip of paper. It is almost enough.

⌒

While other women have become extensions of their husbands, dulled and spread thin by their children, made common and insubstantial by the daily toil of jobs they detest,
Caro has, somehow, managed to stay simply herself. She
does not imagine herself affected by other people's whims or
desires. She has seen her future so clearly—as crisp and perfect as the yellow wing of a bird in the sky—that she will
not do anything now to compromise it.

"Nice to meet you under better circumstances." He had
appeared on Hilltown, right at the corner where the clock
lilted and waited, made the moments of the day move more
slowly.

Caro said, "And what circumstances are these? What
brings you all this way up Hilltown?" She did not even have
the new blue taffeta on; it was still in pieces on the parlour
floor.

Desmond gestured to the clear Wednesday sky. "A nice
afternoon for a walk." He had smiled as he said it, as if it
sounded false even to him.

"I suppose." Caro shifted the weight of her grocery bag
from one foot to the other.

That is what she remembers later about their meeting:
the dull ache on the balls of her feet when she shifted from
one to the other. She will only vaguely remember Desmond
offering to walk her home—which she would decline—or
his offer to meet her that night. Yet she understood that his
innocent offer of sitting atop the Law was not so innocent;
Caro knew what she was agreeing to. The first, specific

moment when she moved a foot closer to him. When she said yes. The breath of a word, the exhalation.

"You'll have to fib for me tonight," Caro says to Wallis. Caro is putting the margarine and bread from her afternoon grocery trip in the icebox. Milk. Sugar. Everything white, flawless, bland.

"Why?"

"You just will." White sausage. Oatmeal. Flour.

Wallis is silent, watching Caro as she places the things in the cupboard, moves back to the icebox, stops with her hands on her hips. She knows what Wallis is thinking, can see it as clearly as if it has been written across the flat's wall.

Caro is suddenly voracious for something bright, something brilliant like a sliced tomato, the peeled rind of an orange. She thinks, briefly, that she was never meant to live here at all; there had been some mistake, surely.

"Caro."

"Oh, Wallis, it's only a few hours." Wallis's judgment weighs on her like a hundred-pound bag of flour, just as sudden.

Wallis tilts her head to the side and finally says with a slight smile, "Fine."

Caro is glad for Wallis. Her dependability, her reliable simplicity. Wallis would never understand about Caro's shimmering tunnel of escape; her brilliant, purple-edged view ahead. Wallis would not understand about this kind of secret.

Imogen makes a list in her mind of places to visit: her grave out on Arbroath Road; Park Avenue; the harbour; the Law; the river in Perth, if she can manage to get there; the butcher shop; Clepington Church, where she will speak to Reverend McWilliam. He is gentle and wise; he will know what to do, he will certainly know things.

Imogen sketches a map of these places on a small scrap of paper. Jagged lines drawn, erased, drawn again.

"Imogen?"

She snaps her head up. Mrs. Wesley is staring at her, waiting for her to answer a question Imogen has not heard. She says, "I don't know, ma'am."

Mrs. Wesley looks away from her and Imogen bends her head back down to the map. Mrs. Wesley will think her strange, again, think she is immersed in her own, odd world. Does she wonder what Imogen daydreams about? Where she goes for those moments when she should be studying geography, learning about kings long gone? Imogen can be anywhere, really: in the room with Brigid and her glistening white glove; on the tracks of the new Tay Bridge, hovering; right there in the twist of a plait. Aileen sits in front of her, the long plait of her red hair hanging down against the back of her seat. Imogen touches the end of the plait with her pencil and wishes she could draw that too, the specific curve and lilt of it.

⁓

His hand slipping into hers. The delicate, heady sensation. This is the first intimate act Caro knows with Desmond.

They drive in his car to a dark field. He brings a bottle of whisky, which Caro tilts up to her mouth and gulps. She likes the sudden heat, the lingering burn down her throat. This amber bottle under moonlight.

He runs his hand across her back as they walk across an abandoned field and she feels her life change. It is split open and laid bare, fraught with possibility. In the distance, she can see the soft glow of light in a farmhouse window. A sole witness. This sudden reminder of normalcy, of houses and farms and children settling into beds, calms her. She lets his hand rest on the curve of her waist as they walk.

"You are beautiful," he says.

And she says, "Thank you."

She is silent, waiting for him to speak. She imagines what she could say to fill the heavy, quiet air between them. *My mother works at your jute mill. My cousin has been orphaned and sleeps beside me.* Finally, she says, "My father was killed at Neuve-Chapelle."

"I'm sorry to hear that."

Caro does not want to show the hate for her father that shimmers beneath the surface, her relief when he died, so she is silent in the thick, dark night. Nods. Desmond must think this is something he can be compassionate for, as if empathy might bind them.

Desmond tips the whisky bottle up to his lips. She watches the slow churn of alcohol down his throat and imagines reaching out and touching the bulge of his Adam's apple. What would the skin there feel like? Skin toughened daily by a razor. But so vulnerable that one slip—a gasp at the wrong moment—would be the end of him.

They walk over wet grass, the shuffling of their shoes the only sound in the night. There are stars, the night is so clear, and Desmond stops to look up to them. He has not remembered a blanket so they must stand with their necks bent to look up. A midnight blue sky, a silver flash. A shooting star. Caro thinks if she were a different kind of woman, she might see this as a sign.

"Did you make a wish?" Desmond asks.

"No," Caro says, "I never remember to." Then, "Do you believe in wishes?"

"Yes. Of course. Don't you?"

"No."

"A girl so young, and you don't believe in wishes?" His voice is slick, sugary. She does not want to look at his face, see his smirk. He thinks she is beautiful, and young, but that is all. She is anonymous, except for this strange disbelief in wishes.

"Wishes are for children and fools," she says.

They walk farther into the fields, sharing the bottle between them. Finally, he says, "You are beautiful in the moonlight. Let's sit and admire the view."

Desmond looks for someplace to stop, someplace that might afford them some relief from the damp grass, but Caro simply sits down. She stares up at him with her young, beautiful face full of determination. Desmond laughs softly and sits beside her. They stare up into the sky for a moment before he takes her face in his hands and kisses her. Hard. There is no gentle yield, no softness and melting. Caro lets him kiss her, lets herself press against him under the bright sky. She lets his hands roam over her body, feeling his frustration over her layers.

Later, Caro will not remember his hands or his mouth so much but the way the stars hung atop the inky blackness. Still and composed as a painting, something unreal.

Imogen walks down Thistle Street, away from the flat and Morag. She does not like to think about what would have happened to her if it weren't for Morag. Imogen would have been put in an orphanage, or perhaps in the convent in Lochee with the nuns. Would this have been so bad? There is always the security of a habit and the hymns, always the warmth of dozens of bodies in one small room. Nor can Imogen imagine what her life would have been like if she had grown up with Oliver and Brigid; she would have been exposed to something raw and uncomfortable, that strange, hard love that had been apparent between her parents. Imogen's memories of Oliver and Brigid are not blissful, not all coloured with the blues and reds and yellows of a child; she has been privy to the messy bits of their love: her mother's nails down her father's arms, Oliver's purposeful silence. Imogen had always known that Brigid would leave her. She was always leaving, pulling and tugging away from her toward something else, something far away and long gone. Imogen just waited. The absence of Brigid arrived like something Imogen had always known, like a dream realized. Brigid was haunting her from the moment she was conceived.

Was that possible? To be haunted before birth?

Yes, Imogen thinks without hesitation or doubt. Of course it was possible, it just made things more difficult.

Where Imogen can recall everything about Oliver—his scent, the way his hair fell down over one eye, the uneven, brilliant smile that made people do things they might not otherwise do—she has no real memories of Brigid after Oliver left. She has simply adopted the stories she's heard about her mother since.

Why don't you remember her?

Imogen turns the corner onto Park Avenue, pushing the nagging voice from her mind. She remembers walking down this street with Oliver, walking away to throw shillings in the Tay, to look down over Dundee from the Law, to search out wild rabbits at Camperdown Park. This street has known the sound of their feet, the sudden rush of Imogen running ahead of Oliver, beckoning for him to hurry. *Hurry.* She moves down Park Avenue until she stands directly across from the black-terraced building in which they had all lived. From the street, she can see the window of the sitting room. The days when she had left the flat with Oliver, they left Brigid behind, her face slim and milky in the flat's window. Imogen looked up at Brigid, searched for the small movement of her gloved hand against the windowpane.

She cannot remember if Brigid waved, if her white glove appeared in the window. Imogen imagined her sinking into the bed, relishing the cool space vacated by her husband and daughter, the day stretching long with possibility. Brigid was distant, often melancholy. She was not beautiful in the aggressive manner of Caro, but delicate: golden-white hair, skin the colour of fresh milk, something fragile and unreal about her. As if she might break if pressed too hard or shouted at. Imogen stares at the window and thinks that her mother could exist in the shimmering glaze of a window;

something that temporary. She wills herself to remember. Anything. Just remember one thing.

Why can't you remember?

Those few slim months after Oliver left, before Imogen came to live with Morag, now seem like a haze; Imogen remembers nothing, save for one afternoon in the butcher's when Brigid was cruel. Mostly, Imogen remembers the smooth surfaces of the cabinets, the slabs of meat behind the glass, red and, not so long before, throbbing. She remembers crying, suddenly and unstoppably, but not precisely why. Her face wet when they left the butcher shop and strode out into the late-afternoon chill.

These memories do not, really, seem to belong to Imogen at all. They belong to that other Imogen, the one who was present during the fugue but now refuses to resurface.

Come back. I need you to come back.

After a moment, Imogen turns away from the flat's dark window. She puts one foot in front of the other and begins to walk home.

⌐

They meet as often as possible. Dark, secret places. Abandoned pavilions. Smooth arcs of land shaded by trees. Caro learns the small desires that he has secreted away from his wife. *She won't let me touch her, only once a fortnight.* In this manner, Caro learns the woman he wants her to be: sexually free, youthful, voracious. She stares beyond the roof of the car, at the hanging sky above. At first, she only let him touch her through the crisp layers of her clothing; she revelled in his desperation, his obvious need for her. There was the sight of her white breasts, the shock of her bare knees. Then, the promise of a thigh, that soft female territory. He fumbles with her skirts, with the tiny buttons of her blouse, and grunts and grinds away at her. Leaves her unsettled by it all.

Caro is sprawled, prone, on the back seat of Desmond's car, her breasts exposed to the cool night air. There are goosebumps across her chest, which Desmond now traces with his tongue as he finds her nipple. The shrill edge of his teeth against the skin there.

For a man with a past so littered and cluttered with women, he is not artistic in his seduction. He rushes, pressing his hand up between her legs. He seems unconcerned with the possibility of her pleasure; he uses her body as if it is his right. It makes her feel distanced from it all, as if she is watching the awkward angles of their bodies from somewhere far off.

She moves slightly against the car's seat, trying to make herself more comfortable, and he takes this as encouragement. Desmond pushes her skirts up around her waist, and then busies himself with undoing his pants. It only takes a few moments and he is inside her; a few more and he is heaving, breathless, collapsing on her. He has the weight of men well fed, men who have compliant and doting wives at home, men who have two helpings of pudding after dinner. Caro breathes in shallow breaths beneath him.

"You are beautiful," he says later, while he tucks his shirt back into his pants and buttons up. Caro smiles, all the while trying to keep her face composed, to keep him shielded from her knowledge of routine.

Caro sees Desmond at night, driving out to abandoned fields or other places where they will not be caught. Caro wants him to crave her, her tight, willing body and her adoring smile. Already, she can feel him easing into her, pleased with her face below him. He has already become accustomed to her scent. That, she thinks, is the real beginning. When the smell of her lasts on his fingers, his chest, so that he can smell her later in his house in the Ferry.

Their meetings never last long; just long enough to drive to a secluded spot, long enough for him to jostle her into submission, long enough to drive back to Hilltown, where he leaves her on the corner.

"When will I see you next?" Caro asks. She moves from one foot to the other. The air is crisp, full with the promise of rain.

"Soon," he says. He is vague. This is a small moment of assumption: he assumes he can be cavalier, that Caro is his alone; Caro assumes he will miss her when he drives away, that he will watch her in the rear-view mirror, squinting until he can no longer make out her figure.

Desmond will soon ask his wife to leave. He will want to wake to Caro's pale face and thick, dark hair, to find her in his rooms in the Ferry when he comes home from the Mill. Caro imagines a drive of white heather up the front walk. *White heather for luck.*

When Wallis comes back to the corner, Caro is standing serene. Her hand is at her collar, cutting her off from the wind, and she is looking up to the Hilltown clock, though it never keeps time. She is always alone. This worries Wallis more than if a man remained at her sister's side, touching her elbow in a sadly possessive manner.

Wallis has watched and worried about Caro since they were young, hiding behind Morag's skirts. Watched her from afar, watched James's hand against Caro's cheek, watched Caro's small, taut anger come to the surface. Caro has become secretive, though; she does not share anything with Wallis, even when she begs Wallis to be her ally. It has been years since Caro really asked Wallis anything about her life.

Caro holds her hand to her hair, brushing stray strands back. When they meet, not looking at each other or touching, they are two halves of a whole. They do not speak but begin their walk home. Caro links her arm through Wallis's and grasps for her hand. Wallis is glad for the warmth, for this shred of intimacy. It lulls her into disbelief, suddenly sure that they are years younger and still confidantes. That they could be the kind of sisters who brush each other's hair and tell each other secrets.

"Tell me," Wallis says suddenly.

"Tell you what?" Caro is coy, a leftover from her time with the man. It does not suit her, Wallis thinks; it makes her seem obvious and plain.

"Tell me."

They walk in silence. A nail in Wallis's boot heel digs at her. With each step she feels the pressure and dig. "Caro."

Caro sighs. Even her sighs are complicated, elegant, formal, Wallis thinks. "Oh, Wallis, I've nothing to tell."

"Who is he? Who are you meeting?"

Caro tugs at Wallis's arm. "Who said I was meeting anyone?"

Wallis is mocked into silence. Caro thinks her foolish, somehow still childish, simple. She will never ask Wallis what she does in the hours while she waits; Caro assumes she knows everything there is to know about Wallis.

Wallis makes a pact with herself. She will stop trying to help Caro, stop trying to protect her from her own narrow destruction. She will let her sister's life play out exactly as it was meant to: messy and irreparable and mooned over. Wallis will not even try to mop up what's left of it.

Imogen puts on her brown cap, buttons her heavy navy coat, and walks the three flights of stairs down to Caldrum Street. On the way, she passes Bessie Lyon, who has her arms laden with groceries. Small parcels tied with string peek out of the paper bag. Imogen smiles and nods and moves into the spring air, full of cold, bright sunlight, and then on into the courtyard.

Windows are shut, barren of women leaning out, hoping for companionship or laughter. But Imogen knows there are eyes watching everywhere inside the tenements. Imogen strides across the close to Mrs. McArthur's small patch of flowers. Tulips and hyacinth already in bloom. The scent greets Imogen while she is still some steps away.

Imogen bends, fingers the new blooms and tugs. She clutches the flowers in her fist. It's not much, but it will be enough. Imogen wants flowers for Brigid's grave. The other graves—unadorned, cold stone—seem lonely to her. Sad and solitary.

Imogen simply bends, grasps and tugs.

Years ago, when Imogen first came to live with Morag and the girls, they all used to go to the cemetery to visit the graves: first, Morag's mum's and then Brigid's. Imogen can remember the first time she went to Brigid's grave. They took the slow, loping tramcar from Dundee out to the open fields surrounding the city. No matter which way Imogen turned, she saw green. Green and the smell of fresh-cut grass; this smell would linger and settle within her to remind her of Brigid's death every time spring came. Green has become Imogen's least favourite colour. It is sickly and over-whelming. It is a solid, unwavering reminder of that April day in 1911 when Imogen held Morag's hand and stared at the headstone that was to represent her mother. So unlike Brigid's memory; if it was meant to be like Brigid, then it should be a wavering, floating bit of chiffon. Torn lace. A melting ice sculpture. Not the piece of stone inscribed with her mother's name and the dates of her birth and death. The moment when Imogen learned the word *beloved*. It was weighted, heavy in her mouth and mind. For the rest of the day she repeated, "Beloved, beloved," but quietly enough that no one else could hear her. *Beloved, beloved, beloved,* until the word was almost unrecognizable. Blurred and crumbled and flattened. Until it was just consonants, thick in her mouth.

Imogen used to carry sprigs of broom and white heather to leave on the grave, sometimes fancy cut-out cards that Caro would help her make. Then, Imogen never wondered what happened to those cards and paper dolls; did they glide away effortlessly, or did someone collect them and read them, Imogen's childish bereavement? It makes her flush now to imagine someone else being privy to those thoughts. Her grief was real and unharnessed and unending. When did it grow tame, she wonders? When had she stopped crying for the lost memory of Brigid?

"Beloved," Imogen breathes. The woman beside her on the tramcar looks sideways at her. Imogen covers her mouth with her hand, pressing back the beginnings of laughter. The woman must think she is mad, talking to herself on a tramcar. Imogen smiles. People think she is delicate, broken since her mother's death. What they don't understand is that something in her was freed when her mother died; Imogen sees things, hears things, that no one else seems to notice. Singing along to silence. Imogen made the mistake, though, of telling Morag once that she saw Brigid out the window. Brigid, pale and soft and wordless amidst the sound of wind. Morag's face contorted and then went unbearably still. She understood the power and proximity of ghosts. Imogen had said it calmly; she was used to the wavering image of Brigid. It had been with her since the morning after her mother's death. When Imogen woke and had to remind herself that Brigid had ever existed at all. Brigid's breath on her face when she slept. Waking to her smell.

The tramcar slows and then stops. Imogen can't quite see the cemetery yet, but she knows it is close. Can feel it as much as anything. She steps down from the tramcar with her fistful of stolen flowers and her smart brown hat and starts the walk up Arbroath Road toward the cemetery. This moment is what she loves best about these trips: the cemetery still just beyond, the sound of the earth beneath her feet, the heady scent of hyacinth curling up to greet her. Well before the stark lettering of the headstone becomes apparent, when Imogen feels the pull of her mother. She might be standing at the side of the road, holding her hair away from her face with her slight white hand.

I'm coming, I'm coming.

Imogen hurries her step.

Now, only Imogen visits the grave. Imogen with her hands full of whatever she can find: wild roses, hyacinth, heather or, sometimes, a fragrant, perfect rose from a private garden. Flowers for weddings and funerals. But it's long since Brigid's funeral now, long since she and Morag and Caro and Wallis stood dripping as the minister spoke at Brigid's grave. Morag touching the top of Imogen's head, surprising her again by the gentle weight of her hand. Imogen, who had become used to not being touched.

She moves through the cemetery arches and past all the high Celtic crosses. The small angels and tiny lambs. She weaves her way through the other graves until Brigid's comes into sight.

BRIGID SULLIVAN

1881–1911

The headstone is so plain, unadorned, that it becomes the exact opposite of Brigid. As if no one wanted to remember her as she was: uncommon and painfully lovely. She has nothing more than her name. She has become forgettable.

That is not entirely true now, is it?

Imogen brushes the voice away. Her fugue has had small lapses as of late. She remembers the colour of her dress when Morag came to fetch her. She can smell the lemony polish scent of Brigid's flat. She remembers her hand on Brigid's bedroom doorknob. The feel of cold metal.

The sun is high today, dry for April, and birds cluster on the high branches of a tree. They twitter and coo to one another, raising their wings every so often. It seems that, lately, Imogen notices birds everywhere. Waiting.

Now, death is all anyone will speak of; the War, Brigid, all the diseases with horrible, beautiful names. Death seems to follow Imogen like a shy playmate, hovering around but never managing to stretch its hand out.

It is Imogen's secret wish that Oliver would return and rescue her. She never mentions this wish, knows it would be hurtful to Morag, after all she's done. But Imogen can't help it; she sees the wish as if it is an old photograph, an event that already occurred and was documented.

The Return of Oliver.

She imagines that Oliver snuck onto a boat destined for some exotic place. He might return the same way, casually leaning on a sack of raw jute, a dark woman beside him. Of course, by now he would have a new wife, perhaps like one of the few Indian women Imogen has seen, fragrant and shadowy. She might be wrapped in silk—royal blue, startling purple, vehement red—and covered with strange Indian gold bangles. The sounds of music when she bent to take Imogen in her arms. The scent of cooking and something else, bathing oils or perfume sprayed on the backs of knees and elbows. Imogen would let herself be folded into her darkness, tucked in like a coin.

Imogen feels a sudden swell of guilt. She is standing on her mother's grave, imagining a new wife for her father, a new life for herself. Imogen closes her eyes to the birds and the spring sun and Oliver. She is sorry for imagining a happiness without Brigid. For loving Oliver just a little more. For not being enough to keep all the pieces whole and safe in her hands.

Imogen looks down the row. Brigid is buried next to her mother, one grave farther from her father. Imogen does not visit the other graves; she saves this time for Brigid alone. She wipes off the headstone with her palm, as if she were smoothing Brigid's hair, places the flowers at the base of the stone and then sits cross-legged on the grass as she always does, regardless of the weather. Oftentimes she leaves with the soggy imprint of the grave on the backs of her thighs.

At once, Imogen is sorry and not sorry at all. It is all so confusing. She is two girls under one skin, forever tearing and uncertain. She crouches on her mother's grave and tries to suture herself whole. She breathes in the scent of grass and cement headstones and faltering blooms and opens her mouth.

To the men and women passing by, Imogen is a sorrowful sight. A wisp of a girl sitting on her mother's grave. Still. A sad frail girl in a lonely cemetery in the middle of the day. The white rope of her hair caught in the wind, up and flipping on the breeze, landing momentarily on her shoulder. Soft as insect wings. What no one notices is her mouth moving. This small girl with her rosy mouth caught in a conversation with her dead mother.

A War to End All Wars

WHEN THEY OPEN the *Courier*, it is with held breath. The War has changed everything. No more long sigh in and out. Instead, the tight constriction of lungs, the collapse. The crisp sound of the paper opening, the snap and crinkle. All this is now part of the War.

Morag stares at the *Courier* on the table in front of her. She does not need to open it, does not need to see the black smudges of newsprint on her fingers. The front page is enough: trench warfare, men slowly dying, lists of the dead. Morag stares at the paper. No more can she pick up a paper with ease; now there is expectation. Morag used to open the paper to see Oliver's name below articles, the alphabet of his name staring back out at her. Oliver and his wit. These years have changed everyone. Sleep is less peaceful, reading might become traumatic, people do not smile in photos any more. Morag sighs as she opens the paper, ready for more macabre news.

The Germans have advanced fourteen miles to the Somme River.

Morag closes her eyes. Coughs into the handkerchief in her hand. She is sick of the War, sick of the men who return broken. It seems this war will never end. A war that was only to last until Christmas has now been dragging on, bringing with it the dying, for four long years. Four years. Morag thinks she has become a different person in that time. A weaver. A provider. A widow. The coldness of the word: *widow*. Morag folds the paper and sets it on the table. She takes a sip of tea and looks out the window to the tenement courtyard. There are sprigs of greenery, the new blooms. Always green with this formidable rain. It is spring, Morag can feel it upon her. There is always something hopeful about spring. It has been a long time since Morag felt hopeful at all, before she noticed the persistent ache in her lungs, the increasingly frequent coughing fits. Hope died just a little then, when she realized what it meant. Mill fever.

Morag coughs again, pressing her hand to her mouth. Trying to choke back the rattle, the quiver of bone to breath. *Just breathe. Breathe.*

She has not yet admitted the illness to her daughters or Imogen. She cannot seem to tell them. Many times, she has opened her mouth with the words poised on her tongue and felt herself swallow them back. *Not yet. Tomorrow. Perhaps the next day.* Morag knows that, soon, she won't be able to keep it a secret. There is no miracle to be had here.

Dreams full of her mother's gentle face.

Maryfield Post Office's storefront is painted a brilliant red with stark white letters. The paint is peeling in some spots, affected by the dampness of Dundee and the sometimes blistering wind, but it still stands out against the other grey buildings. Caro wonders if the audacity of the red storefront was what drew her to it in the first place; something in it might have reminded her of herself, of the things she might be. Like a solitary gas lamp at night, something you cannot look away from. Something to do with wind and water and a restless nature.

She stares out the large front windows at people who pass by the shop. She has witnessed messy fights, screaming children and quick, secretive kisses; Caro hopes for something interesting this morning. Ruth will come in the afternoons when it gets busier, but for the morning hours Caro is alone. Quiet and still, full of thought, on her small stool behind the counter. Later, Caro sorts through letters and sells stamps while Ruth speaks to anyone who comes through the dark door, ushering them in and out with news dispatched or received. By now, Caro can tell if a letter holds good or bad news by its weight; people do not feel the need to write line upon line when they feel joy. Sentiment is for the abandoned and the devastated. She weighs envelopes in her hands before dropping them into the sack behind the counter.

People speak freely when they enter the shop, allowing Caro in on secrets they would not reveal to their neighbours. It becomes a confessional, as if stepping into the office makes everything clear and free of confusion. Caro was the first to know that Reverend Robertson was retiring, and the first to know that Reverend McWilliam had arrived. She was the first to know that James was presumed dead at Neuve-Chapelle. She was the first to know that Angus Lyon had been killed in battle. She does not give away too much, instead holds herself quiet and full with stolen knowledge.

She does not expect many people to come into the office this morning; the streets are slick with rain, and people scurry past beneath wide, dripping umbrellas. Caro has settled onto her hard wooden stool, prepared for boredom, when the girl comes in.

She is soaking, red-cheeked, immensely plain. These are the first things Caro notices about her; then, the low, round belly coming ahead of the girl. She moves awkwardly from the door to the desk behind which Caro sits. The girl wipes at her nose, and hands Caro an envelope.

"For post, please." The girl's voice is young, betraying her belly. Caro checks the girl's hand for a wedding ring but sees none. Bare hands slick with rain and swollen. Her knuckles have almost lost themselves within her fingers. She catches Caro looking at the round bulk of her body and says, "My husband is in France."

Caro takes the envelope. It is soggy, made thinner and transparent by the rain. Heavy, though. Not a letter of joy. She looks at the girl's belly, and the girl pulls her worn coat closer around her frame. As if she is still uncomfortable with this eruption of flesh, still uncertain about her body's mass, even after these long months.

Caro glances at the address. Words and numbers melt together. "For the Ferry?" she asks, certain that somehow she has read wrong.

"Yes."

Caro looks up at the girl and tries again. "For a Mr. and Mrs. Lindsay?"

"No." The answer is swift. "Just for Mr. Lindsay." The girl touches the mess of her ropy brown hair and water falls onto the counter. Without thinking, Caro reaches over and wipes it away. Cleans the spot in front of her before laying the envelope down.

"Right then."

The girl hands Caro cold coins, waits to see Caro press a stamp to the envelope, then retreats, pausing before stepping back out into the wet afternoon. Caro watches her as she moves down the street, tidal.

Caro knows what the letter will say before she tears the envelope open and unfolds the papers.

Dear Desmond,

Why have you not answered me? Why have you not been to see me? I fear what will happen if you ignore me . . .

Caro does not read any further, but instead closes her eyes and holds the damp pages in her hand. She considers folding them back up, putting them in a new, crisp envelope and sending it away to him, perhaps hoping that his wife might find it and allow curiosity to take over. Imagines the look on Mary Lindsay's face when she realizes there will be a child.

Instead, Caro crumples the letter into a ball and tucks it into the waste bin. She tells herself that she cannot let this young, foolish girl come between her and Desmond, that the girl will be better off with a future wiped clean of him, but she does not believe herself, even then. These fractures of the mind, incomplete lies one tells oneself.

She pushes the letter to the bottom of the bin, where it will not be found.

The man steps off the tramcar and sets his suitcase—slightly battered, showing age and travel at the seams—on the damp ground. Dampness reaches into him, right through to the core, like a fist and stays there. He rubs his hands together and then bends to pick up the suitcase again and start his walk away from the city.

~

The meeting has gone long; it's edging on eleven o'clock. The small room is loud, boisterous, full of women. Voices rise above one another as they talk, again, about half-time.

"They need to be in school. They have their whole lives to die in a mill," Margaret Nealy says.

"Lindsay and the others will never agree, the greedy bastards."

"Then we'll make them." There is the pounding of fists on tables, the clinking of half-empty glasses, and the room vibrates with their determination. Wallis loves the pulse here; each woman speaks unguardedly, confident and full of the bright light of idealism in the room. They are committed to ending half-time, to forcing the jute barons to let the children remain in school instead of tearing them from their studies to pull jute. She thinks she can almost see the excitement flicker between these worn-down women.

Wallis closes her eyes for a moment and wishes. A simple, plain wish: *Give them that much more time to be children. There is so much time to be broken down by the mills and the smoke and the horrible, unending days.*

Jean Grant says, "Will we strike, then?"

"We should burn the bloody mill down."

"That would leave us all in fine form, wouldn't it?"

Laughter erupts in the room, safe, relieved laughter. They will not burn a mill, but will have to decide what action they will take.

What would they do in Ireland?

Wallis thinks it before she even realizes she means to; she squints at the faces of women around her, and tries to imagine what the Citizen Army might do in a similar situation. But then, she thinks, we don't have rifles and women hiding out in country farmhouses.

"Wallis?"

She looks up to Jean's face. Her pale cheeks are red, brightened with anger and excitement. Wallis says, "We could march."

There are murmurs of agreement, discussions of where would be the most effective; Victoria Road? Or perhaps through Murraygate? And when?

After the Union meeting, Wallis comes out into the crisp evening. She stands with Jean and Mary O'Keefe, the young, pretty new carder, energized from the electricity in the room, the quickness of passionate debate. Wallis thinks her body hums, vibrates into the night despite the late hour.

"Night, then. I'm off." Wallis pulls her coat tighter around her and starts her walk home. One foot ahead of the next. Each step a small movement closer home. Home. She wishes she were elsewhere. The scene is so vivid in her mind—opening a door and smiling, feeling herself waver and fall away from herself a bit—that she believes, for a moment, that all the secrecy might be behind her already.

Then there is the strike of the Hilltown clock—even from this far away, she can hear it, the hollow clang and ring—to bring her back to this real moment: her feet on a Dundee street, her mind full of an alternate life that is not hers. She is only this: a woman walking up a street, leaving an evening meeting, full of heavy thoughts.

Wallis turns onto Dens Street and feels herself stiffen just a bit; she is that much closer to home, that much closer to stepping into a room where she will have to lie to her family. There is so much to lie about lately—Paddy and John and the rosary beneath her bed—that it makes Wallis feel suddenly weak. If only she could break away from this small, tight life. She listens to her footsteps as she turns up Isla and sees the bulk of Clepington Church ahead. She hears the click of her heels and reminds herself that it will only be a little while longer—she might be bold enough, soon, to count the days—before she understands the beauty of light on water, the impossible freedom of standing on the deck of a boat.

On April 13th, Imogen answers a persistent knocking at the door. She opens the door without any sense of dread or anxiety or surprise. She expects Mrs. Lyon, or perhaps one of the Union women for Wallis. What she does not expect is Oliver standing tall and handsome in the corridor. He smiles at her and her heart breaks again.

Imogen faints.

BOOK TWO

Disasters

Missing Photos

IF THERE WERE A PHOTOGRAPH of the day, it would reveal a sky so open and plain, so hopeful a blue that happiness should have been guaranteed. An attractive couple coming out the open doors of Clepington Church into the sun. His hand is on the small of her back, that modest landscape of the female body where men lay claim to territory. It is at once pleasing—the reassuring weight of his hand—and possessive. Then, even possession had the taste of something sweet.

The photo would not capture Morag's memory of the delicate beauty of the girl standing in a frock embroidered by her own hands; tiny roses across the bodice would be lost by the camera. As would the scars covering her mottled fingers. This is the one part of Brigid's body that she will never hold up for inspection or admiration. She wears white gloves—soft lambskin in the fall and winter, and thin cotton for spring and summer, always.

Behind them, almost hidden by the large church doors, would be the dour wedding party. Morag in what looks like a grey dress, but it could have been almost anything: blue, purple, green.

Morag would stand stiff and strained beside James, who looks awkward, uncomfortable. He was not one for sentimentality, disbelieving the promises of unending love and contentment. A young woman in grey and a man who should never have married. These are the two witnesses to the impetuous marriage of the attractive couple plagued by the woes of the beautiful: joy too tight to contain; insecurity; jealousy; black moods; entitlement. They smile shyly, anticipating a life full of other beautiful things. All the messiness to come is not apparent yet. It is still buried and patiently waiting.

But there is no photo of the wedding day in July 1903. The sole photo to mark the day is again taken at Walton's Photographic Studio some weeks later. In it, Oliver wears a slightly wrinkled suit, and Brigid is in a summer frock and matching hat. Perhaps outside there was sun. Her fingers, hidden behind white cotton, lie still in her lap.

Morag closes the photo album and leans her head back against the sofa. This is not the photo that remains in Morag's mind. Morag remembers her sister's wedding day as one might remember a painting: a glimpse of something beautiful and terrible all caught up in one, and the memory of it flitting through her mind. A light and gauzy figure, her white hand up at her face, touching the edge of her mouth or her cheek. Standing in the wind of the Law, her skirt lifted by the breeze. Turning to look at the dark man, her face pulled into a sudden smile, flashing joy and something primal.

Brigid.

Her clavicle, that low hollow cave. That place where a finger may rest, where lips might graze.

Memory is unreliable but steadfast.

Morag looks again at the photo of Brigid and Oliver and feels something turn over within her. Oliver is a man who has had an easy life; he has floated through on his good looks, his quick wit and charm. His eyes glimmer. His hands are soft and manicured and delicate. The worst Morag has seen them suffer is inky smudges from his writing for the *Dundee Courier.* He is a good writer, she thinks. He is intelligent and persuasive. He is also handsome. She wishes she could feel goodwill for him, but her jealousy boils over when she imagines his easy, charmed life. Nothing like weaving at the Works, where your hands turn into a callused, bloody mess.

Morag thinks of her life with James and her eyes go small and cold. Thank God for her girls, for the clean scent of their skin and the softness of their hair beneath her hands. She is proud of herself, suddenly, for her belief in God, her nightly prayers. Words whispered in the dark. Her daughters—giggling now with their heads leaned in together—make James tolerable.

When Morag looks at Brigid's hand, gentle on Oliver's cheek, she longs to make another sort of bargain with God: a bargain to take James away and leave the three of them happy, but she is afraid to ask for too much. There must be a limit to these small, midnight agreements with God. Morag knows God's vengeance can be swift and harsh. He makes bridges collapse and leaves children orphaned.

If Morag closes her eyes, she can still smell the awful scent of sulphur.

The morning is still and unwavering, hanging around Morag and Brigid like an old woman's shawl. There is that same dark, dank smell Morag associates with the women who have held her to their weighty bulk, letting their compassionate sorrow spill over. Morag, only six years old, wants to hold herself strong against the steely morning, wants to let the light soothe them into believing everything is normal.

Morag pushes the kitchen curtains open. The little light that comes through is filtered, impure. She turns into the curve of the kitchen—this spot by the sink where her mother once stood, her hands wavering in water—and finds the gas lamps.

Brigid moans from the sitting room, "It's dark." She is only three, so small she can tuck herself in her white nightgown into the small chair, like a little, bent angel. She says again, "Morag, it's dark."

Morag searches for the matches, pressing against the kitchen countertop, running her hands over the teapot, wishing the grey day away. A rush of sulphur and then the area around Morag glows a faint, shimmering yellow. She touches the match to the lamp's wick and is engulfed in warm light. She carries the lamp to the parlour, sets it on the small round table. Brigid's smile appears in the new light. Morag feels a rush of joy, a sense of accomplishment. She has done it; for a moment, Brigid has smiled as though her mother is not gone. In the light, the room is less sombre, less weighted with sadness. Morag turns back to light the second lamp. She settles into burning glow and smells the sulphur again as she strikes the match.

Morag has her back turned, so she must imagine what happens next: Brigid sitting up in the chair, drawn by the light. She reaches toward the flame. She might think the flame is gentle, something to love. She reaches too close and the draping white sleeve of her nightgown is caught in flames.

There is a strange hypnotic beauty to fire, and this is why, Morag believes, it took Brigid so long to cry out. Then, only a stifled, "Oh."

Morag turns to see Brigid's arm—fingertips to elbow— engulfed in flame. A column of flame, a spiralling fire entranced by a child's white cotton nightgown. Morag rushes into the parlour with a damp tea towel. She looks at Brigid's face—startled by the fire, stunned into stillness—as she wraps the towel around her sister's arm. The flames extinguish and the girls are left with only the mingling scents of burned skin and smoke. Brigid begins to scream. Her screams fill the acrid flat as Morag runs next door to Mrs. O'Neill's. After that, Morag is hushed, held away from Brigid, turned away while Brigid's arm is covered with salve and gauze. Women from the tenements filter into the flat, petting Brigid's hair, suggesting eucalyptus or heavy medicinal creams.

Morag is just six years old when she sees her sister on fire. She is almost seven when she goes with her Aunt Elspeth to buy Brigid a pair of white gloves. Brigid puts them on solemnly, covering up her scars. A small smile, a quick flash of solace. As if it might be a wish.

Every year, Brigid has a new pair of gloves. Her hands are never seen. Only the whiteness of the gloves, startling in their brilliance.

Everything changed in the moments after Morag's mother plunged into the Tay and left them all in a sad state with their father, Niall, who slowly understood that he could not care for the two small girls. After Brigid was deceived by the beauty of flame. Shuffled from one house to another, tucked tight into beds with other children and their similar scraped knees, Morag and Brigid become like gypsies, less than that even. They had been unwanted, forgotten, something left out in the rain to ruin.

Morag was not comfortable with the constant change. She envied Brigid's ease with new people, her chameleon nature. Each time they moved—aunties or friends or relatives having cited money troubles or illness as reasons for why the girls had to go—Brigid evolved. A continual moth into a butterfly.

Brigid had an uncanny knack for understanding what other people wanted her to be: a lovely, shining child to observe like a fine painting or a jewel. *Pleasant. Beautiful. Cunning.* Morag was never much good at being anything other than herself: solemn, unhappy, grieving for big and small losses. She missed her mother desperately; she missed the house they had all shared; she missed the sudden yellow-grey rays of light through high clouds streaming in through their mother's kitchen window. The threat of them bursting, exploding high above.

Morag busied herself everywhere they were moved, dutifully putting the wash out to dry or stirring large pots of stew, while Brigid played with someone else's favourite doll. They never stayed anywhere long enough for people to see Brigid tarnish; she saved her mean, lacklustre side for Morag alone. She pinched Morag's arm when Morag would not share a sweet with her, tried to pull their dolls' heads off, tore Morag's favourite frock. The one with the burgundy edging, far more lovely than anything else Morag had known. She felt pretty in it, pretty for the first time in her young life, the moment cut short by Brigid's surprisingly strong hands.

Morag learned her sister and her complicated moods better than anyone else; she could tell Brigid was angry when her eyes became a blue-black, darker than the depths of the North Sea. Morag learned from Brigid how to avoid people's foul moods, their petty annoyances, and float by like an unattached kite.

Once they were old enough to no longer be called *girls,* Morag and Brigid were bundled up, their things packed into worn trunks, and sent back to their father. Morag remembers the sight of her father's small body in the door frame of the cottage. He had shrunk, she was sure, and turned a strange ashy shade. He smiled at them with crooked, brown teeth and old eyes. Surely he wasn't that old; he had been young when they had left.

But that was fourteen years ago.

When Niall had come to visit over those fourteen years, he sometimes brought with him rock candy even when they were too old for it, and sat with them in stale, uncomfortable rooms. They had behaved well, polite as strangers, and drank cups of tea, the darkening of which marked the passing of years from mostly milk to a dark, deep brown. Morag kept her eyes on the bottom of her teacup as Brigid told Niall about her friends, her teachers at school, the kind minister at church. Niall had visited them in Perth, in Kirriemuir, in Carnoustie, in Glamis. Learning the countryside of eastern Scotland. He had seemed uncomfortable, uncertain of what to say to them or how to speak of anything but his absence and their mother. Conversations disintegrated into his teary grief for his dead wife. Morag handed him handkerchiefs, surprised each time at the unfurling of his heart, while Brigid busied herself with something out the window, perhaps someone on the street or the rain.

Niall had kept a room for them with a bed and a chest of drawers. There was a window above the bed, and out and beyond, a willow tree. It bent and blew in the slight wind, tapping the glass with a sound like tutting tongues.

"It's not much," Niall said.

It was more than Morag could have expected, the familiarity of the same window and sight of a tree each morning, but she did not know how to say this to her father. "It's grand," Morag reassured him, trying to make this new rawness between them more bearable.

At sunset, the sky had seemed purple, mauves settling into blue and back again. Morag stood at the window, admiring the sky outside and the deep roots of the tree below.

Morag pulled the curtains tight and settled into bed next to Brigid. She watched her sister's small body rise and fall steadily beneath her crisp white nightgown. Morag leaned closer to Brigid to breathe in the sharp, clean scent of her sister. The room smelled of Niall, smoky and musty, bereft of women for all those years.

The next morning, Morag set about changing the house: she washed and dried every pot, pan and dinner plate; she scrubbed and scoured every surface until the dull gleam of Niall's years alone faded away; she opened windows and let the afternoon air in. She breathed in deeply, feeling spring and Dundee all coming back into her.

As she cleaned, Morag found photos of her mother, old and creased, scattered about the house. Some were under Niall's mattress, some in the bureau drawers, others in plain view on the kitchen table. She had never realized there were so many photos, that Niall had needed to hold on to the image of her so badly. She could see some of the oily prints left by his thumb and forefinger, and could smell his smoke on them. He must have sat in this chair by the window, or there in front of the fire, smoking his pipe and gazing at the pictures on his lap like shy gifts.

That night, Morag sat with Niall in the living room and listened as he talked about the first moment when he saw her mother.

"It was a summer picnic in the Ferry. She was wearing a white hat, I remember, and she held a glass of lemonade."

Morag felt as if she were intruding on something intimate.

"I asked her her name, and when she said Davina, I thought it was a song."

Niall's eyes were bright and alert, unfazed by the late hour or the many glasses of whisky he had consumed. He leaned his head down and wept, and this embarrassed Morag. She could not put her arms around him, and she did not know how to console him. She had learned years ago how to bundle and pack away her own grief, and was shocked at the intensity of Niall's feelings. As if fourteen years had not passed at all.

"It's all right, Father." Morag tried to make her voice sound convincing. She pleaded with him to stop, to go to bed, to forget for just a little while.

Morag sat up alone with Niall and watched the night slip into the morning. Pale blue skies crept in through the windows, settling into the room. Niall finally fell asleep, exhausted, and Morag laid a quilt across him.

When she crawled into bed, Morag looked out at her tree, its leafy greenness against the bands of blue sky, and curled down next to Brigid. Brigid stirred only slightly, still drifting listlessly, perhaps dreaming.

⁓

Niall used to talk about his dream of becoming a farmer: him and the girls living on land out near Arbroath. The long, vivid fields of golden rapeseed. The heavy weight of a long day's work, his body aching but satisfied from working his own land. The evening beacon of the lit windows of the farmhouse: Morag hanging laundry on the line, Brigid setting out steaming plates of potatoes, carrots and thick slabs of beef, all collected from their land. Niall imagined himself healthy and proud on the porch of the farmhouse, successful in his land and his daughters.

Niall worked his whole life as an ironsmith. The closest

he came to the lush life of a farmer was the vegetable patch he planted in the courtyard of their building. Lettuce, potatoes and carrots, in the summer, red and black berries. Tended lovingly with his sore hands, even when they shook. Morag watched as he became unable to even hold his teacup steady; she watched as his eyes turned dull from shame. Couldn't button his own clothes, never mind work the day in his shack, hammering and shaping the pipe. By then, Morag had become accustomed to his weeping fits, his lapses of memory, his hot fury at his own useless body. Morag learned his body in a way that saddened her; he was the first man she saw naked. He was thin, shrivelled and prone when she sponged his body. He turned his head away, unable to meet her eyes.

"Right then," she said as she folded a towel around him, patting him dry as she went. It was her relentless precision, her inscrutable efficiency that made the difference; she was as direct as a hardened nurse, working on an anonymous patient. "Come on, Dad." She lifted him from the bed, the astonishing weight of his torso against her hands. She tucked him into a shirt, her fingers working quickly up the long row of buttons. Stealthily. The pants were more difficult, often a challenge; bending his legs into the columns of trousers, tugging and pulling and fastening the trousers as quickly as she could. The buttons there were the worst, the soft slack of his penis behind the fabric. *Quickly.*

While Morag scrubbed her hands of any traces of Niall's body, Brigid sat in the cool bedroom staring out the window searching for something else, something less horrifying than Morag's hands roaming over Niall. In her hands—hands as

innocent of an old man's body, as of the grit inside a pot—
Brigid held one of her plain frocks. She added flowers, edges
of lace to cuffs and collars. She adorned herself while Morag
washed their father's body. Brigid sewed tiny flowers while
Morag fed Niall. He could no longer hold his own spoon
without his whole body shaking.

There would be no harvests to crop.

Once, he had been infinitely stronger. The cords in his
wrists had been tough as rope, just as thick, the remnants of
a lifetime of work. Morag turned his wrists in her hands as
she fastened the buttons there. *I could snap these.* How
quickly the body turned on itself.

Morag was not surprised the morning she came in to
find Niall dead. He had been sleeping in the alcove of the
kitchen since she and Brigid had moved in; he claimed he
liked the heat, the comforting odours of a kitchen. Niall
would have drifted off to sleep dreaming of boiled potatoes,
mushy peas, the fatty ends of tough meat.

"He's gone," she said to Brigid. She nudged Brigid from
sleep, and was careful to hold her face still when she spoke.
Morag had learned how to face death: clean like a freshly
washed windowpane. That clear and blameless.

Morag prepared the body wordlessly. Brigid cried all
afternoon and kept to her bed. Always dramatic, always
sensitive, always leaving the messy bits to Morag.

Morag got a job at the Bowbridge Works shortly after
Niall's death. Brigid made some money from odd jobs as a
seamstress, but she was too slow, too particular to really
make a success of it. Brigid with her ridiculous lace and
flowers when they needed money for the gas meter.

Years later, Morag will not often let her mind travel back to the years before her mother sank into the Tay. Instead, she thinks about the quiet of a house in a field, where her sister once sewed roses onto the collar of Morag's frock.

Unanswered Prayers

WHILE SHE IS PREGNANT with Imogen—with the tiny thing in her womb that will become Imogen—Brigid cries incessantly. And when she is not crying, she craves travel. Any kind. Riding around Dundee in a tramcar. Going to Broughty Ferry for the day. This is why, one afternoon, six-year-old Caro and five-year-old Wallis are bundled up and told they are going to Reekie Linn Falls.

The Falls. Nothing falls there, Caro thinks, the water only tumbles down the crest to reach the stream.

"Why do we have to go?" Caro asks her mother.

"Your auntie wants the Falls. Button your coat."

Brigid's tiny body has expanded; she walks slowly with the weight. Each footstep more determined than the last. Caro holds her hand, happy that Brigid is momentarily not crying. Caro thinks there must be a limit to tears, a moment when your body decides it has given enough. But Brigid's seem to be limitless.

Caro squeezes Brigid's hand as they walk across the small bridge toward the Falls. The bridge is ancient with its greens and browns and memories of moss. Caro slows a bit, peering down into the water below.

"Any trolls?" Brigid's voice is as crisp and clear as the water. Caro smiles. "No."

"Banshees?"

"No." Caro feels the beginnings of laughter somewhere in her stomach. Slowly spreading.

"Leprechauns, then?"

Caro does not answer; she is consumed with giggles. She loves Brigid like this: easy and serene and teasing. Brigid, who is held away from all of them by her otherworldliness. Caro looks up at Brigid and sees the kind of woman that she wishes she might one day become: lovely and golden and floating above them all. Caro waits for Brigid's light voice again, tries to think of more monsters or ghouls, but Brigid is tugging at her hand, bored already with the notion of demons.

Ahead, Morag and Wallis ease up the incline toward the crown of the Falls. Wallis has pressed her hands on her ears to block the rushing sound of the water. Brigid and Caro trail behind, still engulfed by the silence in the fields around the Falls.

Caro points to a solitary farmhouse. "Who do you suppose lives there?"

Brigid's gift is the magic of things that Morag calls nonsense. The tall tales, pretend, lies, anything make-believe that Caro loves, perfectly and unashamedly.

"That one," Brigid says above the new shushing of the water around them, "that one belongs to a lovely young woman and her awful, awful father."

"Why is he so awful?"

"He wants her to marry the old farmer in that house." Brigid points to a farmhouse farther out than the first. Small and squat and brown, some natural shade of brown found in sticks and earth. The door painted a whimsical yellow.

"Why?"

"So he can have all this land." Brigid squeezes Caro's hand confidentially. "Men always want land and *things*. Property and ploughing. But don't worry, she's been praying, right on this bridge, for her true love to come and save her from it all."

Caro can almost see the girl, just after dusk, standing on the centre of the bridge, praying and praying. Her hands silvery in the moonlight. "Will he come?"

Brigid's answer will stay with Caro for years to come. "Of course. He always does."

"Is Oliver your true love?"

Brigid's smile breaks into a wide, thick grin, eclipsing her face. She lights up. "I think so."

"Come on, hens." Morag is at the crown of the crest, cupping her hands around her mouth to call down to them. "We're waiting."

Caro thinks her mother is always waiting. Not doing, but waiting for them, for someone, for anyone.

Brigid and Caro move up the incline, past the deep green thickets of trees, and the sound of water overtakes them. It's like something unleashed, this great fury.

"It's lovely." Brigid rests against a tree, closing her eyes. Caro watches, waits for Brigid to open her eyes again. And waits.

"Can we go to the edge?" Wallis hollers to Morag. Her ears are still hidden by her hands. Morag tugs a hand free and says, "Yes. But with your sister."

Caro is still staring up at Brigid's peaceful face. "Do I have to?"

"Yes." Morag's hard voice against the trees.

Caro leads Wallis forward over loose greenery toward the edge of the crest. From here, she can see straight down to where the water churns into the stream. The water is a cold, bubbling grey-white. Foam explodes and then quiets again, searching out a home farther downstream.

"Look," Wallis yells.

Caro turns and, with one swift motion, tugs Wallis's hands free from her ears. "Oh, stop it."

Wallis puts her hands back on her ears.

"Don't jump." Brigid's stomach brushes lightly against Caro's back. Morag and Brigid stand behind them, staring down into the water. There is stillness, their bodies patient and overwhelmed by the sound of the Falls.

Caro holds her arms up and feigns a leap. Anything to break this moment.

"Terrible," Brigid says. She peers over Caro and down. Stares into the frothing water. "But it would be easy, wouldn't it?"

"It would have to be a big jump," Caro says.

"Mmm."

"It would hurt," Caro says. She ponders Brigid's face, her intent profile in the afternoon light.

"It's supposed to," Brigid murmurs.

"Enough of that," Morag says. "You're being morbid." She moves away, tugging Wallis's arm in the process. Wallis follows dutifully behind her mother, her hands deafening her to the water and their voices. Caro thinks that

Wallis misses everything with her back turned and her ears covered.

Brigid is still at the edge of the crest.

"Auntie Brigid?" Caro's voice is smaller than she intends. Brigid looks so strange like that, one hand on her stomach as she stares and stares at the water below.

"Brigid?" Caro is aware that she is witnessing something, but she can't say what. *Water, water everywhere.*

Her face has gone all milky. There is a small motion, Brigid's foot just a few inches forward. Caro turns in sudden desperation to her mother, who has stopped and stands a few yards away, watching. Waiting.

"Brigid." Morag's voice is sharp. Brigid snaps her head up to look at Morag.

"I was imagining Ophelia," Brigid offers.

Caro walks back with Brigid, down the incline, past the farmhouses, over the banshee bridge, wondering who Ophelia is. She waits for Brigid to speak, but she is silent now, with her hand on the mass of her stomach.

Rosemary Hennessey is Wallis's first real friend. Something of Wallis's to have alone, something for which she can be wholly selfish and unapologetic. The Hennesseys live across the close behind Wallis, near enough that the girls can move seamlessly between the two flats. Sometimes they meet halfway, in the common courtyard, and pretend to be ancient princesses. Rosemary speaks in Irish Gaelic and pretends to be Guinevere, and Wallis makes up words she thinks might sound like Scots Gaelic and pretends to be William Wallace's doomed wife.

Rosemary is a great wealth of all things ancient and fabulous to Wallis. Camelot. Avalon. Mysterious, magical beings that once roamed Ireland. Tristan and Isolde. St. Brigid. (This makes Wallis believe that Brigid must be a saint as well, with her forsaken hands and spotless, white gloves.) Rosemary was born in Ireland but later came to Scotland with her mum and dad and four brothers. They came over the Irish Sea where, Rosemary said, her mother was ill every single day and by the time they reached the port in Troon, so happy to see land that she dropped to her knees and thanked God. Rosemary re-enacted this to Wallis one afternoon, her hands flying from her head to her chest and both shoulders. The flight of a small bird. Something that elegant and full of momentary silent grace.

"She prayed to St. Christopher every day," Rosemary says. She says it in an excitable, breathless manner, and Wallis understands she is being let into something precious to Rosemary.

"Up you come for your tea, Rosemary," Mrs. Hennessey calls from her open window. It's a bright day and her face is whitened against the sun. "Come up too if you like, Wallis."

Wallis follows Rosemary across the courtyard and up the back steps to the flat. Wallis loves the Hennessey flat: there is a cross on the wall; a big, dark painting of Jesus with a holy glow; a three-foot statue of Mary, looking serene and docile in blue robes; a small bowl of holy water at the front door. As Rosemary enters or leaves the flat, she dips her fingers into the holy water and crosses herself. Wallis is a little bit in love with the statue, with the blue folds of Mary's robe and, especially, the slight smile on her lips. Second only to the statue is Mrs. Hennessey. Mrs. Hennessey is thin and pale and always smoking. She laughs often, tosses her dark hair and kisses Mr. Hennessy full on the mouth when he comes home from the harbour. Wallis loves to listen to her talk, to the rise and fall of language within her mouth.

It's quiet with Mr. Hennessey gone off to work, and the boys—all older than Wallis and Rosemary—at school. They will not go to the French Commercial, but to Domestic. The Hennesseys need the boys to begin working as soon as possible. Padraig, Michael, Sean and Mark will all go to the harbour or the Works, at least. Wallis thinks it is terrible that Paddy will not be able to stay in school longer, that his hands will soon become callused and stained with fish blood like his father's.

Some days, Wallis watches from across Hilltown as the Hennesseys walk toward their church, watches the strict lines of their spines. She watches Paddy march down Ann Street and then up the steps into St. Mary's Forebank. He disappears through the doors and she has to imagine him placing his finger into cool holy water and crossing himself.

Rosemary Hennessey wants to be a nun when she grows up, and for this Wallis envies her. There is nothing so perfect, so deliberate and selfless, to Wallis, as the decorative life of Rosemary and the Roman Catholic Church, or the lives of nuns, austere and crisp in their wimples and robes. Mr. Hennessey also wants Rosemary to be a nun, but Mrs. Hennessey will have none of it. Wallis longs to volunteer to take Rosemary's place.

Mrs. Hennessey gives them both cups of tea laden with milk and slabs of bread covered in margarine. Wallis traces her finger through it and it leaves a thick, deep line.

"After our tea we can play the Great Hunger," Rosemary says.

"What's the Great Hunger?"

"The Famine," Rosemary says with a dismissive twist of her hand. "You see, it wasn't really a famine—there were loads of other things to eat, just not the potato. The *Hunger.*"

Paddy says, "What a show-off."

Rosemary turns to look at him, bent over a schoolbook at the tiny table. "Away with you," she says.

Wallis puts her tongue on the margarine for the thrill: sweet, heavy. She licks. She wants to ask Paddy more about it, feels certain that he would know more, but feels her stomach clench and quiver at the thought. Wallis has only heard about the Great Hunger from Rosemary and school. She knows it happened in 1847, and that people died or left Ireland all together, but other than that, it is a silent movie in her head. People walking about dazed, thin, moaning. It all seems very tragic and terrible to Wallis. She balks at the notion of turning it into a game.

"It's not something to *play,*" Paddy says.

"Don't be so serious, Paddy. We're just pretending."

Wallis watches Paddy shake his head, then push his hair from his eye. Before she really intends to, she says, "Can you tell me about Ireland?"

Paddy looks at her, perhaps considering if she is being sincere. He tilts his head to the side a little, and she sees his gaze relax. "It's lovely," he says. "Our flat had a big window and we could see out to the Liffey. Our church was across the street and Father Greeley used to give us sweets after Mass." He smiles at Wallis and she feels herself lurch a little. She thinks, *One day I will see that.* She looks down at her bread and puts her finger in the cleft of margarine. Paddy says, "Once we went out to the country with my gran."

"Hush, Paddy," Rosemary interrupts. "We're playing now."

"Oh, Rosemary," Mrs. Hennessey sighs. She is standing at the window with her hand at the back of her neck. She might be waiting for someone to come up the road, or she might be wishing herself down the road. Either way, she sounds weary when she speaks her daughter's name. "Must you be so morbid?"

"Don't worry," Rosemary says. "I won't be the one to die. Wallis will die, won't you, Wallis?"

Wallis's attention is turned to Mrs. Hennessey; she is waiting for Mrs. Hennessey to turn and look at her, perhaps to refill her cup with tea and milk. Mrs. Hennessey is beautiful and delicate, with the lovely pallor and disposition of someone patiently waiting for tragedy. She is also often sad, which, to Wallis, makes her even more lovely.

Wallis nods, eager for a shy look from Mrs. Hennessey or a glance of pure pleasure from Rosemary. She does not dare to look at Paddy; instead, Wallis volunteers herself to be murdered.

"Rosemary." Mrs. Hennessey's voice is cool, final. Rosemary rumples a bit and then brightens.

"We can play the Howff then."

This, Wallis is familiar with. No one will have to die, but there is the lingering question of who will be the landowner—

one of the Greyfriar Monks who oversee their gardens—and who will be Mary. Of course, Rosemary is Catholic like Mary, Queen of Scots, but Wallis was born in Scotland. Wallis knows, even at seven, that religion will win out over geography.

"I'll be Mary," Rosemary says.

Wallis's hopes of rising in ranks from the poor dead and the dull monks are dashed. She says, "Right."

For the rest of the afternoon, under the peaceful canopy of the Hennessey flat, Wallis moons about with a sheet wrapped around her, and Rosemary wears her mother's jewellery and pronounces, "These shall be burial grounds."

Wallis crosses the courtyard and arrives home in time for dinner. James is asleep in the tapestry chair, his mouth slack and pink. Morag is busy heating a meat pie and a kettle of tea on the gas ring. Morag turns at the sound of Wallis with her hands full of the silver gleam of cutlery. Morag does not like it when Wallis goes to the Hennesseys, though Wallis cannot say why. Her mother turns cold and stiff when Mrs. Hennessey comes around, though Mrs. Hennessey is always kind and laughing.

"We played Hunger and the Howff," Wallis offers.

"The Hunger?"

"Yes, I was supposed to die because of the blight, but Mrs. Hennessey wouldn't let us. So then Rosemary was Mary Queen of Scots and I was the poor Greyfriars monk who lost my garden."

"And what would you know about the Hunger?"

"Rosemary told me about it. How all the poor Irish families were hungry and sick and died because no one helped them when the potatoes got the blight."

Morag shakes her head and lets the kettle whistle whine into the room. James stirs in his chair. His eyes are open, watching Wallis.

"The what?" he says.

"She was playing with Rosemary Hennessey," Morag says. "She knows all about the Famine now, and our Queen Mary."

"Can you not find friends other than those bloody Hennesseys? You'll be praying to Mary and crying for the Pope if they have any say in it."

Wallis does not like when her father speaks like this, as if there is something hot on his tongue and he is trying to spit it out.

"Good Catholics with all five children and nowhere to put them. Mister always off in the pub with a full pint while his children eat nothing but bread."

"Do you see him there?" Wallis asks innocently.

Wallis, until now, has managed to escape her father's temper. She feels his hand hard at the side of her head, and her ears ring. "I'm not a bloody Hennessey," he says.

Wallis does not know it then—she does not know anything except the loud clanging in her head and the throb across her skull and ear—but this has been her first lesson in politics and religion. A different sort of history lesson, but valuable nonetheless.

Where Wallis learns about politics, Caro understands the surprise of a fist reflected in a spoon. Caro believes she is the first person to pray for her father's death.

"Mush," she said as potato billowed through the metal spikes of her fork.

"What was that?" James's hard voice. A spike in the room.

Caro felt his anger in the tone of his voice. A voice something like the bummer that called Morag to work in the morning: demanding, unrelenting, making you hurry just a bit more.

"Nothing."

"What did you say?"

"Leave her be," Morag said. She sat across from Caro and her plate of mush and abandoned cutlery.

"Smart mouth on her," James said. He pushed his plate away and looked at Caro. Caro watched his grey eyes squint small and then relax. He squinted again and Caro looked to Morag, who was watching James's stillness.

The clock on the mantel ticked. There was taut silence in the room; Caro thought she could hear neighbours through the walls. She suddenly wanted noise. Her fork on the plate. Morag's voice. Anything.

"Well, then." Caro closed her eyes. James's voice was hard, full of the contortion of false patience, a startling blue-orange behind eyes. A flame too close.

Caro did not see her father raise his hand, pull back and then strike her full across the face. But she felt it. She felt it under her skin and through to her bones. Her cheekbone seemed to shatter with his single punctuated blow. She opened her eyes slowly, painfully, as if somehow her eyes had been welded shut with the heat of his hand.

"Anything else smart to say?"

Morag was still and pale. Caro looked to her, hoped for her voice in the room, her arms suddenly around her.

Instead, there was stillness. Morag sitting still with her hands in her lap. James staring at Caro.

"No," Caro mumbled.

"What was that?"

"No," she repeated. "No, Father."

James went back to his plate of potatoes and peas. Mush, Caro thought, even if she could not say it aloud again.

James methodically chewed and swallowed in the horrible manner he had. A man so patient he could wait, weighing the time between the moment when he considered striking you and when his hand made contact.

"Off you go, hen," Morag said and took Caro's plate of peas and potato.

Caro flopped on the bed—still smelling of sleep, of Wallis's hair on the pillow—and squeezed her eyes closed. Held them closed so tight that there was pain just there, just behind her eyelids. She whispered, "I hate him. I hate him. Please take him away."

She touched her cheek and knew that there would be a bruise, something turning from purple to blue to yellow and back. She was tired of her father's mean eyes, his demanding presence, his fists. Life would be so much better—she would be safe from his rage, her mother might smile—if James was simply gone. *Gone.* A prayer for a swift excising. A prayer close to death.

⁓

Wallis falls in love first with Rosemary, then with Mrs. Hennessey and her dark, tragic beauty, her flagrant faith and altars, and lastly with Padraig. Padraig—*Paddy*—is Rosemary's eldest brother, four years older than Wallis, with freckles across the bridge of his nose and a hard slant to his eyes. Wallis falls in love at seven with the uncompromising nature of an adult. Small and round and soft but with the flinty heart of an ancient woman.

Wallis memorizes small pieces of Paddy's life: his laugh as it comes across the close; the squint of his eyes when he is angry; the way his hands make themselves busy during even silent moments. A young boy with restless hands.

In the early morning, Wallis watches from the bedroom window as Paddy crosses the close. There is something predatory about his movements; she thinks he is stalking the morning. He is fierce for a boy of eleven. Wallis watches him and thinks she can see, in his face, what he might be like in fifteen years. A man of angles and fierce reactions. Unpredictable. A man who might walk out of your house in the morning and never return.

From above, she watches the top of his head as he passes. The soft brown hair parted on the left, that lovely white patch of scalp showing through.

Only the afternoon before, Wallis had crouched in the courtyard with Rosemary, their fingers quick and busy with glossy marbles. They did not know how to play properly; instead, they rolled the globes between them, giggling at the cool shock when they bumped against their bare knees. Other children skipped across the close; some older boys stood in a corner with a stick and a grimy ball. Rosemary rolled a perfect blue globe toward Wallis as Paddy appeared at her side. There were the sounds of the other children's voices, the girls' high squeals and the boys' low laughs, but Wallis was acutely aware that Paddy stood watching as she pushed a pale green marble across to Rosemary.

"That's not how you play."

Wallis felt her cheeks flush and redden with shame. He would think her childish, foolish.

Rosemary said, "Yes, it is. You don't know."

Paddy squatted down between them. "You're daft. That's not the way to play marbles." He took a shimmering black marble from Wallis's pile, his hand briefly brushing against hers. She looked down at her hand, as if she might be able to see the imprint of his fingers just there.

Paddy drew a faint circle in the dirt, then arranged their marbles within it. He shook Wallis's black marble in his hand and then rolled it forward. It bumped up against Rosemary's pale blue marble, then the pale green one, and they rolled outside of the border of the circle.

"There," Paddy said. "That's how you play taw." He bent to grab the blue and green marbles, and Wallis stared at the pale line in his dark hair. Paddy handed Wallis the two marbles. "These are yours now."

Wallis stared at the marbles in her hand. They were warm, still, from Paddy's palm. She closed her fingers over them.

"Ach, you're not letting a mick teach you, are you?"

Three older boys stood behind Paddy; Wallis recognized her neighbour Ian Lyon, passing the dirty ball between his hands. The blond boy laughed and the other, the one who had spoken to her, leaned on the stick. Wallis swallowed.

Paddy turned around. "Leave her alone. They're just playing."

The boy with the stick smiled. "And so are we." He took a step closer to Paddy.

Rosemary said, "Paddy?"

The boy with the stick said, "Now surely you can play with someone else, lass. There's better than the likes of them."

Wallis looked at the boy, then to Ian Lyon, who quickly looked at the ground beneath him. Wallis thought, Coward.

"She can play with whoever she likes." Paddy stared evenly at the boy. His hands had closed into fists as he clenched and unclenched them. "Now leave them be."

The boy with the stick looked back to his friends; Ian Lyon was still staring at the ground and the blond boy stared at Paddy's fists. "Come on, lads," the boy said, scraping the stick against the dirt. "We've better things to do than this."

Wallis watched the three boys walk away, back the way they had come, and resume their game. They hit the ball against the side of the tenement building, and the sound of it echoed through the close. Paddy watched them for a moment, then turned back to the girls. Wallis noticed his hands relaxing, his body stiff and straight.

"Don't let them bother you," he said before he walked away. Long, even strides. The shattering sound of the ball against the stone.

Rosemary said, "Come on, Wallis. Let's play our game again." She rubbed out the circle from the dirt and rolled a marble toward Wallis's exposed knee.

Imogen is born in June 1904. Brigid screams and cries and whimpers and then stays in bed for days after Imogen is finally pulled from her body by the midwife. Brigid is wan and lifeless, but it all seems worthwhile: Imogen is perfect, all pink and cream and bubbling with happiness. She is beautiful, like her mother, and this makes Morag worry even more. Beauty like this leads to desperation and disappointment. She says a quick prayer for Imogen, and gets on with waiting for something to happen.

The Knowledge of Letters

1906 IS A YEAR of whimpers. The year brings rain and chills, a few moments of sunlight, the hours of waiting and wishing, until a cold October day when Mrs. Hennessey puts her head in the gas stove. Simple and decisive: five small children are left motherless. They still have a father, of course, but that is little reassurance to anyone. What would Charlie Hennessey know about raising five children? Until they can take the boat back across to Ireland and their granny, the other women in the tenements help, taking the children in for meals and walking them down to the baths once a week. This will be perfect practice for other orphans to come.

After the Hennesseys leave, Wallis stares out the window facing the close searching for Paddy. Listens for Rosemary's laugh, for Mrs. Hennessey's voice, clear and high like a singsong, between the tenements. Wallis is set adrift in silence.

She watches another family move into the Hennessey place. Stands at the opposite end of the hall and watches as they pass a chair, small teacups, a mantel clock, through the doorway. All these items disappear into the cavern of the Hennessey flat. Wallis aches to step inside and search the walls for traces of them: a nail hook, the smatter of kitchen grease, small stains from feet on the carpet. The shadow of the Bible with its burgundy leather on the side table.

Wallis dreams of Mrs. Hennessey and her terrible, beautiful face forever frozen still. A baroque painting, the colours muddied. She wishes she could see her as she wants to remember her: standing in the flat, holding the curtain back to watch the road. Something wistful in her expression, as if all her future, all her possibility lay in that road.

Then, her head turned away. The curtain dropped. The sound of her son's voice. The moment broken.

Months after they leave, the first letter comes from Rosemary. Stiff, starched cream-coloured paper. Wallis reads it with trembling hands.

December 11, 1906

Dear Wallis,

We have moved in with my granny, who says that we
make an awful noise and need to start minding her. I try
to be good, but the boys do not. Paddy got sick on the
boat to come across because the water was very rocky . . .

After this, Wallis daydreams about the Irish Sea with new zeal. Promises herself to it like a sacrifice.

⌒

The countryside is dotted with ruins, crumbled places of worship, magnificent memories of vanished monarchs in sprawling castles. Wallis is nine the first time she sees

Arbroath Abbey. She feels something tighten and snap within her; there is something too perfect about the way it has crumbled, the way the roof has been lifted up and spirited away. It stands open to the elements now, lying bare and exposed in a manner that makes Wallis feel sudden shame; there is no privacy to the abbey, no corners in which to hide.

The abbey was built in 1178, set far up from the harbour, made solid and strong by bricks in every shade of red. This was where, Wallis knows, in 1320 Abbot Bernard de Linton drafted the "Declaration of Arbroath." She is proud of her diligence in history, her ability to remember things other people forget. De Linton's famous phrase, "as long as but a hundred of us remain alive, never will we on any conditions be brought under English rule," comes back to her in a rush.

Wallis stands in the centre of the west end of the nave, staring up at the clean, hard sheet of blue sky. She feels weightless, overwhelmed by it all, by the day and the blue sky, the sound of her mother's and sister's voices beyond the abbey. She thinks this is what saints must feel like. She wishes for Rosemary's rosary, for the cool feel of the onyx in her hand.

Wallis moves slowly around the interior of the nave, holding her hands to the chilled bricks. She wonders how many people have done this, how many people have found shelter and comfort here.

Wallis thinks of Mrs. Hennessey. She wonders if it is possible to love someone who is entirely separate from you, distanced from you by oceans and death. Even at nine, Wallis keeps her hopes private—her love of the Hennesseys, the rosary against her breastbone—and therefore does not allow herself to be disappointed.

She is not even wounded by James and his indifference, his sporadic nature. Wallis is the kind of child, and later will be the kind of woman, who happily takes what is left for her: the smallest slice of fruitcake, left moist and wrapped in a tea cloth, the shreds of a beautiful, sad mother's attention.

"Come on, then," Caro calls from the nave's gaping door. She has her hands on her almost-apparent hips. Caro will develop early and in a way that Wallis envies; Caro will be shaped like a winding road, while Wallis is plumper, curvier, in the way of older women, even at thirteen. The women in the tenements say she is beyond her years, that she has been here before, as if the shape of her body denotes wisdom.

Caro's dark hair shimmers in the afternoon sunlight. "We're going down to the harbour for smokies."

The idea of the smoked fish makes Wallis's mouth water. The tender flesh falling away like butter, the heavy-sweet taste of the smoking. Wallis follows Caro out of the abbey and down through Arbroath to the harbour. Morag and James walk behind, silent.

"Four smokies," Morag says to the man behind the counter when they arrive. She holds her hand out to James, who stares blankly at her. "James?"

"I've only enough for two," he says. He makes no move to search his pockets; Morag watches him coolly.

"I'm sorry," she apologizes to the man behind the counter. "Just two, for the girls." Within moments, Wallis and Caro hold the haddock in their hands, the smoky scent strong and familiar. They all walk down toward the water, to the small dock crammed tight with boats.

Everything about the afternoon is crisp and clean, pleasing to Wallis: the stretch of blue sky, unmarred by clouds; the fragrant, salty water so close; the sunlight on her arm, through her woollen coat; the smoked fish on her tongue.

Wallis and Caro walk along the sandy shoreline with their smokies. Ahead is the cliff, and the carved stone of St. Ninian's well coming out of its green side. The well where, it was said, St. Ninian baptized the people of Arbroath. No markers to tell you so, just the kind of omniscient knowledge of small cities. Often, Wallis has wished that they lived in Arbroath rather than Dundee; James could be a fisherman, lolling out in the middle of the sea on one of the painted boats, and Morag could certainly find work as a seamstress or a house servant. And then they would always be surrounded by the beauty of this city. They could be distanced from the grey smoke of Dundee's mills. Wallis would feel cleansed here, where she could walk up to the abbey and take solace in its crumbling remains. It brings her closer to the devotion she once felt in the Hennessey flat than the hardness, the strictness she finds in her home now.

Caro stops short of the well and stares out at the sea. She sighs as she bites off a piece of haddock, and Wallis thinks she looks unequivocally happy. Wallis reminds herself to be thankful for what she has. Many people have less, and many less than that even. Wallis tries to be thankful for this day, for Caro's pleasure as she stares out to the sea, for the smokie she holds between her hands. If only they could stay here in the sunlight, stay like this forever.

—

Caro watches the lighthouse that sits out in the middle of the sea. She thinks, Ralph the Rover. She remembers the story of the terrible pirate who stole the lighthouse bell, then washed up dead on the same rocky shore. Caro sighs and bites into her smoked fish. Men. Always stealing things that aren't theirs, mindless of consequences. Caro looks back to James, sitting silent and stony beside Morag. By now his pockets would be empty from too many trips to the pub, and their two smokies. She has yet to meet a man who is honest, who does not thieve and drink and disappoint. A man who enjoys women for more than their soft round bodies and steaming bowls of stew. She looks back to the lighthouse, and imagines the prone body of Ralph the Rover with a certain amount of glee. The quick fate of men.

By the time Imogen is five, she has decided that she loves Caro the best. Imogen can never tell when Caro lies, or when she is being truthful, which inspires Caro to make her stories even more extravagant. Caro is twelve and already an accomplished teller of tall tales. This is the one thing she can give to Imogen, this one link to Brigid.

"Paddy Hennessey is on the Mars because he shoved his mother poor mother in the stove."

"Really?" Imogen's eyes are wide, as she imagines the floating prison.

"No. His mother stuck her head in the oven."

"Really?"

"No."

In this way, Imogen can never be sure of the simplest things, like Mrs. Hennessey's death or her own parents' meeting.

"Your mum was sewing a dress for your dad's fiancée, but instead she stole him away."

"Really?"

"No. Your mum was a woman of ill repute, being an orphan and all, when your dad met her. He saved her."

"Really?"

"No. It was the other way round."

Imogen is the first person to fall in love with Caro. Acutely and accurately, able to list reasons why she is worthy of adoration. The smell of her dark hair, newly washed; the dip of her voice when she tells Imogen stories; the dusky shadow of her sharp chin against her pale neck.

Caro takes Imogen up to the Law to see the city, and is angry when Imogen falls and tears up her stockings and shins.

Between sobs and tears, "I didn't mean to."

"Brigid will be after me now. I can't take you anywhere. You are too little."

Imogen wipes at her damp face and straightens her bloodied stockings. She sets her face and says, "Show me something."

Caro turns Imogen to face the Tay Bridge. "That's where our granny died. That's where her ghost is."

"How did she die?"

"The bridge collapsed. She drowned."

"Oh." Imogen is sad, despite having never known her. Caro softens for this small, pale child. The lovely yellow ribbons in her hair, the careful curls at the ends.

"And that's why my mum had to take care of yours. They had no mother."

"Really?"

Caro nods solemnly. "She taught Brigid to sew. She took care of her for a long time."

"She doesn't any more?"

"No. Your dad is supposed to do that." Even when Caro says this, she knows it is not true. Brigid should be taking care of Imogen and Oliver, but Brigid is not the kind of woman who will ever be much good at caring for other people. Brigid is the kind of woman who needs to be sheltered and softened and consoled.

"Oh." Imogen is thoughtful. "Maybe I could take care of her."

"Can you cook?"

"No."

"Sew?"

"A little."

"Clean, at least?"

"No. But I could learn. You could teach me." Imogen is insistent. She has found, miraculously, the way to be important to her mother and her cousin: caring for Brigid, as if there had been a transformation and she had become the mother.

"No," Caro sighs, "I couldn't. I suppose you won't be much use to Brigid after all."

This comment, though meant in jest and in the joking

tone of Caro's saved solely for Imogen, will cut through Imogen, settle and stay like an unwelcome guest.

"Right then, useless one, let's go down to the harbour." Caro does not wait for Imogen's reply, merely begins walking away. She knows that Imogen will follow her in the same way that small animals are drawn to the scents of food and friendliness.

⁓

February 22, 1912

Dear Wallis,

Today I told Granny that I hate when she speaks to me in Gaelic, and she gave me a box in the ear. She says we must learn Gaelic and must not forget our culture before England took us over. She says it is a shame we aren't going to hedge schools, but why would I want to? I can't think of anything more dull . . .

These are the years before the War changed everything. Wallis opens the *Courier,* and images assault her: suffragettes being forcibly fed while imprisoned; the burning of buildings associated with politicians. Wallis reads that Dr. Elizabeth Smith, the wife of the minister at Calton Parish Church in Glasgow, was caught trying to burn down a west-end house. Telephone lines were cut. Arson attacks on unoccupied mansion houses. Events have been escalating in the past years: in July 1914, Rhoda Fleming jumped in the King's motor car and tried to smash his windows. The Gatty Marine Laboratory in St. Andrews and the Western Meeting

Club in Ayr were torched. Two women hid on the golf course at Lossiemouth to assault the Prime Minister. Wallis hoards these details and catalogues them.

There are few suffragette branches in industrial towns such as Dundee, and for that Wallis grieves. She longs for storefronts selling photos and pamphlets, women in large-brimmed hats and demure dresses demanding the right to vote. Women who might stand a bit taller together, eyes turning fiery and dark. Not just the women confined to illicit, evening meetings and whispered plans. Women whose mouths were always ready, always puckered as if they meant to be kissed instead of whispering directions for torching a home.

Wallis holds the open *Courier* to Caro. "Look," she breathes. The photo shows suffragettes at a storefront, huddled around a long, low table. Pickets and pamphlets surround them.

Wallis and Caro sit in the garden of the tenement yard. The sun touches their shoulders as Caro toys with the end of her long, dark braid. There is a pale green ribbon at the end, securing the plait. Caro peers at the photo.

"Why don't they smile?"

"It's serious."

Caro shrugs. "They would look more lovely if they smiled."

Wallis holds the paper on her lap. This is her own small treasure, a Sunday afternoon with the *Courier* across her knees. Wallis is voracious; she wants to know everything about these women who march in streets and set fire to houses. When the Jute and Flax Workers Union was established in 1906, seven-year-old Wallis had urged Morag to join. The idea of a union just for them; the women of the jute mills joining together to demand something closer to equality. Wallis feels like she grows taller, hardens, when she thinks about it.

Now, her attention and devotion has been sliced in two, to allow in the suffragettes. Even the word seems thick and exotic to her. She wishes she were older so that she might see her own face in the grainy photo. She imagines a white scarf around her neck, her hand at her chin. Meetings under the dark cover of night, as if there were something to be hidden, something to be ashamed of. Rocks thrown through storefronts, leaving a gaping wound as if a gunshot had gone through. Wallis would be proud to be in the photo with her face open and plain to the camera's flash. A moment caught: eyes tired from the late hour, bodies weary from the daily toils of work and then meetings. Restless souls in a restless time.

Wallis says, "I wish I was there." She stares at the picture of the suffragettes, as if she might be able to wish herself into it.

"Oh, Wallis," Caro sighs. "You're not meant for that kind of thing."

Brigid's Face

BRIGID IS CURLED into Oliver's side of the bed. Her eyes are red; her cheeks are puffy; her hair is flat and tangled. She does not look beautiful, as Imogen is used to seeing her.

"Mum?"

Brigid groans and tucks into the bed. She pulls Oliver's pillow closer to her and buries her face in it. She breathes in again and again, her moans obscured by the pillow's weight.

"Mum?" The sound of her voice is tinny in the room, smaller than she means for it to be. "Mum? Mum?" This is the moment Imogen begins to lose her mother, when Imogen's voice is lost, when her mother is busy trying to breathe Oliver back into her.

Later, Imogen will be told that her father had left. That there had been a fight, a loud, messy scene, and then he had gone. Despite her attempts at eavesdropping, Imogen never finds out why her father left. It was an act of mystery, the type of thing other fathers did, but not her own. Her father is the Captain of Grand Adventures. He wasn't supposed to leave.

Once, in Murraygate, as Brigid was trying to decide between mincemeat and black pudding for dinner, Imogen asked why Oliver had gone. Brigid shifted slightly from one foot to the other. In those days she could no longer make the simplest decision. She shifted. Then Imogen asked the question again.

"He's gone," Brigid spat. Her eyes had turned hard, angry blue. Colder even than the North Sea, if that was possible. "He left us, don't forget that. He didn't just leave me, he left you, too." Brigid turned back to the butcher. "Mincemeat."

"Maybe he'll come back," Imogen offered. "He could."

"He won't," Brigid said through clenched teeth. "He doesn't want us."

She was a wounded animal, Imogen would later think, snapping at anything that came close.

Imogen started to cry at the slap of her mother's words, large, obvious tears in the middle of the butcher shop. The room stopped as she cried, all the customers still and staring. Brigid's eyes like saucers. Imogen could feel her mother's body, close, could feel the embarrassed heat coming from her.

"Stop it," Brigid whispered. "Stop it."

Imogen cried and the other women in the shop tutted their tongues.

"Stop it," Brigid said again. Imogen concentrated on the ache behind her eyes, the tightness in her head from unshed tears.

Brigid's hand came down squarely on Imogen's open mouth, trapping her sobs inside. Imogen squirmed and moaned. Brigid ushered Imogen out of the butcher shop, through Murraygate and up Hilltown like that, her hand clamped tight over Imogen's mouth.

She had left behind both the black pudding and the mincemeat; instead they had salty broth, which Imogen was sure contained some of her tears.

Brigid had married Oliver quickly, without much thought as to whether he would make much of a husband, or if she would be much of a wife. Oliver was charming, handsome and unpredictable. He took Brigid to Campbeltown just to look at the Irish Sea. He proposed after knowing her for only two months.

They had Imogen quickly, when they seemed oblivious to anything but themselves. When they were still bright, shiny and selfish. Imogen, everyone said, softened Oliver. No one spoke of Brigid.

Morag watched her sister with Imogen and saw what no one else would admit: hurt, unhappiness, jealousy. Morag watched it fester, boil, die away and start again over the next seven years. She had heard the stories of late-night arguments, saw scratches on Oliver's smooth face. She heard Oliver try to deny it all, pretend he hadn't made a mistake with Brigid. She watched them unravel like a torn hem.

Morag knows Oliver has left when she finds Imogen wide-eyed in the flat. Startled, like something caught.

"What is it, Imo?" Morag moves past her into the house. It smells of sleep, unwashed hair, skin. "Where's your mum?"

Imogen takes her to the bedroom, where Brigid is curled up on the bed. Her eyes are shut tight, but she mews at the sound of the door opening.

"Brigid?" Morag thinks: Oliver's finally done it. He's broken her. Then, she's sick. Paralyzed. "Imo, where's your dad?"

Imogen shrugs.

"How long has he been gone, dear?"

Imogen starts counting on her fingers. *One, two, three, four . . .*

"Right then." Morag has learned in Imogen's seven years to trust her about Oliver. She is his shadow; he adores her recklessly. Morag pulls the blankets from Brigid and lifts her into a sitting position on the bed. She looks like something long forgotten. Morag moves to the sink in the parlour and turns the cold water on full force. She holds her hand still under the stream until it's icy cold. She fills a jug with it and returns to the bedroom, arcing the water onto her sister's unresponsive body. She says, "You should be ashamed," and leaves Brigid like that, shivering and drowned looking, like something already dead.

Morag takes Imogen home with her. She tucks her into bed next to Caro, who curls up to the new warmth. Imogen falls asleep quickly, exhausted, and comforted by her cousin.

Two days later, Brigid comes to the flat looking bathed, though gaunt and pale. She smiles weakly at Morag and says, "Imogen?"

"She's fine. Come in."

Imogen runs to Brigid when she sees her. Morag watches them embrace, watches Imogen cling to her mother.

"Oliver?" Morag asks.

Brigid shakes her head. Imogen holds on, the white of her knuckles disappearing into the folds of her mother's coat.

Morag says, "That man will be the death of you." She watches, still, as Brigid strokes Imogen's hair absently, and Imogen settles into the crook of Brigid's body. It will all be different now, Morag thinks, now that Oliver has gone. There is no barrier between Brigid and Imogen, just this raw joining of those abandoned.

Caro never liked Oliver much, anyway. She is fourteen when he leaves Brigid, and by then she already knows enough to realize he is not the kind of man you hang your hopes on. He is good-looking and charming, of course, but beneath that Caro could see something restless, something shifting that rose to the surface. But Brigid, she thinks, looks at him like Wallis looks at clotted cream: as if the possibility of its sweetness is enough. She has even seen Brigid's scratches on Oliver, as if she were nothing more than a cat marking her territory.

Oliver took Wallis and Imogen and Caro to Broughty Ferry one summer before he left. It was during a hot spell when everything seemed hazy, unclear. For a long time after, Caro wondered if that explained it all.

People wilted all around them; no one was used to the heat, the brightness of the sun. Everyone staggered under the weight of it. Women leaned out tenement windows, but instead of gossiping they fanned themselves, hoped for a breeze. Morag kept the windows open, but the curtains shut so they had to guess who was hanging from their flats. Caro listened for voices, sighs even, convinced she would be able to recognize the women. She squeezed her eyes shut to concentrate.

She was trying to determine if it was Mrs. Sutton's or
Mrs. McCullough's voice when Oliver appeared with
Imogen. They were both smiling, unfazed by the heat and
the dim flat that smelled of sweat.

"Want to come to the beach?" Four-year-old Imogen
had her tiny bathing dress in her hand. It was blue and
white, with a ruffle.

The beach. All that hot sand; Caro would jump into the
crisp, blue water straightaway, not caring about ice cream
shops or her sister. She would let the water erase the heat of
the day, the tiny smudges she imagined it left on her skin.

"Can we?" Wallis asked Morag. Wallis with her big,
pleading eyes. Caro glared at her as she waited for Morag to
answer.

Please. Please.

Morag looked at Oliver. Let her eyes stay on him for a
moment too long. She sighed a little. "I suppose."

Wallis went into the bedroom with Caro. Morag spoke
to Oliver in the parlour, her voice tense.

"Mind them, then."

"Oh, aye."

"No, Oliver." Her voice hard. Shellacked. "Mind them.
I don't want to hear about anyone being lost, or nearly
drowned, or forgotten."

Morag said nothing about the beach or the trolley there,
or the long pier that stood up from the water. Morag had to
ruin it by assuming the day would be disastrous. Caro grit-
ted her teeth until her cheeks ached.

"They'll be fine, Morag," Oliver said in his easy voice.
"It will be a laugh."

Oliver had borrowed a car from someone, and they all piled in. Caro had been to the Ferry before, but it was different with Oliver, who let them run and swim out a bit. He watched from a rock on the beach, waving to them every so often. He was handsome with his hand raised to protect his eyes from the sun.

"Watch!" Imogen had discovered she could hold her breath and was now obsessed with going underwater. She still swam in the shallow bit, where she could stand if she wanted to. She came up quickly, cheeks puffed.

"That's lovely," Wallis said as she dog-paddled beside Imogen. Her hair was dry, piled on top of her head.

"That's nothing," Caro said. "Watch." She plunged herself underwater and treaded as she counted. She could see Wallis's pale legs kicking, her feet looking boneless at the tips. Imogen was standing, tired already from swimming. Caro poked her bony knee. Imogen squealed, muffled for Caro by the water, then laughed. Caro broke the water's surface.

"Do it again," Imogen said. Her wet braids had turned from pale blonde to a muddied brown. She sucked on the end of one absently.

"No. It's not the same again." Caro was already climbing out of the water, waiting for the delicious feeling of water evaporating from her skin. Being warmed again.

She scanned the beach for Oliver, for his dark hair, but saw nothing. Families. Children at the edge of the water. Women on beach chairs with their skirts pulled up, exposing pale shins. No Oliver.

Wallis and Imogen still played in the shallow water, splashing and shouting. Caro started down the shore, toward the pier. Her shadow stretched out beside her, dark and thin. She watched as it crossed children playing with pails, piling sand into small mountains, or fathers having their toes buried. No Oliver.

No Oliver ahead. No Oliver behind. No Oliver.

The shore became blurry as Caro felt her eyes fill. *Don't be so daft. It's just Oliver.* But everywhere there were families huddled, children calling to their fathers. No other children left alone.

Caro's mind raced. How would they get back to Dundee? They had no money. It was too far to walk. Caro felt her head swell, swoon with disastrous visions of being abandoned.

And then there he was; up the shore, crouching on the sand beside two women on beach chairs. One had pink shins turned up to the sun and the other had her legs curled under her as she spoke to Oliver. He laughed, showing his white teeth, and ran his hand though his hair. Caro watched the way it fell, one coil curling over his forehead.

She walked up the beach toward them, concentrating so hard on Oliver, she was sure he would burst.

"There you are."

Oliver turned at her voice. Hard, prickly, like Morag's.

"Here I am." He glanced at the girl beside him. She wasn't even pretty, Caro thought, nothing like Aunt Brigid. He looked back at Caro.

Caro was blank, unwilling to admit fear. "Imo," she said. "She wanted to show you . . . she can hold her breath."

"I've seen it. Yes, she can, can't she?" Oliver could see through her lie, she was sure, but he got up from the sand.

Brushed his hands on his shorts. He gave a small bow to the girl, which made her laugh.

Fool, Caro thought.

"It was grand," Oliver said. "Truly grand."

The girl blushed and nodded. "Yes." Her voice was breathy, almost lost in the roar of the ocean, in other voices littering the beach.

"Let's go watch Imo drown," Oliver said as he put his hand on Caro's shoulder. She moved away from his hand, from the grit of sand on his fingers, from the possibility that it might have touched the girl. That somehow he might pass that moment on to Caro and she would be responsible for it.

⌒

Morag and Brigid stand at the edge of the Law, the lip where it extends over the city. The Firth of Tay lies ahead, to the side, everywhere. And there, visible enough to make Morag's heart ache, suspend, wilt and then sigh, is the Tay Bridge. Her mother's true resting place, the grey-green depths of the Tay, stunned and stilted. Filled with witches' hair and buried men. Not the headstone simply detailed with her name, the dates of her birth and death. *Loving Wife and Mother.*

Brigid hugs herself against the wind. "I think Oliver might not come back," she says.

Morag hears her sister but does not respond. Brigid's voice moves and shifts like the wind, and cuts her sister cold.

"Did you hear me?" Brigid asks. "I said he might be gone for good."

"I heard you."

"Morag."

Morag turns to Brigid and her face is pale, stony and shocked into something stiff and unwavering. Brigid is already grieving him. "Why do you think he is gone?" Morag is weary. Brigid is too much for her.

"I just know."

"Brigid."

"I do. I just know."

"What about Imo? He wouldn't just leave her."

Brigid shrugs.

They look out at the city, so still and serene below them. It is 1911, and around them the world is changing. Women are marching for the right to vote. The Triangle Shirtwaist Fire kills 146 workers in New York. Suffragettes huddle in midnight meetings in rooms in Nethergate. But the city is the same, the grid of streets and tenements and the high stacks of mills and factories. A city under a blanket of smoke. This is what stays the same, what Morag can hold her hand over and claim as true. There are so few things that remained reliable. The city and her past and her sister at her side.

The wind nudges them closer together and nearer the edge. Brigid's blonde hair comes loose. A strand coming onto Morag's cheek so that she has to brush it away. Brigid confessing her worst fear. Standing on the lip of abandonment, testing it with her toe.

"I think he met someone."

"Why?"

"A woman *knows,* Morag. Wouldn't you?"

Morag doubts it. Then thinks, perhaps, if only by the relief James's absence would offer. A new empty space where his pipe once sat, lit and smouldering. "I don't know," she finally says.

Brigid sighs. She runs a hand over her hair. She is vulnerable in the faltering afternoon light with her tiny body and loose hair. She is pale, Morag thinks. Frail as a paper doll. "Have you been eating?"

"How can I eat when my husband is leaving me?" Brigid snaps.

He has already left you, Morag thinks. "You'll have dinner with us then." Morag knows not to dismiss her sister's fears straightaway. It is best to move around them, distract her. "We'll have a nice meat pie. Walk down to the snug later, perhaps." Morag moves away from the edge and back toward the walkway. Brigid stays, staring down and down.

"Brigid."

Brigid comes like something drawn limp from the sea.

On April 11, 1911, Wallis sits in the paisley chair and opens the *Courier* to see a photo of the suffragettes at a midnight gathering in Nethergate. Their stiff collars, elaborate hats, mouths set stony. She stares at the women until their faces blur; these women who even managed to push Churchill out when he came to Dundee. She tries to imagine their power, the fresh buzz of electricity around them. The quick snap and shutter of the camera as they sit, bored, at the small table. Waiting.

"Maybe one day I'll be a suffragette," she says to Morag.

Morag looks at her with sharp eyes.

"Well, why not?" Wallis asks. "Why shouldn't we vote?"

"I suppose next you will be in favour of Home Rule."

"What's that?"

"Letting Ireland rule itself."

Wallis says again, but now cautiously, "Well, why not?"

Morag goes back to drying teacups. They chatter and clink in a language all their own, intimacy forged between the teacups and the soap while Wallis stares at the suffragettes, wishing herself into the photo.

November 9, 1915

Dear Wallis,

Isn't this a terrible War? They said it would be over by this time last year—I feel terrible for all the boys who are fighting. Another Christmas away from home. Mrs. McCallum from downstairs has lost her youngest son, and the older one is being sent home having been shot in the leg. It's a terrible, terrible War. Michael and Mark have gone over now, and I pray for them every night. Before this, we were all worried with Home Rule, with trying to keep Ireland whole, but now we are all worried about dying . . .

Rebel Hearts

WALLIS'S HEART FLUTTERS and drops when she opens the *Courier* and reads the news. On Easter Monday 1916, Irish rebels set out to capture the most prominent buildings in Dublin: the South Dublin Union, the Four Courts, St. Stephen's Green and Boland's Flour Mill.

Paddy.

She has no way to know if Paddy would be involved in the uprising, but she feels it like the beginnings of a bruise. Paddy walking through Dublin holding fast to the ideals of a hero. Holes in the soles of his shoes, letting in the rain. She runs her fingers over the article until her fingertips are black. Remembers a day when she sat in the Hennessey flat amidst the smells of fried eggs and lye soap, a strand of hair coming free and sliding across her cheek, and ran her fingertips over the oil painting of Jesus with his sacred heart. Felt the prick of thickened paint and understood why the Hennesseys were different from her: they had something to hold in their hands, something to remind them of their faith.

She collects the rosary from under the bed and pins it to the inside of her dress, so that it hangs in the space between her breasts. She looks out the window to see Caro sitting down in the courtyard with her knees drawn up to her chest.

"There's an uprising in Dublin," Wallis says as she steps into the courtyard and into the space next to Caro. Wallis needs the heat of another body to keep herself contained.

Caro nods. She has not made the leap to the Hennesseys, to the stark possibility that Paddy may already be dead. Wallis stubs her toe at the ground. Still damp from the night's rainfall.

"I wonder if Paddy would be there."

"He's not terrible enough."

"They're not terrible, Caro."

"That's not what I meant," Caro says. "I mean, he is not the kind of boy to be able to shoot someone. To imagine dying in a street. They were not *political* enough."

"Paddy might be. Now."

"Now that what? That his mother is dead, and his father has probably drunk himself into a grave, and Paddy will have to care for all the other children?"

Wallis says, "Now that he is a man. He would be twenty-one now, Caro. He might be different." Wallis has an image of Paddy in her mind that is unwavering; the same brown eyes with crinkles in the edges from smiling, the same dark mop of hair, the same crooked smile. But his face would be different somehow, older and leaner and more calculated in its angles and degrees. She can imagine Paddy as clearly as she sees Caro before her with her knees jutting into the air.

"He isn't that kind. He'll wait for someone else to sort it out and then go along," Caro says.

Wallis says, "I remember asking him about Ireland, about where they grew up, and his eyes got soft and sad. I think he might be the kind of man to fight for it."

Caro is silent. She plucks a blade of grass from the damp earth. She says quietly, "But he was just a boy."

Wallis is silent.

Finally, Caro says, "What are they fighting for?"

Wallis does not answer, does not know how to take this small gift of concern from her sister, or how to explain it to her. Colonization. Geography. Protestantism. Catholicism. None of the words seem enough alone, yet Wallis can think of no others. Wallis is not patriotic, nor is she an unfaltering romantic, but she can imagine the weight of a rifle in her hand as she walks through Dublin. She rubs her fingertips against her palms and looks at the black streaks they leave behind.

After a week of fighting, British troops once again take control of Dublin. Wallis imagines a strange, dull quiet over a city newly accustomed to gunshots and crumbling buildings. A sky lit up by gunfire.

All the men involved are arrested. Wallis reads each day for news of Paddy, but his name doesn't appear in the reports. Still, she imagines him locked in a small stone cell, all of Dublin patiently waiting for him outside of Kilmainham Gaol's walls. A quiet city filled with retribution. Wallis learns the names of men she's never met, never imagined. Their faces are blank.

Eleven days later, the executions begin. The seven men who signed the Republican Declaration—Padraig Pearse, James Connolly, Thomas Clarke, Thomas MacDonagh, Sean

MacDiermada, Joseph Plunkett and Eamonn Ceannt—are executed in Kilmainham Gaol's courtyard. James Connolly has to be tied to a chair to keep him upright.

Wallis hears only gunshots for days.

⁓

Morag remembers a day so bright the sky seemed to be split by the sun. A strange day for late summer, when the thick, dry scent of fall was in the air. Morag thought, then, that the day must be what India was like: so bright it hurt your eyes, so fragrant you forgot there was any other smell besides weather. Morag had considered, many times, creeping onto one of the jute boats and travelling across the sea to places like India or Africa. Places with names that sat heavy on your tongue, sticky like marmalade.

That day, a quiet morning in 1911, she chose to walk to Brigid's flat instead of taking a tramcar, despite her anxiety. The beauty of the day did not soothe her or soften her as it might someone else; it was too solid, too uncompromising. Later, Morag will think that she chose to walk because she already knew. She will think she walked to delay the inevitable just a little while longer.

Brigid's flat was closer to the water, so Morag had to skirt the Tay as she walked. The water again caught her attention, the tense body of the bridge passing from Dundee and away, turning small in the distance.

Mother.

The sight made Morag's chest tighten; it seemed unreal, too brilliant in the hard glow of the sun. Those straight, thick legs disappearing into the water. Morag shut her eyes and hoped that she was wrong, that the sick, unbalanced feeling in her stomach was unreliable. Morag prayed.

Hours later, when Morag went back to Brigid's flat, she stood still in the middle of the room, trying to memorize everything around her. Small photos of Brigid and Oliver, taken before Imogen was born; the delicate lace doilies under porcelain figurines; a vase with wilting flowers. The scent of petals dying, stale water. Morag touched the surface of everything, letting Brigid in through her fingertips, and grieved alone for her sister.

Morag folded Brigid's clothes, her brassieres and under-clothes, into tiny squares. She held her blouses and sweaters to her face for a moment, smelling Brigid's perfume and her skin. Soon, she thought, the clothes would be free of scent altogether; they would be mere clothes, nothing extravagant or intricate, plain and dependable, the kind of clothes found in any woman's cupboards. The very essence of Brigid would be lost.

Morag had so much to do, so much to plan in the next few days. Brigid's funeral, Imogen's new life. Morag never once wondered what would become of her niece. Imogen would, of course, stay with Morag and James and the girls. She would fit seamlessly into the family, keep them whole, keep Morag from surrendering as the women before her had.

Morag took Brigid's photos, a few of the most elaborate doilies and Brigid's wedding ring. That, she tucked into her pocket where it would remain every day after. As she sat on the tramcar, she fingered the ring, the unending circle, let-ting her fingers work it around and around.

～

June 27, 1917

Dear Wallis,

Paddy has been released from prison, and has come
home. He says he couldn't wait to get out of England
and come home to a pint. He was home briefly, but then
went to meet some of his mates who had also been
released from jail. Wallis, I am so worried about him.
If he keeps up with all this, with the Citizen Army and all
this fighting, he will surely be sent back to jail or, worse,
he'll be killed . . .

～

After, Morag will think that perhaps she did the kind thing,
but at the time she was not conscious of kindness or sorrow
or guilt. She found the scissors in the kitchen—where they
would have been stained and bloodied had they been
Morag's scissors, from cutting into kidneys for kidney pie—
but Brigid's were mercilessly clean. Still shining silver.
Morag walked calmly back into Brigid's bedroom.

Morag did not have much time. Brigid might still be
buried on the church grounds. Morag would have to see
Reverend Robertson. She would have to find a way to
explain it to him, to have him allow Brigid a real death and a
real burial. When she was finished tending to her sister,
Morag took the scissors back to the kitchen and put them
back in the drawer, and sat on the kitchen chair with her head
in her hands, the smell of jute rope fresh against her face.

BOOK THREE

Shipwrecks

Dreaming of India

BLUEBELLS IN A VASE. Sunlight touching the crystal and bursting into a thousand prisms. The beauty of it makes Imogen's head ache and her eyes narrow.

"Imo." Caro's voice, diffused by the heat of the sunlight and Imogen's slim view. Caro sounds softer, as if she has been flattened and then filled with air again, reshaped. "Imo, your dad's here."

Imogen remembers: the knock at the door, the sight of Oliver, the blackness. How had it been Oliver who returned when all this time she had been waiting for Brigid?

"Hullo, Imo." His voice is unaffected by time, by age, by the sunlight and warmth in the room. She is six again, tugging at his hand when they search out rabbits in Camperdown Park; Imogen and the Captain of Grand Adventures. He is looming and brilliant and lovely. Imogen opens her eyes.

"Dad." It is all she can manage. Her heart has travelled up to her throat at the sight of him in his charcoal suit. His hair is still inky, slightly greying at the temples, shining from pomade when the light falls on it. He looks tanned, healthy, his teeth white against his lips. He smiles down at her awakening on the sofa, and she feels the absence in her fill, her heart suddenly whole again. "Dad."

Oliver bends down to her, resting his hand on hers. "Hullo, Imo." He smells like peppermint and the staleness of beer. She wants him to bend farther and kiss her forehead, as he did when she was small. She forgets for a moment that seven years have passed. He might find her foreign now, changed. She has not felt changed until now, under the scrutiny of Oliver.

Imogen takes in the room like a dreamer dreams. Everything is slightly unreal, slightly hazy. This could be a watercolour: *Return of the Father.* Look at how fine, how elegant his hands are; as if he has never had to work but has somehow been granted a fine life. A fine life with a fine young daughter suddenly struck ill. See how she holds her head up to him, looks at him as a heathen might look when first seeing God. Something close to awe but more raw, damaged and unflinching.

"Been quite a while, Oliver." Morag's voice is pointed. Measured. Thoughtful of the joy spreading across Imogen's face.

"Well, now," Oliver says, "I'm here now."

"You look well. Rested."

Oliver smiles again, showing his white teeth and his tanned face. "Yes," he says. He is not apologetic. He does not offer an explanation and this changes him from long-lost father to something more magical. Imogen thinks Oliver has become someone else, a hero in a story; certainly he *had* to be gone this long. Something must have kept him—he has returned as soon as he could.

"Where have you been, on a ship to India?" Caro teases.

"Yes." The answer is so plain, so simple, that Imogen immediately knows that he is telling the truth. She sits up on the sofa.

"Really?" She searches him for any traces of foreign countries. There should be something to mark him. She searches his hands, his neck, his face.

"Yes. For a few years."

This is all Morag needs. The small door opens and she says, "You have been gone for seven. What did you do the rest of the time?"

Oliver winks at Imogen before turning to Morag. "I was sorry to hear about James. It must have been difficult for you. You've done a lovely job with the girls," he says instead of an answer. His trousers have been pressed to hide the fact that they are well worn; he has been careful with his appearance. Imogen wonders if he was nervous coming back after all these years.

"Will you stay then?" Imogen asks.

"I've a room. For now."

Happiness swells within her even when he says he must be off, he has other things to attend to. What things? A job. A bigger flat, perhaps rooms in a house. He plans to make his life here. Imogen cannot help but smile wide, the smile consuming the rest of her face. Imogen walks him to the door, hugs him emphatically, then watches him walk down Caldrum from the window. She watches and watches until he is nothing more than a small grey shadow in the late-afternoon light.

The Whiteness of the Sky

A SHOCK OF WHITE against the blue horizon causes
Imogen to stop and stare. A surprise in the verdant of this
farmer's field. The whiteness curling and unfurling as the
man bends and hammers spikes into the earth below. She
watches as he hits the spike once, twice, three times, before
stepping back and admiring his work. There is one spike left,
and the last corner of the tent flips up, caught on the wind.

Always the wind.

Ahead, just up the road, the Eastern Necropolis, the
cemetery, awaits. She knows she should continue on her
walk; the small bunch of wild pink roses in her hand are
wilting, the petals scattering when the wind tears them free.
She looks down as they flutter to the ground.

He hammers the last spike in, and the whiteness is
finally contained. Imogen feels an inexplicable sorrow for
the restless flutter of the white tent in the wind. She moves
away from the dark man and his white tent, thinking only
the word *Caught*.

It is hard for Caro to recall when she first thought of Wallis as
political. It could have been when she watched Wallis open

the *Courier* and become entranced with the suffragettes. The way her face changed, as if light suddenly had come upon it with the crisp snap of the paper opening. Perhaps it was when Wallis first learned about Home Rule and tried to understand if that would stop the fighting in Ireland. As if civil war was ever indebted to morality. When she sat beside Caro in the close and spoke of the Easter Uprising. Then, Caro could see the shadow of the Hennesseys behind Wallis's eyes, the fear of Paddy dying in a street immediate.

Or, Caro thinks, when Wallis, as a member of the Jute and Flax Workers Union, demanded an end to half-time work. She wanted children to be in school for the few years afforded them, not standing stunned by exhaustion in the mills, slowly falling deaf and ill. Wallis, whose eyes lit up in a way Caro had not seen since Mrs. Hennessey's death and the children's swift disappearance.

Wallis had become active in the Union as soon as she could. She went to meetings in the evening, coming home breathless and full of ideals. Better conditions for the workers; Wallis was not fooled by the barons' attempts at philanthropy with the donations of parks, Lochee or Baxter, and their grand pavilions. She walked through those parks, navigating the dark shade of the trees, the thick bolts of green below her feet with a cynical eye. Parks would not save lives; she wanted ventilation in the mills, shorter working hours, perhaps even something to protect their ears from the incessant din.

"But it's always been this way," Caro said.

"You say that because it does not affect you."

"No, because I am a realist. I don't believe you can change this."

"Caro, I'm tired of it all—the coffins, the unattended looms. And the faces of the children. It's horrible." Caro watched Wallis leave the flat, touching her hair in a last moment of vanity, her cheeks brightened with excitement. Wallis was no longer meek, plain, apologetic; she was simply a woman with dark hair, bowed lips, beauty shimmering just below the surface. As if there was a new fire somewhere within her.

Now, Caro's relationship with Desmond has aligned her with the barons, with the people Wallis is busy rallying against. She wonders if Wallis can smell Desmond on her— the tangible link to the excesses of the rich, those men in grand houses plotting out bits of land to give away in mock generosity—when she returns from meeting him.

Caro smells her wrist but is greeted only by the lingering of lavender soap. The crispness there.

The tent wavers in the wind, looking like a bedsheet caught up in the breeze across the unending green. Morag stands at the side of the road, her hands in her coat pockets, her shoes coated with dust from the walk. She had not wanted to be seen getting off the tramcar so close to the site. She walked, instead, along the dirt road that wound up and behind, until the tent came into sight. She stands at the side of Arbroath Road, considering.

Psychics and mediums and clairvoyants are not unusual in Dundee. They arrive, having travelled through England and then up, layered in shawls and overcoats against the cold. Sometimes they hold séances in homes, and sometimes they can be found at the outdoor fairs, shaded by pavilions and makeshift tents. Morag has never submitted herself to anyone of the sort. When she heard the girls in the weaving warehouse talking about this new healer, the room had gone quiet. *A healer. Out near the cemetery.*

Morag's hand comes up to her throat. She takes a step onto the grass.

Morag sits with the others on the makeshift wooden-plank pews, waiting. The terrible nature of waiting, the small deceptions and avenues your mind might travel, the precise moment when hope floats away. Soon, anticipation turns into something more pedantic: the unravelling thread on the coat of the man in front of her; the wet sounds coming from another woman's lips; the way the sky is slanting, falling away from time and place, and into the basin of the tent. The man's dark face appears against the heavy draperies of the white tent, a small portrait of his bones and skin. There is something reassuring, pleasant even, about the angle of his head when he speaks, the reverberation of his voice. She feels his voice more than hears it.

The healer takes the hand of a woman on the first pew and helps her to stand before the dozens of people. He closes his eyes and holds her hand between his; to Morag, it looks as though he is praying.

He says, "Your hands. When could you last use them?"

The woman gasps and holds her one free, gnarled hand to her mouth. Whispers filter through the crowd as the healer continues to grasp the woman's hand. Finally, she manages, "More than two years."

The healer does not move. Morag watches for the slightest suggestion of breath from him, but it appears to her that he is utterly still, concentrating only on the misformed hand of the woman.

After a few stilted moments, he lets the woman's hand drop and opens his eyes. "You will use your hands again."

Morag watches with the rest of the crowd as the healer mixes liquids together into a small bowl; he grinds herbs with a pestle; he pauses, considers and then adds more. He transfers the liquid into a thin, clear jar and then holds it to the woman's lips. "Drink."

The column of the woman's neck is exposed suddenly, a creamy flash against the deep brown of her collar. She takes three sips.

The healer takes her hands in his and begins to massage them. Slowly, deliberately, he works on each of her fingers, from base to tip; index finger through to pinkie, the healer's gaze does not waver from the woman's hands. At last, he pours the remainder of the liquid from the jar into his palms and works it into her hands. He steps backward, two small steps, and says, "Try."

The woman does not move for a moment. She stares straight ahead at the healer, as if she does not yet understand what he is asking of her.

He repeats, "Try."

She looks down to her hands as though she has never seen them before. She makes the smallest, most tentative motion with her left hand.

Morag thinks, She does not yet want to be disappointed. She wants to hold the possibility for another moment.

The woman cries out and snaps her gaze back to the healer. He nods slightly, smiles. She turns to face the crowd in the pews and holds her hands up; painfully, slowly, she makes the smallest of movements with her fingers. There is a communal inhalation of breath, and whispers, again, roll around to the doubtful face of Morag.

The acts at first continue to be small: A man can almost hear now, after years of deafness. A small child's face begins to clear of sores. Morag thinks of them as something closer to coincidence than miracles. Anything is possible when you have opened your mind to it. She watches people press bills and coins into the small gold bowl beside the dark healer.

On the third day that Morag sits in the tent, still feeling anticipation coiled somewhere at her feet, the man heals a woman of her hate for her son. Morag watches him touch the woman's chest, just above her breast, and imagines the pressure against her own. All his force pushing against her, propelling the anger from her. The woman sobs and col-lapses against her husband. Morag watches with all the oth-ers seated in the tent and then watches as they stand and disperse. She smooths her skirt and steps out from the dim light of the tent into the sun of the afternoon.

"Wait."

The man, the healer, is behind her, coming across the grass to her. He holds his hand in the air as if in protest. He smiles at her.

"You've come three times and not spoken," he says.

"Yes."

"Why?"

Morag says, "I haven't decided."

He seems to warm to her confession. He touches her arm and she feels her own pulse. His hands are small for a

beyond the blue

man, almost womanish, but strong. He grips her lightly.
"Why do you come then, if you don't believe?"

Morag is not sure how to answer. Desperation is such
an easy response, predictable, and something about his
smooth, dark face with its wide eyes makes her want to be
unusual. "Because there is nothing else for me."

He nods slowly, and she is pleased. She thinks, He
understands, he knows what I cannot say.

"Perhaps we should meet alone," he says. "If you aren't
comfortable here."

Morag looks back to the white tent and its graceful
movements in the breeze. "Perhaps."

"I have a room on Arbroath Road. You could come one
night, and we'll talk about what brings you here."

"It's the Fever," Morag admits. "I'm dying."

He touches her arm again. She thinks he might be the
gentlest man she has ever known; his hand, this time, is a
slight weight on her forearm. "My name is Godfrey," he
begins.

After, Morag moves away from him and back down to
the road. She walks past fields of rapeseed and their brazen
yellow brilliance; she sees men bending in the fields, their
hands occupied with the earth. She smells summer coming,
the thick and full perfume of the air. She walks halfway
back to Dundee, then steps up and onto the tramcar and lets
it carry her home.

Villains and Angels

IMOGEN CRAVES OLIVER LIKE SWEETS, or salt, or something tart to make your tongue burn. He takes Imogen to look at the ships pulling in and out of the port, to the bathing ponds where Imogen dives under again and again, to the cinema where they see *The Adventurer*. Imogen loves the black theatre, the hush and awe, the way she and Oliver can escape for a while together, anonymous and laughing in the dark.

In the theatre, she watches her father. He is the most handsome man she has ever seen and, she thinks now, the kindest. Her eyes are huge, demanding globes; she is terrified that he might disappear again, just as easily as he had slid back in. He could be the man on the screen, the man seeking adventure and heroism. Imogen has already forgiven the abandonment because he has entranced her, the way a movie star might, all bright and burning.

After the movie, they come out onto Hilltown and Imogen's eyes water in the afternoon sun; she dabs at them impatiently. "What shall we do now?" she says.

Oliver smiles down at her, and she thinks she must perplex him. Perhaps her need is overwhelming. She says cautiously, "The graveyard?"

"The graveyard?"

"Well, I thought you might like to go. You probably haven't had the chance."

"I don't think so. No."

They walk up Hilltown in silence, save for the sound of his shoes—polished black, shining enough that Imogen imagines she could see her face in them if she bent down to peer—clacking on the cobblestones. It is a strange sound that worries Imogen. Like someone walking away. Imogen dabs at her eyes again, not so much from the sun but from Oliver's clipped response. She dabs and dabs, but the tears keep coming. She turns her head away, embarrassed.

"Imo," Oliver says when they reach Caldrum. "I said everything I had to say to your mother. I didn't come back for her." He hands her his handkerchief. There is a line of gold embroidery at the edge, lacy and drooping. Imogen wipes her eyes quickly, definitively.

"It's lovely," she says as she hands him back the damp handkerchief. She smiles to show him that she has forgiven him again, though this time she is not sure what she has forgiven him for.

"Yes," he says, gazing at the cloth. He rubs it between his fingers thoughtfully. "I brought it with me from India."

"Did someone make it for you?"

"Yes."

"Oh." Imogen imagines the woman who must have made the handkerchief. She can imagine her fingers with the scrap between them, carefully stitching on the gold edging. Nothing plain like blue or white, but dazzling yellow gold. She imagines the woman stitching and stitching until she has stitched her own finger into the cloth, a thin gold band attaching it there.

Imogen wants to ask Oliver about the time he's spent away, about India and his life there. A high, unflinching sun. Beautiful brown women in dresses light as air. Cities thick with sweat and bodies and mud running from the previous night's rainfall. Holding your palms up to capture the rain. Hands wet when he reaches his fingers through the woman's ebony hair. Uncoiling it and then turning it damp, slick as oil or melting tar. His hands in her hair, searching. He might have memorized the shape of her skull. Could have recognized her if he went suddenly blind.

Imogen stops and says to him, "I missed you. I think I missed you."

"You're not certain."

"No. But, then, there are so many things I'm not sure of any more."

Oliver is pensive, cool, when staring at her. He waits.

"I can't remember Mum."

"You must."

"Yes. No, I mean, I remember her before you left."

Oliver says carefully, "And after?"

"No. Nothing much at all from after." As simply as that, Imogen has laid her life out before Oliver. Before. After. The two girls within her. Her uncertainty, her fugue, her sudden snap. She says, "Will I see you tomorrow?"

Oliver shrugs. "If you're lucky." He winks.

Imogen throws her arms around him; there is so much she wants to ask him—when she will be coming to live with

him, when they can be a real family again, about Brigid—
but she does not want to rush him. He must find a flat, and
settle himself in before she can follow. She squeezes him in
her arms.

"You are going to break me in half," he laughs. He pulls
back from her and kisses her on the top of the head. "Be
good for Morag," he says.

Imogen watches him walk back down Caldrum, the
way they had come, as if he were going back to the theatre
to see Charlie Chaplin rescue the two women from death
again. There was always laughter and misunderstandings.
There was always someone to rescue.

Some days Imogen lets Wallis walk down Caldrum and out
of her sight. Other days, Imogen pads silently down the
road after her. She writes lists of where Wallis goes, what
she might see there: Victoria Road where she looked at the
sky; the Howff where she held her hand to the gate; Ann
Street where she watched the sun on church spires.

Imogen follows Wallis and watches her climb the steps
into St. Mary's Lochee. Wallis with a man who holds her
elbow like she is sea-glass. Their heads tilt close to one
another, conspiratorial. Imogen thinks she can see Wallis's
hair touch the man's shoulder. They move into the church
and are quickly lost.

Imogen sits on the small bench across the street from
the church. She crosses her legs at the ankles, aware of their
protruding bones. It's a clear day. Imogen turns her head up
to the sky and sees Brigid in the few, benign clouds.
Something in the consistency so like Brigid.

She searches the sky for Brigid's gloved hand. She searches for the perfect cloud, the right tilt of wavering whiteness. She thinks, *Glove.* Most clouds are too thick to be anything like Brigid's slim hand. *Glove, glove, glove.* She leans back and the cloud shows itself to her, a long, slim sliver of white that could be Brigid's arched finger. *Glove.* The word shifts and coils in her mind until it might be something else entirely; it could be the name of a river, a foreign port, the curved valley of an ancient battlefield. *Glove.* The word becomes unknown to her. Had she ever known what it meant? She mouths the word slowly, cautiously.

Wallis and the man step out of St. Mary's. Imogen follows them to Lochee Park, where they move away from her quickly, heading toward the privacy and shade of the trees and the pale cream pavilion. Imogen leans against the iron gate of the park and watches as Wallis and the man become smaller, slighter. She can still make out the pale grey of Wallis's coat, but from this distance, Wallis could be anyone. Imogen covers one eye and then the other. Wallis could be a stranger walking with her lover, on a Sunday afternoon. Imogen considers Wallis, her expression unguarded as she walks beside the man, and feels suddenly that she is intruding. She moves away from the thick gates and leaves Wallis under the shade of the pavilion.

The girl has walked out to the middle of the new Tay Bridge. It is late afternoon, that time just before sunset when water is shifting and sinister. A train will not come for another hour or so. The bridge is quiet, save for the sound of her feet on the metal.

She walks in bare feet, her nightgown ballooning out around her. People in the street have stared at her, whispered to one another, but no one touched her arm. No one offered to help her home, ask if she is lost. Such a strange girl, she looks unwashed in her dirty nightgown with that immense bulge beneath.

She stands at the edge of the bridge, her toes peeking over the edge.

The girl looks down to the churning Tay below. She does not speak, does not even let out a cry as she heaves herself from the bridge.

(He does not have time to yell to the other men on the dock. They have their backs turned as they tug containers from the newly docked ship. He alone has been staring out across the water, thinking of the disaster and, perhaps, of India. There is the scent of fish, the damaged salt scent that will cling to the man's hands later, even after he has scrubbed them raw. And the monotonous grief of these men on the dock who spend all day lifting and moving and wishing themselves elsewhere.

He thinks he has seen an angel falling from the bridge, that perhaps one of the ghosts of the disaster has come back to haunt them. He sees her swoop down toward the water and disappear.)

A Walk of Heather

WALLIS LOVES EVERYTHING about St. Mary's Lochee, but most of all, she loves the windows, all in blues and reds. She can imagine the patience, the exactitude required of the men who bent over long tables of glass. Dyes and lead nearby, a vision in their heads. This is the kind of man Wallis imagines John might be—John, who never was able to fight the Germans, but instead learned to pray for God's help to save all the young men lost to the War.

She knows that John is this kind of man: faithful and solemn, dependable in a way men in her family have never been. John is steadfast and unwavering. He does not want much: a small flat and fragrant bread and Wallis.

Lately, John has become more serious with her about marrying soon. She has never imagined her life tethered to any man but Paddy. Never has she imagined that any other man would want her, would imagine her as the centre of his small life. John's love for her makes her feel weightless, hopeful and guilty at the same time. Mostly, she feels foolish, daft in her unflagging childhood love; would Paddy feel the same? Would he even recognize her after all these years? Could he have met someone else while fighting, pining for her in jail?

When she drifts into these dark corridors, Wallis must shake herself free. It is not only Paddy, but the journey itself: standing on a deck of a boat, knowing that she would reach Ireland and a new life. This quick grip on her heart is so strong that it must be true. Foolish or not, she knows she must make that journey. She thinks this is part of why she has not told anyone her plan, or about John; she fears the cynicism, Morag's cold eyes when she sees the cross about John's neck. Another cross, another quick disapproval. Morag would disapprove of John—his faith, his limp, his motherless children—but even more, she would scoff at Wallis leaving for Ireland and Wallis would have to hold her tongue taut in her mouth. Feeling the ridges of the roof of her mouth.

And Paddy.

Today, Wallis sits in the pew and stares at the window of Mary with the child. Outside, it is raining. Her shoes have got wet, soaked right through, and her feet sit now in cool pools of water. She does not want to leave the church and start the walk home, so instead she sits and stares and imagines how her life might be different if she just said yes to John, without thought of consequence or the looming wave of regret.

Wallis is sure that her life would become something pleasant and reliable. A hand to hold in the dark. Of course, she would have to abandon her family for the cross that hangs on the wall of John's flat, for the three-foot statue of the Virgin Mary in the window. Wallis would have more to explain than the rosary beads tucked under her bed.

Certainly, Imogen would visit her, enjoying the mirth of Lochee. She might see Caro once in a while, bump into her on Hilltown or maybe in the din of Murraygate, but certainly she would not come to the flat for a cup of tea. Caro and her new exasperation at pews and hymns and prayer books. Caro would be put off by the oil painting of Jesus with his fierce red heart. And Morag would have to become a memory, something from Wallis's past that sat with her like a photograph. Something like James.

Wallis squishes her feet in her shoes and feels water pool between her toes. Small lakes just there, keeping her uncomfortable and chilled even in the warmth of the church.

The church is quiet, almost deserted. Most people are tucked away in their flats, comforted by warm teacups and blankets over their knees in the spring rain. A few candles flicker and turn the cavernous room amber, that soft shade of twilight. A woman behind Wallis, just a few pews back, prays softly, her words like a muttered song. Wallis strains to hear her, lulled by the repetition. She touches the rosary in her pocket and is reassured by the cool beads. Wallis folds her hands, but she does not know what to pray for.

She has deposited more money, has watched her account grow and blossom in the past few months. Each time she hands money across the wicket to the teller, she thinks it is a small puncture into her tentative relationship with John. She wants to tell him—to explain her love for Paddy—but cannot imagine his face if she spoke the words.

Yet there is still some flint in her heart. She fears she would dissolve—simply and unequivocally disappear—if she gave up John, and Paddy did not return her feelings. Dissolve like something left out in the rain.

Finally, she bends her head and prays for an answer.

Wallis is successful: half-time has been abolished. The small room in Nethergate reverberates, hums with excitement. Children will go to school full-time until they are fourteen. Wallis does not think of the families who depend on the wages that have now been secreted away, replaced by the long strain of school chairs and knowledge useless to those who cannot afford bread or milk.

"Here, Wallis." Elaine Gillan fills her glass and Wallis tips back a drink of whisky in celebration.

Wallis has relaxed into the intimate atmosphere of the Union—she folds herself into warm rooms filled with the scent of women: perfume, newly washed skin and hair. She listens to conversations, sometimes laughs. "Another, Wallis?" The deep-amber whisky flows, her glass quickly refilled. There are Jean Grant's small hands, Mary O'Keefe's pretty brooch at her collar. The women of the Union celebrate by having photos taken with small children holding up signs proclaiming victory. The smiles on their faces. The cap and fringe of dark hair.

John meets her later, on the darkened steps of the McManus Galleries. The Gothic nature of the building is enhanced by the dim light, the glow of night around them. He greets her with a smile, his arms coming around her.

"Ah, my fierce Union member."

Wallis lets herself smile back at him, proud of herself, content now with his pleasure at having her by his side. She is warm, fluid from the whisky and the celebration.

"Let's walk."

beyond the blue

They walk into the evening streams of people in Murraygate and Wallis relaxes. John still does not understand her strange fits of silence but allows her to have them nonetheless. Sometimes they walk without talking at all, their bodies hard against the stiff wind and misty rain. Their shoes murmur in a hushed language of leather and nails over cobblestones, train tracks, loose stones. John's limp makes his walk recognizable even in storms.

"Cup of tea then?" John asks her as they approach his building. He always asks, even though she continually refuses. Shakes her head and looks at her feet, unwilling to admit her reluctance at immersing herself in his life. His flat, his teacups, his children.

John's children are a blank canvas to Wallis; she cannot imagine their faces; she cannot imagine the impression of their mother on them. The prospect of their disapproval, their dislike or dismay, leaves Wallis staring at the worn brown leather of her shoes. The small humps of her toes. Bessie Lyon says that you can judge a woman by her shoes; what, then, would people say of her? Reliable, plain, perhaps overused and pinching. Yes, she decides, you can judge someone by their shoes.

"Not tonight." Wallis is too happy, too proud of the evening's events to stumble into the flat and meet his children.

She knows John does not expect anything else of her; he will go up to his flat and relieve his neighbour, Mrs. Brady, from minding the children, as Wallis begins the long walk, up the slow angle of the hill and then to the right, a few more blocks and then up the stairs and home. There, Wallis will tell a bold-faced lie to Morag and not feel one

199

glimmer of guilt about it. Her guilt, for once, will not lie with Morag, but with John and his serene, sleeping body in Lochee. Wallis will say she went to church after the Union gathering, meeting with some of the other women or practising with the choir, and she will think that she has not really lied. She could have been at church, she could have been singing. A church, a memory, a man. So, she does not lie to Morag, simply forgets to tell her what kind of church she means.

On the road outside of the school, Imogen sees her mother in a new spring daffodil: the lilt and dip of the petal, sagging toward the ground. Her mother's shoulders after Oliver left.

She can see Brigid anywhere, she just has to look. Beneath the broom branches. In the smeared handprint on the bedroom window. But she cannot find her in her mind; her mother's face is the face in a photograph she has seen. Always the same, her thin, angled face turned up to the sun. One strand of hair coming across her face. Sectioning away her forehead and right eyebrow. The innocence of that arch.

When the Baxter Park pavilion was built, men stood at the top of the sloped roof and could see all of Dundee before them. That freedom. The taste of air so high. The sight of the striped pavilion roof below them.

Now, when Caro looks up to the roof, she imagines how it must have felt to be one of those men. How it must feel to be anything but this small, this insignificant, in a pavilion beside a man. She pulls her skirts down in a flash of modesty.

Desmond smiles at her. "Shy, are we?" He reaches over from his position on the bench beside her to cover one of her breasts with his hand. She pulls away slightly and he says, "It's dark. No one will see." His hand trails down from her breast to her thigh, where he begins to pull up her skirts again.

Caro flattens her hand on his. "No."

"You weren't so shy a minute ago."

The slick words make something snap in her: ice off the eaves melting in her hand as a child, that same chill. She stands.

"Desmond, I want to lie in a bed with you. Not a pavilion bench or a farmer's field."

He sighs and looks away from her, out into the silence of the park's grass. She wonders, suddenly, how many other couples have come to parks like this, lain on the grass or sat in this pavilion. She looks at Desmond. She wonders how many other girls he has brought here.

"Caro, you know that's not possible."

"Why? We could go to your house. I've never even seen it. I'd love to lie in your bed and wake to you in the morning."

Desmond snorts. "I have a wife."

"But you could arrange it."

"No."

"I'm sure you—"

"No." His voice is hard, final, under the cone of the pavilion roof. There is a slight echo and Caro hears the word come back to her.

No.

She turns away from him and stands looking out to Arbroath Road. At night the park is desolate, solitary, predatory. She wishes for the loudness of day: birds in tree branches; motor cars on Arbroath Road; children with kites running across the park. What she has is this dark, shadowy corner. A wooden bench and cool air.

Desmond's hands catch her waist. "Caro," he mumbles into her neck. "You know I want to see you." He presses against her. "I need to. But we've got to be careful. For now."

For now. A promise of a possibility. The slightest chance. Anything and everything all at once in those small words.

For now.

Caro spins around to face Desmond. A hole has been punctured in the future; there is possibility. It waits there, glimmering just ahead of her. She must have patience.

"Yes," she says. "Of course."

Desmond smiles at her and she can tell he is pleased. Pleased with the sight of her, with her waist in his hands, with the fortune of this shaded pavilion.

⌒

The two children stand at the steps of St. Mary's Lochee, and Wallis is transported back a dozen years: Paddy at the gate of St. Mary's Forebank, staring up at the small statue of the Madonna and child mounted on the church's exterior, high above his head. The children do not look up to the Madonna at St. Mary's Lochee, but they are just as still and serious. They have been dressed in their good clothes, washed up and tidied as best John can. Anne's shoes—once white—are clouded by remnants of dirt; even her hair sash has a dull, grey cast to it. And tiny Stephen with his large blue eyes stands at Anne's side. Holding her hand as if she, at six, might be able to shelter him. They move slowly up the stairs and into the church, a small, strangled family.

Wallis stands across Methven Street, hidden away from John and the children. Behind her is the fishmonger, beside that the butcher. She looks down High Street and sees this curved little street much like Hilltown. Twinned streets divided by nothing more than religion. There is no reason to leave this street. John wants her to live here. Where both a convent and a park donated by jute barons are monuments.

Wallis can see herself walking up High Street with her arms full of groceries, the music of the church bells melodic and true. John's flat is close to the church, in tenements set up by St. Mary's. She could get a job at Cox's Mill; here, per-haps she could be happy. John would treat her well; she has already blossomed under his devotion. Needing his attention and love but wanting another man. She feels a fraud.

But still. Only a possibility.

She has seen other futures slip away—a head in the stove, a quick departure—and is suddenly afraid to inno-cently let another go.

She steps into Methven Street and toward St. Mary's Lochee.

⌐

April 23, 1918

Dear Wallis,

Mark and Michael are still off in this horrible war.
Sean has not signed up, and Paddy says he won't
fight for Britain. He will go with the Irish Volunteer
Force, but not with the Ulster Volunteer Force. I know
he has joined the Citizen Army, but he won't admit it.
He goes to meetings late at night, disappears for
hours, but he won't tell me anything. He talks and
talks about Éamon de Valera until I can't stand
it any more . . .

Rosemary writes that the War has put the Irish cause on
hold; Britain is afraid that if nationalists fight in the War,
they will have too much access to knowledge of arms, of
warfare, of tactics. So instead they form their own divisions.
Irish independence has been forced into silence and inactiv-
ity. Wallis imagines it is a time when political lines are
drawn, thick and unwavering. When nations align and fight
one another only to realign again later. When geography is
marred by gunshots and boots in mud.

A fortnight of rain. Incessant rain that tears at the founda-
tion of things.

Imogen watches from the bedroom window. Behind her,
Caro and Wallis sleep, unaffected by weather. She holds her
hand to the windowpane, feels her fingertips slick against
the glass. She writes the word *Mother*, secure in its invisibility

and anonymity. Traces the letters again where she imagines them to be.

The windowpane shudders slightly. Imogen is not certain what woke her, but thinks now it could be the wind. She pines for something dry and arid, a release from the damp. The chill of the windowpane reminds her that they are on an island, that they are forever surrounded by water. *Water, water everywhere.*

Imogen's mind snaps like a winter branch and she is six years old again. Oliver has not left. Brigid is sturdy in her ambiguity. On a good day—a day when the sun shines—Brigid takes her to Perth. They walk through the city and out to where the River Tay lopes and languishes. Imogen bristles with heat.

Imogen remembers her mother's face reflected in the water. Something dreamed or wished upon. Brigid putting her hand in the river, breaking the reflection. Imogen has put out her hand to stop her mother, but it is too late. Her face is split in two, and then forgotten entirely.

Imogen steps into the cool water. A shock travels up her legs, finds a home at the top of her spine. Imogen is motionless, aware of the late-summer breeze, as she watches Brigid peel her clothes off. She reveals a slim white arm, a bangle at the wrist. The bird crest of her shoulder blade. Brigid piles her clothes beside the river in a small heap. In her bare legs, white slip and gloves, she slides into the water wordlessly. She turns onto her back and floats, her breasts and the pale moon of her face breaking the surface of the water. Imogen watches as her mother, partially submerged, flutters her white hands away down the river.

Imogen moves quickly along the edge of the riverbank, watching Brigid sink. Brigid letting the river take her over, letting her body be settled and cupped by its slippery warmth.

Brigid finally stops and drags herself out of the water. She moves sleepily, as if she were dreaming. She wrings her hair out and Imogen watches the flecks of gold waver against the sun. Sees through the thin veil of Brigid's hair the open fields beyond. She watches Brigid walk back the way she had come, put her blouse and skirt back on, her hands moving swiftly along the buttons.

"You look as though you have seen a ghost."

Imogen stares. Brigid twists her hair up and pins it on top of her head. She turns and Imogen stares at the wet patch in the small of her mother's back. Brigid walks away from Imogen, toward the low sun.

Why did I always follow? Where was she going?

Imogen's hand is still on the windowsill, gracing the edge of the cool pane. Outside, a robin flies between the tenement buildings. Imogen watches its gentle flight, the curve and arc of the bird's small body across the air. That sweet, perfect moment when the robin's wings unfolded in the air and crested to the sky; this is what Imogen wishes for. To be weightless, lifted momentarily from the heaviness of Brigid.

Morag's dreams of her mother increase with the coughing fits. Soon she is dreaming of her every night, waking to the greasy scent of the kitchen and the moonlight coming through the window.

Morag's hands reach out to tug the wool blanket up to her chin. She is reluctant to come out of sleep, out of the safety of that gauzy phase where anything might be possible. She fingers the rough edge, comforted by the slight fraying. The reminder of things falling apart. Morag's dreams have changed from the innocent memory of her mother's face into the dream of the bridge's collapse, of her mother's face against the window, of the plunge. Every night, the terrible creak of the bridge surrendering to the train's weight. The dream does not encompass beauty, but there is surrendering and ownership, as Morag claims the memory as hers.

Every morning, she wakes to coughing and the sight of blood in her handkerchief. Some days the shape of a rose in bloom. Some macabre beauty in it after all.

A Little Bird Named Enza

On Sunday afternoon, Morag watches the men as they spray the streets in lazy and loping twists of the wrist. These men wear masks over their faces as they trail behind the chemical trucks, long hoses reaching out like trunks. As they pass, the streets dampen with the chemical mixture, as if it has been raining for days. The scent is so strong, Morag holds her palm over her face to avoid the stinging in her nostrils.

The first cases of influenza appeared in Glasgow in May. Until then, it remained across the North Sea, safely tucked away in France, Germany. They have all heard of it, *the Spanish flu,* of course, the bluish colour of people's skin, the quick, violent deaths. A sudden wave of death across countries, a long train of bodies laid out like train tracks. It comes in a rush, bringing with it fierce fear, false diagnoses. Suddenly streets all across Scotland are sprayed by men behind masks. Everyone eats mounds of porridge after being told that it may save them from the illness.

Morag hears that tobacco smoke keeps you healthy, so she smokes even more than usual, despite the irritation to her lungs; the flat is hazy with her smoke. "I'll stay strong," she insists and snaps a match. The cigarette makes a crumpling sound as it begins to burn. "Mark my words." Because of this, Morag does not fear influenza like the others. With her lungs so tight, her nights so full of dreams of her dead mother, she does not fear it much at all.

"At it again," Morag says. Caro has gone into Murraygate, but Wallis and Imogen are beside her in the flat. Imogen is bored and wilted on the chesterfield, staring blankly at the watercolour on the wall. It's of the Highlands, hills covered with broom and patches of heather. Green and gold-yellow and purple, all melting into the blue of the sky.

Imogen sighs. "In flew Enza," she says absently.

"What?"

Imogen looks up at Morag. She smiles a little. "Nothing. A silly nursery rhyme. Nothing."

"Say it then."

"It's silly."

"Imogen." Morag does not have patience for games like these. She is irritated by anything so trivial, so coy and irrational.

Imogen sighs again and sets her head in her hands. She says lazily, "I had a little bird—its name was Enza—I opened up the window—and in-flu-enza."

Wallis gasps. Morag tuts her tongue against the roof of her mouth.

Imogen says innocently, "What?"

"It's shameful, Imogen. Think of all those people who are dying," Wallis says. Her face is puckered with her distaste for the rhyme.

"Ridiculous is what it is," Morag says. "You are too old for nursery rhymes." This is not entirely true; there is still something childlike and unaffected about Imogen, something fresh and crisp.

"I just heard it from some of the girls in the courtyard. They sang it while they skipped rope."

Wallis says, "It's horrible. Girls skipping rope to a song about death."

Morag shuts her eyes for a moment. She does not want to think about the Spanish flu, about girls singing such songs, about Imogen's fragility; about the rhythm of shoes skipping on cobblestones. "Tea then, Wallis?" she says.

Wallis stands in the kitchen with her back to Morag and Imogen. She turns the water on and the rushing sound fills the small room. Morag settles into it, into this familiarity and comfort. This is what her life has become: Bowbridge during the week, tea on Sunday afternoons, her daughters resentful and angry, sometimes loving her just a little. And Imogen. Morag never does know what really goes on in her mind.

Morag begins to cough and cannot stop. She reaches for her handkerchief, the small white one with the embroidered flowers at the edge, and presses it quickly to her mouth. It might muffle the sound, the harsh rattling in her chest. When the fit subsides, she finds blood on her handkerchief.

"Are you all right?" Imogen is crouching at her side and patting her back gently. Her eyes are too big for her face, blue saucers rimmed with white, staring into her aunt.

"Yes, yes. I'll be fine." The rattling is still there—now, it is always there—though she has managed to stifle it. She takes a few deep breaths and lights another cigarette. Wallis has been preoccupied with the tea, with halving scones and setting teacups on saucers, but now turns to Morag. Her eyes are hard on her mother. Morag hopes she will assume it is an uncommon coughing fit, perhaps from all the smoke and having the windows closed against the wafting chemicals outside. Hopes that she won't yet realize what it is, what it means.

Morag looks at Imogen and her big blue eyes, and she knows that Imogen somehow understands.

Don't say it. Don't let on that you know.

More than anything, Morag fears the thought of pity, that deep dark well of good intentions turned into something sickly sweet and cloying. That sad, relentless look that suggests compassion, but is closer to curiosity. People who are thankful, suddenly, that they never had the fortune to work in the mills, that they had to scrape together a living as a cook or a housekeeper. She has not really let herself believe that this is what God has in mind for her. After everything: her mother, James, Brigid.

It's all too much.

Morag regrets the thought the moment she has it. She does not even have a gold wedding band; James thieved it and sold it long ago, no doubt to warm his belly with a few more pints. In these moments between her coughing fit and Imogen now straightening up beside her, Morag's life has been boiled down into something she could fit into her palm, something that small and easily misplaced.

May 12, 1918

Dear Wallis,

Joseph and I are engaged to be married! Wallis, I wish
you could be here to meet him. Imagine—I'll soon be
Rosemary Devine. *How divine!* We will be married in six
weeks, and then I will move with him to his flat. I won't
be too far from Granny, so I will be able to look in on
her. She needs someone to help her with the smallest
tasks now. It's terrible to see, really. Everyone loves
Joseph, even Paddy, who can be so difficult to please . . .

Wallis walks down Caldrum Street, cozying herself in her
coat against the winds. Though it is May, today is cold and
crisp. She wishes she had worn something heavier, her green
winter coat with the small polished buttons, but she has
dressed as if trying to hurry summer. Summer with all its
promises: longer, brighter days; new buds siding the streets;
the pure possibility that comes with the season. Another
season closer to it all.

Wallis does not fear Morag, not precisely, but she would
like to avoid the inevitable ill will, anything negative Morag
would have to say about her choices. Morag can't, surely,
expect that Wallis would stay in the flat, in her worn paisley
chair, for years upon years to come, knitting until all she
wants to do is gouge her eyes out with the needles. Wallis does
not like to admit it, but she thinks that perhaps that is exactly
what Morag expects of her. Caro would be the one to marry
and have lovely, small children, and Imogen would do something dramatic or courageous and Wallis would be the one to
stay with Morag, nurse her into death with comforting words

and capable hands. Morag has never asked Wallis what she wants; no one has thought that Wallis has real plans for herself, plans as dramatic and drastic as this journey to Ireland.

Wallis does not think she is lying, really, if no one bothers to ask her the question. Would she answer if Morag said to her suddenly, "Tell me your fondest wish, Wallis"? But Morag would never ask such a question. No one believes that Wallis is the kind of woman to have wishes or wants.

She turns down Isla Street and Clepington Church comes into sight. She is still comforted by the sight of it. The brown bulk is reassuring; its spire rises high into the sky. She sighs a little, feels her body ease at the prospect of tugging open the heavy doors and walking into the quiet and calm of the kirk. The stillness of a church soothes Wallis. She feels the daily aches, the pressure of holding back her own truths and plans, slide from her. She wishes she could step into St. Mary's Forebank, but knows this would be impossible. A Church of Scotland girl sliding into a Catholic pew? No. She could never do it alone. For now she will have to be content with Clepington, with the church she has known since she was a child. Her heels click on the low stairs up to the kirk.

Clepington is almost deserted at this morning hour. It's only Saturday, and most people won't be coming for prayer until Sunday. Wallis loves the few Saturdays she does not work at the mill. Everything seems calmer, more quiet and placid. Wallis would slip past Clepington and into St. Mary's every day if she could; her faith has been strengthened by John and their trips to church together. She is embarrassed to have doubted at all. She will say an extra prayer to give thanks, and another for her omissions to Morag. She fingers the rosary in her pocket and chews on her bottom lip, considering. Could she do it? Could she leave Clepington, walk the short way down to St. Mary's and step in, brazen in the light of day? Two small red marks appear on her lip.

Perhaps she will say two prayers for all the omissions.

She sits in a pew near the back. The air is slightly fragrant, thick and cloistering around her. She breathes in and shrugs her coat from her shoulders before bowing her head. She tries to concentrate on her prayers, on being truthful and repentant, but she can only think ahead to John. She will meet him this afternoon and they will stroll through Camperdown Park. Just the thought of it thrills her. Trailing after this thrill, though, is guilt. She should not enjoy her time with him so much. She should not let him believe that there is possibility for them. She should not want to see him so that she might look up to him and see Paddy's eyes.

Wallis notices the woman rise from her pew at the front, mostly because she has only seen her in the kirk a few times before; Wallis always assumed that they must worship at the kirk in the Ferry. Mary Lindsay approaches, with her long, sad face and her crisp clothes. She wears a heavy tan coat, and the impeccable hem of a navy skirt peeks out from the bottom. She moves quickly down the centre aisle, her shoes silent on the carpet. Wallis smiles up at her as she passes, but Mary Lindsay stares straight ahead. When she passes, Wallis smells something clean, almost clinically so. She has the sterile smell of someone who does not have to cook her own meals, clean her own floors or launder her own clothes.

As if something essential is missing. Wallis turns to watch Mary Lindsay as she leaves the church; she holds a hand to her head as she pushes the kirk door open and goes out into the cold, windy morning.

⁓

Imogen and Caro walk up Main Street to Hilltown for a small package of minced meat. They have left Wallis in the flat with the water boiling and small coins of carrots spread out around her.

Every time Caro comes onto Hilltown, she is pleasantly overwhelmed. The hum of a busy street, the cluster of immigrants, the slight notion of sliding into something foreign yet familiar. Caro and Imogen move with ease down the street, pausing to admire the new bolts of fabric in Davies Dress Shop's window. Imogen, who is always drawn to the dress designs on parchment paper, small sketches of lithe women. Their backs are turned when a procession comes up behind them, pulsing and humming. Caro turns her head slowly, prepared for anything from a sudden fair to a funeral to a bridegroom with his feet printed with treacle and ink.

Imogen breathes, "Look."

There is a tiny, plain pine coffin between a spectacled man and a woman shrouded in black. A dozen mourners follow them, with mouths moving in hymns or prayers or random despair, Caro can't be sure. Mostly women, of course, and a few men. Old men with weepy eyes. Young men with limps and hidden deformities. Windows to flats above the shops open wide and faces appear, becoming part of the moving funeral.

Imogen says, "It's so tiny."

Handkerchiefs are held to mouths, either to trap sobs or protect them from influenza.

Caro thinks, In flew Enza. She closes her eyes and can almost hear Imogen's feet on the pavement, a hasty hopscotch drawn below her. Feet in squares, words on lips: *Influ-enza. Open the window and in-flu-enza.* Caro wants to hold her hand out and stop Imogen—hold her in place as the procession moves past—just stop her in the middle of the street. Keep them both still in this moment.

The procession moves down Hilltown, progressive wailing trailing them. Grief is muttered into the street from open windows. People step from the shops to join the mourners until they bulge to fill the street. Caro watches women cross themselves, their hands moving in a secret language. Eyes close. Heads lower. The street is dark and moving with bodies.

"Come on," Caro says. She tugs Imogen away from the sight of the funeral march, up toward the clock and the butcher. She is suddenly desperate to get away from the flagrant sorrow she has witnessed, the weight of a faith she does not share. Caro leads Imogen away, longing for the isolated nature of grief that she is accustomed to: dour faces and dry eyes, sorrow only freed behind closed doors.

No Rest for the Wicked

PASTEL BLUE DRESS with a dark blue sash at her waist. The tart scent of lemons, making her nose twitch and her throat clench. Making her think of summer and the beach and Oliver, with tall, sweating glasses of lemonade. That shock of cold metal on her fingertips, the possibility of turning the doorknob.

What is behind the door, Imo?

Imogen wakes to the night sky coming in the window, the voices leaving her head. Did she open the door? She cannot remember if she had, either in her dream state or the actual day she was whisked away by Morag. The doorknob is the last image to flee from her mind; her own reflection there in the gleam of silver. Her large eyes, cool globes of strange blue, unrecognizable to her.

Open the door.

Caro sleeps solidly beside Imogen, her face quiet and peaceful. Imogen reaches out and holds her hand above Caro's mouth, feeling the warmth of her breath. This bit of Caro escaping to land on Imogen's palm soothes her. Wallis snores lightly, bunched and bundled under the quilt. Imogen wiggles her toes into the chill of the room.

Since the outbreak of influenza, they have slept with the window slightly open, despite Imogen's silent fear that ghosts could enter through that slim slice. Morag insists that cool air is good for them, will keep their lungs fresh and young and working in their chests. Imogen holds her hand to her own chest to feel it rise within her breath and fall, then rise again. She imagines the expansion that happens inside the cavity of her chest and is reassured.

Imogen moves silently from the bed and stands at the open window. Clotheslines still hang across the close, with stray garments glowing in the moonlight: a pair of white knickers flicker; a baby's blanket; a stiff petticoat, unfazed by wind or rain. Imogen watches the clothes shiver slightly in the night air. She holds her hand up to the windowpane as if she might be able to touch the petticoat, feels her fingers prickle and gasp at the starched sharpness.

Imo.

She squeezes her eyes shut. She does not want to hear the voice, does not want to fall back into the dream. She does not want to see what is behind the door.

Are you certain, Imo? Just one peek.

"No," she says aloud, then spins quickly to see if she has awoken Caro or Wallis. Wallis shifts in her sleep and mumbles, but neither of the girls stirs. Imogen turns back to the window and the innocent clotheslines, willing the voice away. She doesn't want this any more. She wants to be free of ghosts, free of visions, just one whole, simple girl.

There is a flash as she turns back to the window—could it have been a trick of light? A figure she would recognize anywhere, in photos or reflected in the Tay or fragmented in her own mind.

Mother.

Imogen squints and searches the navy night. Nothing but undergarments and baby clothes. Tenement windows. Cobblestones and newly lush vegetable patches. Nothing.

Imogen stands at the window for another moment before crawling back into bed beside Caro. Her feet and hands have turned icy. She shuts her eyes and curls up next to Caro, sinking into her heat and her silence. She thinks, Just go away.

Imogen sleeps.

Goodness is a concept wasted on Caro. Goodness twinned with the expectations of faith burdens her every time she sets foot into Clepington. It makes her suddenly weary; she does not believe that anyone is ever good, all the time. Caro can only really believe in her own ability to determine her future. She glances over at Wallis, sitting quietly in the pew. Even she is not unabashedly wholesome and altruistic. Certainly she has had impure thoughts, she has lied about where she goes at night, she has been jealous and gluttonous. It relieves Caro a little to remind herself that, really, she is no worse than her sister.

Just different.

Caro sits beside Imogen and watches as the kirk fills up. Mary Lindsay comes down the aisle, looking thin and smart in a muted brown dress and shoes. Desmond follows her in a dark suit. Mary slips into a pew and bows her head. She is too thin, thinner now even than before, and Caro suddenly wonders if she knows Desmond is seeing someone. Perhaps he has been distant, perhaps he has been awkward with her. The thought makes Caro smile a little.

After the sermon, Caro watches the Lindsays step out of the kirk. Desmond does not touch his wife's arm, does not hold her close. Caro watches as they step gently around each other, as they move in the same direction but as entirely separate beings. Mary Lindsay in her brown dress. Desmond with his dark suit. Two simple, unattached people leaving a church on a Sunday morning.

Caro follows quickly behind them, leaving Imogen and Morag and Wallis behind her in the church. They will speak to one another, speak to Bessie and the other members of the congregation, will not notice her push open the doors of the church with her slender force and go out into the pale light of the day. Nor will they see her stride toward Desmond with determination.

Caro moves past the others who have stopped outside the church doors and who now litter the church grounds. A child climbs the wrought-iron fence and is called to by his mother. Caro moves around the dark coats that occupy the front garden to stand closer to the Lindsays. Mary Lindsay speaks to another woman; her head is tilted away to the side when Desmond notices Caro. Caro smiles and is surprised at his ability to hold his face still; not one muscle betrays that he knows her, that he has lain on damp grass with her body curled small and tight beside him.

Look at me.

Caro moves slowly around to position herself closer still to them. Desmond has turned back to his wife; he is speaking quietly to a gaunt woman with his hands in his pockets.

Caro is aware of each step she takes, each moment when her foot rises from the cement and then comes down again. *One, two, three.*

Look at me.

Caro weaves until, finally, she stands behind the Lindsays. She breathes in—a long, deep breath—and then steps forward, passing between Mary Lindsay and her husband.

"Excuse me," she says. She smiles at Desmond, then at Mary Lindsay, as she squeezes between the two.

"Of course," Desmond says as he moves slightly to the side for her.

Mary Lindsay glances at Caro, then Desmond. Caro sees her eyes crinkle, the spot between her brows furrow. Caro wonders if she can recognize it, if she can see the slight sway in Desmond's body when he is close to her. Mary turns her head—perhaps a bit too sharply—back to the woman she had been speaking to. Caro smiles again at Desmond before she walks away from them. She feels as though she is stepping out of something, stepping out of a deep well or a rushing river. She continues out onto Isla Street, where she stands, waiting for her family.

"Was that the man in the car?" Imogen asks when she appears beside Caro.

"No," Caro says.

"I'm sure I recognize him from that day . . ."

"No." Caro glances at Morag, trying to determine if she has caught something, understood the hard edge behind Caro's words as the certainty of a lie. "Let's go," Caro finally says. "Don't dawdle, Imo."

—

Morag takes the tramcar, then walks up Arbroath Road to the open field. She stares at the wavering of the tent, as if she might be able to see a sign from this distance. She shifts her weight from one foot to another, promising herself that she will go into the tent in a moment.

One more minute.

The minutes go by and Morag still stands outside. She can hear the voices from across the field, then long pauses of silence. In those silent moments, Morag shuffles from one foot to the next, listens to the birds in the trees above.

Just another moment.

Morag is not afraid of the possibility of being healed; rather, she is afraid of the tight thrill that went up her chest the last time she saw Godfrey. She imagines giving herself over to the healer, feeling his fingers touch her again as they had touched the others, then feels shame blossom over her.

Foolishness. Damn foolishness.

Morag walks back down Arbroath Road and then takes the tramcar back to Dundee. She walks home up Hilltown, and climbs the stairs to the flat. She fills the fire with coal, lights the fire, lights the gas lamps, makes herself a pot of tea before the girls come home. Morag sits alone in the flat with her cup of tea and her embarrassment.

Wallis steps out of St. Mary's Lochee with John at her side. The cool evening air touches her as she looks quickly to the left and the right. She cannot help but check for any familiar faces, for anyone who might ask Morag what her youngest daughter was doing in a Catholic church. Those few words so like a spear, a hard point pushed swiftly in. *A Catholic church.*

"The park for a walk?" John asks.

Wallis turns to him, smiles and nods. She would like the shelter of the trees and the pavilion right now. They walk toward Lochee park, John's limp punctuating the silence between them.

The park is lush, green from all the new rain. They step onto the grass and Wallis takes a deep breath, thinks, *This is it. This exact smell is green. This is what Ireland will smell like.*

"Wallis?" John sounds perplexed, put off, ignored by his sudden omission from her thoughts. She smiles.

"Oh, I was away. What were you saying?"

"It would be lovely to have a picnic here. You and me and the children."

"Mmm."

"I'd like you to meet them."

"I know."

"And St. Mary's is always lovely for a wedding."

She is sure it is imperceptible to John, but her body sags, weakens just a little. She does not want to talk about this, does not want to have to find a new way to get around the subject without wounding him.

"Wallis?"

"Yes, John, I am listening." Her voice is more weary than she means it to be. All she had hoped for tonight was a walk in the park in the evening air, a few moments to think and stand under the sky before going home to the noise of the flat and her family.

"Don't you think it would be lovely?"

Wallis looks at his face and sees what she had hoped would not be there: love, expectation, patience. "I'm sure," she says, hoping to avoid the pinpoint of the discussion. She steps into the park, moves delicately across the grass.

"Well, then?"

"Oh, John." She sighs. "Can't we just walk?"

John does not reply but walks beside her in the evening light. She can feel his disappointment as surely as an elbow against her ribs. She loops her arm through his, knowing that this is not enough, it is not what John was hoping for when he uttered the words *It would be lovely*. Yet she cannot think of anything else, any other way to attempt to suture this new wound between them. So, instead, she walks with him across the darkening park and says, "I would love to meet Stephen and Anne."

John straightens, brightens, and she feels absolved.

A bright yellow sun infuses the blue sky and the blue ocean with a shimmering light as Caro walks along the low rocks that line the shore of the Tay. Behind her stands the new Tay Bridge and ahead of her, sitting on one of the low benches, is Desmond. He looks uncomfortable, his trousered legs crossed as he waits for her. He checks his watch, then looks out to the sea; he is impatient in the brightness. Caro moves more quickly along the stones toward him. She calls out, "Desmond."

He turns at the sound of her voice, his face full and carved in the sun. He does not stand but watches as she comes down the beach.

"Hello," she says.

"You're late."

She picks up his arm to read his watch; this finery, its leather strap and golden face. She says, "I suppose I am."

"I've been waiting."

Caro says, "It's a lovely day, isn't it?" Instinctively, she holds her hand up toward the sun to feel the warmth. A bright day in June and Caro sitting on a bench next to Desmond, staring at the sea. She feels suddenly, inexplicably, happy; content as the sun warms her knees under her dark skirt. She puts her hand on Desmond's leg.

For now.

Desmond says, "You should not have done that the other day."

Caro looks at him.

"At the church. You shouldn't have spoken to my wife."

"I didn't speak to her."

"Caro."

Desmond stands. He paces briefly on the sand, and Caro looks at the small impressions his shoes make. Watches the shadow of him cutting across it all.

"I didn't do anything," Caro says. "I just wanted to see you."

"She is my wife, Caro."

Before she can even think it, Caro says, "For now."

He stops to look at her. He is dark—smaller than she remembered—in the sun. "Caro."

She cannot stop looking at his shadow, watching it shrink as he moves toward her. She takes a deep breath.

Caro says finally, "You didn't tell me about that girl."

Desmond looks at her sharply. He says evenly, "What girl?"

"There was a girl. She came into the post office."

"Caro."

She looks at him and sees something she has never seen before. Not guilt quite, nor shame. Something undone and falling around him.

Caro stands and kisses him swiftly on the lips. She says, "Don't worry so. It was nothing." She takes his hand, quickly, before dropping it again. "When will I see you?"

He says, "Soon."

She moves back up the small beach toward the road. She is aware that as she moves away from Desmond, from the heat and sunlight of the beach, she is leaving behind something else, something difficult to name or place. As she steps up to the spot where the beach meets the road, she turns back, quickly, to look for Desmond's dark figure on the beach. The bench is empty. The beach stretches out yellow and lazy behind her, spotless, forgotten.

⌒

The flat smells of urine, the dark, musty scent of night urine trapped in a bedpan, and rosewater. Rosewater, of course, to mask the scent of urine and unwashed skin. Rosewater in a vain attempt to mimic cleanliness.

Wallis has not been up to the flat before, has not met

John's children or the neighbour who minds them. She has always managed to find an excuse—time, weather, peering eyes—but, since the night in Lochee Park, could think of none. She has not yet told him that she has seen the children, that she has watched them from a distance with their hands secure in their father's.

It is unfair to expect the warmth and comfort of the Hennessey flat. Impossible, but still the image is there floating in her head when she steps from the hallway into John's rooms.

It is not a but-and-ben like her own; instead, this flat has only the small parlour and kitchen, then the bedroom tucked away to the left. The smallness of the flat is amplified by its clutter: photos, small porcelain trinkets, teacups, doilies, papers, candles, matches, pillows, clocks. Not one surface remains clear, unencumbered by odds and ends or dust. Small religious trinkets. Wallis thinks she could lay her hand on a table and come up with a palm full of soft, grey dust. She imagines blowing it into the air and watching it fall hazily, immediately lost in the cluttered mementoes of John's wife. Wallis is so busy looking around the flat, she barely notices the children folded into the wide chair in front of the window. Their hands are in their laps, their legs crossed neatly at the ankles. Big docile eyes after being warned for good behaviour. They have the look of something untended; a garden gone wild. Wallis wonders how long it has been since the children had someone to comb their hair, tie bows at the ends of Anne's plaits. Wallis swallows hard.

"Children," John bends down beside them. The girl stares out the window. "Anne," he says, touching her shoulder. She looks at him, wounded and small. Wallis straightens her coat while John coaxes his children into gentle communication. Anne smiles a little with watery eyes.

"Oh, Daddy, you are finally home from work." She pats his leg as one might pat a dog.

"Yes, Anne. I wanted to come home early so that you could meet a friend."

"Oh, yes," she turns back to the window, smiling to herself. She does not look at Wallis.

It's ridiculous, Wallis thinks, I was frightened to meet these children, and they are so small. She relaxes a little, settles back into herself.

"She has been very excited to meet you," John says as he smooths down Anne's hair. Stephen—wearing short pants, despite the chilled evening—looks at Wallis and smiles shyly. John smiles in relief at Wallis, and her heart breaks open wide. "Tea?"

"Please, please." Wallis will never refuse tea. Like Morag and her belief that tobacco and night air will save them from influenza, Wallis believes that tea can help anything. If nothing else, it will calm her nerves now.

John crosses to light the stovetop. The hiss of gas fills the room. He fills a kettle with water, swirls it twice, pours the water out and refills it. He is methodical, particular in everything he does. He takes four china teacups from the cupboard, wipes them quickly with a tea towel. Wallis watches him with new interest. She is not accustomed to his domestic ease; she does not remember ever seeing James pour water in the kettle, much less wipe out china with a delicate swish. Two quick swipes. She watches John's slim hands work quickly and efficiently, and she is suddenly sorry for Morag and Caro, and perhaps even Imogen one day, as they will never know this structured peace. She can imagine herself and John standing side by side, their soapy hands under the running water as they clean up dinner dishes. The soft chatter of the children playing on the floor. The slow falling feeling of comfort, the peace that she longs for.

The kettle cries out and Wallis's reverie is broken. John pours water into the teapot, dotted with small buds. Matching teacups with tiny handles. A vine pattern on the tea towels. Wallis realizes that John is out of place here, not meant to be surrounded by this choking femininity; these are the trappings of a woman, of a house meant to please and accommodate her. John's wife is still here in this suffocating flat; she has removed anything hard or brash or male about him.

"Here," Wallis offers. She reaches out for the teapot, easily moving between John and the tea set. She is embarrassed at his knowledge of the feminine; he must cook for the children, clean for them, bathe them, dress them. She pours four cups of tea—heavily favouring the children's cups with milk—then wipes her hands swiftly on the tea towel. She thinks of Paddy and his time in English jails, and carries the cups across the room to the children.

Up close, Anne is quite lovely; her eyes are pale and milky, her hair a lovely soft brown. Wallis smiles at her, holds the teacup in front of her. "Tea?"

Anne looks at Wallis. Wallis feels herself shrink; the girl's gaze is too direct, capturing Wallis as if caught in a lie. Her heart quickens. She tries to hold the teacup steady. Surely,

Anne is happy to meet her; why should she feel so pried open? Anne bites her bottom lip, lets her mouth quiver into a slight smile, and Wallis moves the cup toward her.

The girl shrieks, flails her hands out in one swift moment. Wallis is struck dumb and still, her hand coming loose on the cup. She watches the cup tip and fall, terribly slowly, to Anne's lap. Wallis is frozen. The tea springs loose from the cup and splashes across the girl's hands and lap. She shrieks louder, and her brother turns to watch. Wallis watches the tea spread down her stockings, turning them a milky brown. She watches the dark stain spread and does not move.

"Anne!" John is at her side in an instant, pulling her stocking away from her leg. He puts a hand on her face so that she will calm and look at him. "Anne, are you all right?"

Anne sniffs and whimpers a little. She looks up at John with thick, wet eyes. She glances at Wallis, then back to her father. She wipes at her wet cheeks.

John turns to Wallis. She does not see anger in his eyes, but something closer to disappointment. "John?"

"I think it's best if you go now," he says. "Anne will need to get washed."

Wallis nods and stands. She has not yet even removed her coat. She wonders if she ever meant to stay at all. "Of course," she says. John turns back to face his children. He rubs Anne's cheek, smooths some of the hairs that have sprung loose from her plaits. Such tenderness.

Stephen says, "Goodbye, miss." He smiles at her as Wallis backs out of the flat, careful to close the door quietly behind her.

Sinking Stones

HIS BREATH on the back of her neck. The scratch of the stone of St. Mary's Forebank pressed against her cheek. The quiet of the abandoned street. The inky darkness of the night. His breath on the back of her neck as Desmond pushes into her, hard and unforgiving.

Caro does not want to look up to see the looming statue of Mary. She does not want to see anything, does not want Desmond's body hot against her, the sound of his voice as he breathes, *You are beautiful.* The hollowness there. She does not want any of it.

She concentrates, instead, on the texture of stone beneath her fingertips, the nature of roughness. She thinks, *Necessity.*

Wallis does not see John for days after the tea incident. The moment with Anne stretching, as if it were as grave as an epidemic, a death. In the days that follow, Wallis worries, watches Imogen fall back in love with Oliver, feels her own heart turn a little more stony. She has been a fool to imagine that she should have this man in love with her, another man seeing something within her, something beyond her jute-tinged fingertips. Within four days, Wallis has accepted that her short relationship with John is over, that she is meant to be somewhere else. Yet she misses the warm brown of his eyes, the roll of his tongue when he speaks. As if, without him, her memory of Paddy is lessened, pulled flat and airless.

Wallis goes down to the water. She does not know where she is going, only this sudden need for the clarity that comes with summer afternoons and the quality of light on the ocean. She watches the city slant by her as she moves steadily down toward the port: women tugging on the hands of small, stubborn children; shopkeepers leaning in their doorways, bored and tired of shops empty except for their own whistling. Wallis remembers the time before the War, when the streets were cluttered and loud and alive, when men went into the pubs and stayed long after they should, when women still coloured their lips in case they met an attractive man in the street. These same women who have kept the factories going and kept their children just barely fed. Wallis longs for the day when the War is over, and the men can return. The city will seem real then, not a strange, empty reflection.

Wallis has never believed in luck or wishes, but today she takes a coin from her pocket, closes her eyes and prepares to make a flagrant wish and throw it into the Tay.

I wish for a different sort of life. I wish to be the kind of woman who has wishes granted.

Wallis knows she should not be greedy, she should only wish for one thing, but how to have one without the other? She throws the coin as far as she can from the shoreline, then opens her eyes to watch for the splash. She sees nothing, not even the slightest break in the surface of the water, and wonders if she has somehow muddled even this too, the simplest thing there is, a wish.

She walks away, leaving the scent of fish and the sea behind. She continues up and onto Victoria Road, surprised when she hears John's footstep behind her. The pull and drag of his bad leg. Surprised more that she lets him follow her for a while before she turns around.

Have I hardened this much in such a short time?

He smiles. "Hullo."

If anyone were to ask her, she would say he sounded exactly the same; she would say that he seemed to be unchanged. "Hello." Her voice is tight, but she manages to veil her sadness; it had been spoiled, this possibility, and she is left now with something else. A secret, heavy determination; a new resolve. Wallis sees rotting fruit, milk that's turned sour and curdled, and understands her own clumsiness, the necessity of one cup of spilled tea.

"Lovely day."

Wallis wonders why he has followed her. Is he being cruel, reminding her that his love for her has shrivelled and dissipated? She has never thought him cruel before, but she can think of no other explanation.

"Yes," she answers.

"Shall we go for a stroll then?" John holds his arm out to her and Wallis—surprised at her quick reflex—takes his elbow. They walk in silence along Victoria Road, parallel to the flat, grey water of the Tay.

Finally, she says, "I feel terrible about the other day." She needs to say this: a quick explanation so that all might be forgiven. She looks up at him and then looks to the water, feigning interest in the ships. Moments pass. The strangled time of the anxious and the wounded.

"Don't worry," he says. "She can be a bit of a fright sometimes." John is smiling at her—an innocent smile that makes her want to cry. He is so uncomplicated it frightens her. He is not plagued by doubt or fear or memories.

"Oh, John," she says as she would to a child. She leans her head on his shoulder. He is solid, real. His feelings have not changed; he is everything certain and simple. In this moment, walking up Victoria Road, she wishes to love him, wishes it was his face, his name that she thought when she threw coins into the Tay.

In the early-morning light, pre-dawn, Imogen's face is silvery and still, her hand lost in her hair.

She is looking for Brigid.

The window affords a picture of the courtyard—Imogen has always had views of them—with their crumbling stones and leaning trees and small gardens, next to which a few stray vegetables have rooted themselves between broken stones.

Imogen is tired of seeing Brigid everywhere. Broken images, other times the same ones playing themselves over and over. Brigid staring out the sitting-room window. Brigid with her face in her hands. Brigid sinking her face in a basin of water. Silent movies, scratched reels. Moments Imogen has not remembered in years: her shallow sobbing once she realized Oliver was gone. Her feet dragging across the room to light the stove for tea. Scalding her hand, holding the infused pink up for Imogen to see.

Why can't you remember more?

Imogen watches the trees arch and bend again in the morning wind. She looks for birds but sees none. The sky is devoid of flight, of the inky blues of crested breasts or shining eyes. The sky is just the sky, the deepest blue stretching as far as she can see; there is no hint of Brigid or birds or clouds.

She has walked up Park Avenue in search of Brigid. She has stood at the edge of the Law, trying to force her mother back into her mind. She has spent endless hours staring at that photo, wishing she could remember everything, every tiny, meaningless moment with her mother. She has taken flowers to her gravesite, hoping that the new blooms might inspire some new memory. She looks out the window. And still, Brigid only comes to her in flashes, small fits of voices and apparitions.

The knob of a door, a plait of hair, a white glove.

This is not enough. Imogen wants more, wants the whole memory of her mother, the terrible bits, the horrible, beautiful bits that have somehow come unhinged from her mind and flown away like a sparrow.

Imogen will go to see the minister. She will look him in the eye and ask him what happened to her mother.

⁓

It all happens so quickly, the shattering of a dream, a glass jug of milk slipping from the lip of a table. The wide breaking open and spilling.

First her hand on his face, on the lines of his jaw, the strict clenching and unclenching there. Just that one plea, that one plaintive wish that she should have kept silent, *Leave her. We can be together.*

The jaw clenching. Clenching tighter still.

She knew what the answer would be before he spoke; his words were just the spike that pinned them to her heart. A disbelieving chuckle.

No.

Desmond did not love her. She had been just another girl, another young, stupid, willing body, blinded by her own determination. She was no better than those other girls she pitied; those girls who looked used up, thrown aside. She was one of them now.

"Caro," he leans out of the car to call after her. She is already a half-dozen feet away from him, moving through the grass toward the walkway of Camperdown Park. She pauses at the sound of her name from his mouth—only this moment, this cry; he would never say her name with tenderness, with real affection, with gratitude as he said his wife's name. She almost turns to go back, almost convinces herself that she can change his mind, that he will love her if she is patient. Then she remembers the awful sight of the girl in the post office, her eyes old and her body expanding shamelessly. The intimation of love in the slim letter. Caro does not love him. That is the difference between her and all those other simple girls. She does not need him. Caro strides across the park, farther and farther from Desmond and her clouded shame. Cars pass her—one does slow for just a moment, it could be Desmond—but she does not turn her head up. She keeps walking until she is alone, until there are no more cars moving past her, until she can smell the green in the park. Until she can think, *Green*, and really see it.

"Caro. What a surprise." Oliver has caught her elbow. His handsome face, his wide smile, unexpected. Caro pulls her arm away. "Oh," he says by way of apology. "Are you off?"

"Yes." She does not slow down, so he must walk quickly to keep up with her.

"Were you with a friend?"

"No." Caro reconsiders. "Yes, I suppose."

"Could we stop then? Sit, perhaps?" He smiles his charming smile at her and she wills herself to refuse it.

"I've got to be home."

"I'll walk you then."

Caro stops, turns to face him. "What do you want?"

"Nothing, nothing. I just saw you coming across the footpath—" Oliver stops. He says quietly, "I saw you coming from Lindsay's car."

"You were spying on me?"

"No. I just saw you."

Caro feels shame spread over her, feels her cheeks flush and her head go light. She lets herself sink against him and begins to sob. Not for a broken heart, as Oliver might think, but because she has been foolish and more than anything she hates foolish women.

(A starling blue-black bruise on her thigh. Caro presses it to feel the expansion of pain. Thinks, This is aggression. This is what he has left her.)

—

Oliver sits in the paisley chair, spying the flat. "I see something yellow."

Imogen hugs her knees to her chest at his feet and bites at her lip. "Is it bigger than a palm? Smaller than a pea?"

They could go on like this indefinitely; Morag has seen it before. She watches Oliver tease Imogen, watches Imogen's unabashed, joyous response. They have already fallen back into an easy relationship; every day Imogen grows a little more attached, a little more enamoured of her father. Oliver and his charm. Charming and fickle and possibly kind, sometimes cruel. Morag worries her tongue against the back of her teeth when she watches Imogen falling back into Oliver. The kind of man who is dangerous to those around him.

"Is it the sun? The flowers on Wallis's teacup?"

Imogen's eyes drinking in Oliver, thirsty and greedy. Jealous, even, when his gaze strays from objects to Wallis to Caro.

"Is it the broom outside?"

Oliver smiles, pleased with himself. He shakes his head and waits for her next question. He turns back to the newspaper in his lap, while Imogen searches the room. Her eyes flicker from Caro at the window to Wallis on the sofa, balancing her teacup on her knee, to Morag beside her. Imogen smiles a giddy smile at her. Morag smiles, doing her best to hide her worry. They could awake in the morning to find him gone again, having crept onto a ship in the night, or having taken the train to another, more gentle and forgiving town. A more forgiving family.

Morag suddenly wishes that she had learned forgiveness. It is something she admires—see how Imogen can forget so easily, and allow herself to be thrust into the thick of happiness?—but she has never managed it.

"What are you looking at, Caro?" Wallis asks.

"Nothing."

"What are you staring at?"

"Nothing." Caro's voice is flat, final. Wallis is hurt; she is impossibly easy to wound, impossibly fragile despite her appearance of all things sturdy and bland. Caro stays at the window, her hand pressed up to the cool glass. Oliver glances at her, watches her for longer than Morag is comfortable with.

"What are your plans, then?" Morag asks. Oliver turns to Morag, and she finds herself seeing him again at twenty-five with his boyish, exuberant good looks. His hair, now, is just as dark except for the temples, where it has turned a new steel grey; his eyes are still mischievous, though there is something older about them and slight lines appear when he smiles; his smile is still as sudden and welcomed as sunlight in January. Oliver has changed little, and this worries Morag anew. His life has been too soft, too easy for him to have any real character; he avoided Brigid's death and Imogen's grief only to return now when they have been levelled into acceptance. They have been hardened, polished like sea-glass, and are safe now to Oliver.

"I suppose I'll have to find a job. And a flat." He winks at Imogen. "With enough room for two."

"Is it the flour label?"

"Room for two?" Morag asks. She has not thought about Oliver's intentions with Imogen; she has foolishly assumed that he would come to visit, treat her like a favourite niece. It has never occurred to her that Oliver might want to be a real father to Imogen. Morag feels the roll of another coughing fit coming up her throat; she swallows hard, takes a sip of tea to quell it.

"Sure," he says. "But a job now, that's the thing."

"And what will you do?"

"I fancy reporting again. What do you think?" He makes a face and Imogen laughs.

"Reporters would have to move around a lot, wouldn't they now?"

"Not necessarily. Maybe."

"Well, then, better to get it over with sooner than later."

Oliver gives her a strange look. "Better to get what over with, Morag?"

"The leaving." The moment she says it, she recognizes the bitter sound of her own voice. She recognizes that she is being unfair, and cruel, but she cannot help herself. Better for Imogen to know now, she thinks, than for her to get hopeful. There is nothing worse than false hope. She coughs into her hand and the room goes quiet.

Oliver straightens and the remnants of his smile disappear. Morag coughs again, now into her handkerchief, and takes a deep sip of tea, thankful for its slippery warmth. Oliver's face turns dark. "I wouldn't say that," he says evenly. He is being careful, she realizes. He is measuring his words, his response to her accusation.

"I would," she says. She gets up and crosses the room to refill her teacup. "More?"

"Is it alive?" Imogen asks.

Oliver is annoyed now, with the game and with Morag and her cynicism. "It's that bruise on Caro's ankle," he says sharply. They all turn to look at the slim patch of Caro's ankle that is exposed beneath her skirt, the small, round yellow bruise there. There is silence. She looks down herself for a moment, and puts her hand over the bruise.

Private Acts

THE STREETS ARE CLEAR and crisp and fresh when Wallis steps out of the bank. She has a slight, serene smile on her lips. She opens her hand and looks at the small, folded piece of paper. The dark, inky numbers come up to her, stunningly perfect in the afternoon sun. She has enough. Enough for her passage to Ireland, enough for the few weeks when she might be without a job, enough that she does not have to worry. She could go now and pack her bags and take the next train to the port of Troon. Nothing stands between her and Ireland.

Paddy.

Wallis writes the letter in her mind. *Tell him I'm coming, Rosemary. I hope it's not too late. I have been praying for this for so long.*

She will need to stop and buy stamps, a crisp envelope. She can almost see her words on the paper; she can imagine Rosemary's excitement, Paddy's face at the port when she pulls into harbour.

Now that I've done it, it all has to be true. Rosemary, Paddy, all of it.

When Wallis comes up the stairs and steps into the flat,

she still has the smile on her face. She steps out of her boots and shrugs off her coat. She says, "Lovely day, isn't it?"

She watches Imogen turn and smile up at her; she sees the slight furrow in Caro's brow, her lack of understanding of Wallis's joy, her smile. Wallis sees this, runs her hand through her hair and relaxes on the sofa. She says, "It's a perfect day."

Morag has planted her own small patch of vegetables in the courtyard. Until she dug her fingers into the soil, there was nothing in this small patch but forgotten blooms, litter, the ends of cigarettes, footprints from drunken walks home. She saw the potential in the small patch of soil; it was the only thing in the close for ages that could sustain life.

Besides, she thought, we could use some greenery around here.

She brought down potato peelings and planted them far down, covering them with her palm. She made an X in the soil so she would know where she had already planted. She wanted to plant asparagus, but thought it might be too difficult. She settled for potatoes and carrots.

Morag wishes she had apple trees, lettuce, something with lacy edges to remember Niall and his dreams of a quiet farm life. Not a shrine, particularly, but a memorial. She has so little to remind her of him or her mother. They might have disappeared entirely if not for Morag's memory. And Brigid has left Morag a slice of herself with Imogen, whether she intended to or not.

Another coughing fit hits Morag. Her throat is raw, always slightly irritated, intolerant now of salt or spices. She is reduced to bland, boiled food, generous amounts of cream in her tea to soothe her coughs. She coughs and coughs and fears she won't stop; she'll cough herself unconscious and be found, here, face down in the small plot.

"Morag?" Bessie Lyon places a comforting hand on her back. Morag tries to answer but is caught by another fit. She waits for the blood on her hands. Soil and blood mingling together in a macabre harmony.

Bessie waits until Morag is calmed, her breathing more even. "Morag?"

"It's nothing. Just a bit of a tickle."

"Morag." She is saddened by the lie in a friendship unencumbered by lies, filled instead with births and deaths and abandonment.

The women are quiet, sheltered from the sounds of Caldrum and Hilltown by the tenements. Someone has planted purple heather out here; the blooms are starting to sprout. Morag wishes it were white heather, suddenly willing to believe that white heather would indeed bring luck. Soon the streets will be lined with summer blooms and the air will be heavy and lush.

"How long has it been then?"

The words wash everything else away. Morag leans into Bessie's sympathy, softened by it, relieved by the honesty. Bessie strokes Morag's hair as she weeps. Unselfconscious, hearty sobs that wrack her body much like the coughing fit had.

"Oh, Morag."

Morag clings to Bessie, leaving dark trails of soil down her lapel.

At the middle of June, Oliver rents a room from Mrs. March, a widow in Magdalen Yard Green, and Imogen's dream of living with him dissolves. She had not even had the time to really imagine the flat with Oliver, had not yet had time to tie herself to the prospect.

Imogen scolds herself, *A silly wish.*

She moves up the street toward the kirk, her stride purposeful and determined. She does not want to think of wishes, but rather of something more specific. She has left school in the middle of the day so that she might speak to Reverend McWilliam. She wants his voice, his honesty. She wants to hear him say Brigid's name and suddenly make her real.

Will that change it all? Will you remember then?

The kirk is quiet at this hour. Imogen feels like an intruder. She croaks out "Hello?" before moving across the front entryway and holding her hand up to the minister's office door. She takes a deep breath, straightens her coat and knocks.

The minister opens the door and smiles at Imogen. "Well," he says. "Imogen Sullivan. What are you doing here?"

She shuffles from one foot to another, suddenly uncertain of whether she has made the right decision. She bites at her thumb, considers and then says, "I want to talk to you. About my mother."

She thinks she sees the minister's face falter, fall just a little. He says, "Your mother."

"Yes. There is so much I can't remember."

"Well, certainly your aunt could tell you all about her."

"No. No, she can't." Imogen does not want to admit that she has been too cautious, too shy to ask Morag anything about Brigid. "It is all too sad for her."

The minister looks at her. "Yes," he says after a while.

"I want to know about . . ."

"Yes?"

Imogen pauses, then says quickly, "I want to know how she died."

Mr. McWilliam touches her arm, much the way Oliver touches her shoulder. Gentle, certain, heavy in a way that only a man's hand can be. "Ah, Imogen, I wasn't here when your mother died."

"Oh."

"That was Reverend Robertson, I'm afraid."

"But you must know."

The minister's hands meet each other in a gesture that is infinitely gentle, unassuming. Imogen thinks, He knows. He knows and he does not want to tell me.

"Mr. McWilliam?"

"Imogen," he says as he puts his hand on her shoulder and guides her out of the church and into the garden. There is the bright light of the day, the squat shrubs around them, the smoke from the Works overhead. There seems to be everything, suddenly, in this small church garden. He sits on the bench and says, "Imogen, you have a family that cares for you. I understand your father has returned. Speak with him; he can help you more than I can." He adds, "Your mother is missed every day."

"But Mr. McWilliam . . ." Imogen hears the desperation in her voice and tries to mask it. "I need to know . . ."

"Imogen, all things come in time. Patience."

Imogen watches the minister as he looks up to the sky, pleased with the day. After a few moments, he moves away from her and back into the church. She stands in the garden and moves from one foot to the other, watching a small bird fly low above her and take rest in one of the tall trees, twittering in the sun.

Caro comes up the stairs to the sound of music. It greets her like a forgotten lover. She stands at the door for a moment, her hand held up to feel the vibrations through the wood. Lets her face crumble and reassemble before stepping into the complications of music.

Imogen is in Oliver's arms, being spun and flung around the room. The windows are open, letting in the afternoon sunlight. Brilliant. Light coming through Imogen's hair. The flat has never been so alive, so pulsing and loud.

"Look what Oliver brought!" Imogen nods to the gramophone with her face caught in joy. Joy at the music, at the dizzying twist of the dance, of Oliver's proximity. "Isn't it grand?"

Caro nods, smiles and bends to unfasten her shoes. This sudden gift of normalcy: music on a Saturday afternoon.

"Come on then, Morag." Oliver spins Imogen to the chesterfield and wraps his arms around Morag. She pulls back, grimaces, before Oliver lifts her unwilling body.

Moves her around the flat with speed and ease, light coming across her face and then disappearing again. As if they stretch between day and night, Oliver leading in complicated steps, Morag twirls and spins and finds herself clinging to Oliver. She is breathless when she collapses onto the paisley chair.

"Who's next?" Oliver asks. "Wallis, come here."

"Ah, no . . ."

Caro watches as Oliver repeats the performance with Wallis, who is stiff at first, but then relaxes into his arms. Lets herself sink into the music and the dance, and laughs when Oliver twirls her in place, dizzying her spectacularly.

"Me again." Imogen is on her feet, moving toward Oliver. Now that Oliver has rented a room, Imogen seems even more eager for any shred of him. Just the touch of his arm. But Oliver reaches out and grasps Caro's hand. He pulls her to her feet as Imogen's smile fades. Oliver pulls Caro close as they arc across the room.

Caro relaxes into Oliver's sure embrace; she bends and sighs and moves like a willow tree in the wind. Oliver holds his hand steady on the small of her back. The tempo of the music changes and they begin to move more slowly, turning from a celebratory dance into a gentle waltz. There is no space between their bodies, just the shimmer every so often of sunlight easing in and tumbling back out. A sudden brilliance on Oliver's dark hair. Yellow on Caro's forearm. Light cutting the crisp line of Oliver's trousered thigh.

The music stops suddenly as Imogen moves the needle off the record. "Time for a new one," she says. She takes the record off and places it on the side table.

Caro is acutely aware of the closeness of Oliver's body before they part. The heat, the girth, the sheer maleness of him. She realizes suddenly that he is reluctant to let her go; his hand remains on her back for a moment too long, a long moment when the sunlight has captured the two of them.

~

Oliver, Morag thinks, is a coward.

The *Weekly News* and *The Scotsman* both splay news of the War across their pages: RETREAT OF THE GERMANS. It seems that the War might be waning; papers report that German workers are suffering from fuel and food shortages, that there is talk of German revolution. The incessant drafting—old men and young boys—has all but ceased. There are now five million American men in uniform. Finally, the War seems capable of end. Finally, it seems the city might no longer be occupied only by women and the unfit.

And Oliver.

Jute comes from India, oranges come from Spain and now soldiers come from Dundee. While all the other men—fit or not—are being drafted and coerced and bullied into fighting, Oliver has been lazing about Calcutta, tanning his face and resting his body. It is shameful, certainly, but not unexpected. Oliver is not the kind of man made for valour or honour; Oliver will rest on his good looks, and after they have begun to fade, on his charm. The memory of fairness, for some, is enough. Morag is sure that Brigid would have been the same if she hadn't died; Brigid would have found some other man to marry her, and would be full of pride and comfort. Brigid's only injuries were self-imposed: Oliver and small pricks from her sewing needles.

Morag gets off the tram when it slows on Arbroath Road, just up from the Eastern Cemetery. It is melancholy, a home so close to a cemetery. The streets are wet. Morag steps from the tram onto the street and begins to walk.

Past the shops below the flats, now with their windows and awnings pulled tight to the rain, the doors painted in red, blue, green. Lovely alder trees growing along the street. She stands at the side of the street and stares.

It is only half-ten; she has time to turn back and pretend she never got on the tramcar in the rain, full of hope. She is coughing up blood daily now; she cannot stop herself from folding in two with the pain. Bessie is the only one who knows, and Morag wants to keep it that way. She does not want the pity or the fretting of the girls, the sad eyes of Imogen being abandoned again, and continues to walk toward the outer layers of the city where open fields and trees stand bare to the elements.

Houdini Is Coming . . . Where? read signs all over Dundee, making Morag think of Godfrey. Magicians. Healers. This is where they might appear: tied to tram tracks; hanging from pier support beams; stranded high atop one of the spired city churches. Morag longs for something as implausible as Houdini now; smoke, mirrors, tricks of the eye. Anything to clear her lungs like a hand wiping a fogged window.

She does not need to search for long; the street number he has given her appears on a dark-blue door. A bright door knocker. A firefly at night.

She wonders how many others have been invited to his rooms on Arbroath Road. News of a healer travels fast, and it seems since the War began there are endless supplies of wounded and dying people. *Dying.* Morag tries not to think the word. She does not want to be like the other mill workers she has seen, who die from collapsing lungs or tuberculosis or bronchitis. Coughing and hacking their insides up, dying from exhaustion. Morag wishes for another answer.

The door opens. She steps into her hope carefully.

"Hello," Godfrey says.

He smiles at the sight of her. He is slight and dark in the dim light of the afternoon. Morag notices the line of his cheekbone, the taper of his inky eyebrow. The first man since James who stands close enough that she can smell his skin. Sweat and travel and soap. Morag's body bristles even at the possibility of him touching her. An accidental brushing of arms. Trouser against the edges of her skirt.

He says, "You said, the Fever?"

"Yes." Morag nods. She allows Godfrey to look upon her with sorrowful eyes; she hopes she will appear more beautiful in the context of tragedy. She coughs and finds his flesh: his hand swiftly on her throat.

His hand is warm, clammy; pleasant in its weight. She has forgotten the solidity of men's hands.

"Yes," he says, "I can feel it." His hand remains there, measuring and gauging. He cups the roundest section of her neck and then frees her. He says cautiously, "There might be a tonic."

"Yes?"

"I would have to bring it over from France."

Morag stares at his round black eyes. He furrows his brow slightly at her inspection.

He says, "It might be rather expensive."

"Will it work?"

"It might."

Might. A word until now that Morag has associated with strength, with bullish men and the capture of territory. Now she sees it waver, turn less opaque and shiver. "I will find a way. If you can get the tonic, I'll find a way to pay for it."

Godfrey smiles and takes her hands in his. Morag thinks he is truly pleased now, optimistic in his ability to heal, to provide wonder, miracles. They stand like that for a moment longer, and Morag feels something within her dislodge.

Caro is wearing the blue taffeta dress when Oliver comes to collect Imogen. He stands at the dark entrance to the flat while she sits in the sunlit paisley chair, a book in her hands, a blanket across her lap. Caro watches Oliver out the corner of her eye. The memory of Camperdown Park comes back to her; she is ashamed that she let herself be so vulnerable with him. He has seen those slim slices of her life and she is left raw.

Imogen throws her arms around him and breathes excitedly, "Come in, come in."

Oliver removes his coat and crosses the room to the small sofa. Caro watches the swift movements of his body, one leg crossing the other crisply. Imogen sits on the floor at Oliver's feet. Caro touches her sleeve, her hair, the spine of the book in her lap; small efforts at normalcy.

Oliver says, "*Portrait of the Artist as a Young Man?*"

Caro looks at him, startled by the question. She says hesitantly, "Yes. Have you read it?"

He nods. "Do you like Joyce?"

Cautiously, "Yes. Very much."

"People say he is difficult."

For a moment, Caro falters: she cannot tell if he truly wants to speak with her, or if he is mocking her. "I love the way he talks about Ireland. About the places he knows so well." She says it before she realizes she means to. She feels foolish, speaking to Oliver about words and geography, things he must know so much more about. She wonders if he finds her foolish, but she cannot see any trace of it on his face. He is looking at her intently. Considering her.

Imogen says, "Can I read it, Caro?"

"You won't like it yet, Imo," Oliver says distractedly.

Caro feels herself blush at the attention from Oliver; his gaze is so steady. Already he knows so much about her. Past her pale skin and loose dark hair; past the blue lapels of the dress; past the walls she has constructed for herself. She realizes he is not weighing her beauty but instead listening to her. He has heard her speak, has let her words sink into him. He leans toward her.

She watches his face and feels something in her turn light when he smiles.

"Where are we going today?" Imogen asks.

Caro looks away from Oliver. She is still in the same simple room with its thick rugs and lingering scent of tobacco and small trinkets on the windowsills.

"A walk to the Law, perhaps, or maybe the Galleries."

"Oh, the Galleries. The Galleries." Imogen is always pleased, always happy to hear that Oliver has planned something, anything, for her.

Oliver glances over to Caro. "Why don't you join us?"

"Yes," Imogen says. "Come, Caro."

Caro looks at her hands, at her book, then back up at Oliver. He smiles. "Maybe I will. Might do me good to get out."

They walk down Hilltown, turn at Victoria Road and then walk on toward the extravagant building of the McManus Galleries. It is beautiful, even from this distance; Caro has always loved the building; stoic and Gothic, it reminds her of an ancient cathedral more than an art gallery. She thinks that just ascending the steps changes her, moves her closer to something she can't quite name.

Oliver opens the heavy lead-glass door, and Imogen and Caro pass through. Caro is always amazed by the silence of the Galleries—only the swift click of shoes on the polished floors—and the coolness of the building. Even on the warmest summer day, the Galleries are a hush of unending chilled air.

"Let's go up to the watercolours," Imogen says.

"It's always watercolours for you," Oliver replies.

Imogen says, "Water, water everywhere."

Oliver laughs, but Caro looks at Imogen expectantly; she feels as if Imogen has let Brigid into the room, as surely as a northern wind or a small flood.

"And you, Caro?"

Caro turns to Oliver, expecting to see his face broken open, cracked with the reminder of Brigid. Brigid floating down a river, Brigid entranced by the Falls. But Oliver's face is plain, smiling. She says, "*Dante's Dream.*"

"You like Rossetti?"

"Mmm." Caro is still watching Imogen, watching her twirl, hopelessly happy, in the foyer of the Galleries. She has sewn small yellow and blue flowers onto the cuffs of her blouse. Just as Brigid might have once.

Imogen places a foot on the stairs, and Caro feels something heartbreakingly gentle in that movement: her small foot suspended in mid-air, only briefly.

"I love Rossetti's imagery."

"Lovely use of colour."

"Have you seen others?"

"Only in books. I'm not a world traveller like you." Caro does not mean this to come out harshly, but she can tell Oliver has taken offence. As if he can see all his days in India laid out before him. As if Caro has stepped around them, not wanting them to mark her.

Imogen says, "Come on, then." She is on the third step now, waiting for them.

"Let's see the Rossetti first," Oliver says.

Caro says, "It's fine—we can see the watercolours."

"Ah, there are always watercolours. There's only one Rossetti."

Imogen comes down the steps, obedient in her blouse with wildflowers. She takes Oliver's hand as they move through the cool, quiet rooms until they step up to the Rossetti. Oliver drops Imogen's hand to consider the painting.

Dulled light comes through the long side windows to diffuse the room in a creamy glow. Even though it is afternoon, the room seems to be a fresh morning; the moments when light and time combine to reveal the possibilities of the day. Caro steps closer to the painting. She says, "It's lovely." She feels overwhelmed by the stilted intensity of the painting, the capacity of light, something within her cut loose.

"I like the watercolours better," Imogen says.

"You're allowed to. It's subjective," Oliver says.

The huge painting looms back at Caro. There is something about the depths of it—the crimsons and golds and muted browns—that makes Caro want to bend and crumple to the ground. The carpet of roses; the delicate kiss between the two auburn-haired women; the makeshift canopy held above them all. Caro sighs. "Do you know the full name of the piece?"

"*Dante's Dream at the Time of the Death of Beatrice.*"

Imogen says, "Who is Beatrice?"

"The girl Dante loved. He met her when she was a child, and he fell in love with her," Oliver says.

Imogen pulls a face.

"Do you think that is possible?" Caro asks. "To fall in love with someone like that, despite everything?"

Oliver turns away from the painting and looks at her. He pushes the hair from his brow. She thinks for a moment that Oliver must think, standing and staring at this painting in this gallery, she is ridiculous.

"I think it's possible to love something about the person. Kindness. A gentle nature. But to fall in love with her then?" He shrugs. "I don't know."

Caro looks at Oliver for a long moment. His words reverberate within her. A full, gentle answer in this cool room. She looks back to the painting, considering. She considers the reality behind it, this poet who fell in love with a child. She looks to Imogen—barely more than a child herself—and sees Brigid. The floating blonde hair. The translucent skin. The lovely, terrible pink mouth. She wonders if Oliver has fallen in love with that part of Imogen. Caro says, "Let's go to the watercolours."

They walk away from the Rossetti silently, the three of them heavier and full now with the idea of Beatrice, her terrible youth and her perfect death.

⁓

Morag steps off the tramcar and back into the bustle of Dundee with the small bottle in her purse. It tinkles slightly, like a woman's laugh, as she walks.

Godfrey had been so pleased when he produced the bottle. "Look," he'd said. "It's finally here." He had smiled at her, a toothy smile full of pride and wonder.

Morag looked at the bottle—the dark green tinge of it—as he held it in his hands. There was a cork stopper and a wavering liquid line. Godfrey held it out to her, placed it gently in her hand, and she felt a bubbling rise within her. The new familiarity of his skin against hers, the kindness of his eyes, his wide bright smile.

It had cost more than Morag expected—the money she had for the gas meter and the week's parcels of meat—but she did not have the heart to say anything to him. She looked at his teeth behind his lips and felt the warmth of his hand, and could not find her voice at all.

Now, Morag moves up Hilltown with the thought of a prayer on her lips. She can do nothing more than think it; she does not dare utter the words. Instead she hopes—*hope* a safe, certain word—that the tonic clears her lungs, lets her breathe in the smoke of the Works as she has for the past twenty years.

Caro knows it when she sees the pattern of her life changing, rearranging to include him. She finds herself doing small, strange things. Wearing the blue dress when she might see him, remembering that he once said she suited blue.

Her shoulder a white-capped mountain. The rolling crest of the sea. A soft place for him to rest his world-weary mouth. This is the first place his lips touch; periphery, as if she might not notice. Before that she'd never thought shoulders erotic. Now even the word seems enticing to her.

Caro has not expected this. She was stunned when his lips first touched her, after meeting outside the Galleries on a clear afternoon, but she did not pull away. Let herself yield. Melt as if she was without bones. Now she thinks, without conscience.

He said, "Caro."

She heard an evening church bell in the distance. Oliver had not moved his hand from her shoulder, and she was thankful for that; she was surprised and saddened all at once. She has seen the way Imogen looks at Oliver and feels a thief. She has taken something that was not hers to claim: what was left of Oliver's heart.

Caro takes Imogen with her everywhere now. Bakeries. Movies. Walks to the Tay. Staring down on the city from the

Law. Caro feels giant, imposing from this height. As if she might reach down and touch the outline of her life.

"Will you miss me when I'm gone?" Imogen asks her. "I promise to come visit."

Imogen is still convinced that Oliver will soon find a new flat where they will live together. She looks out over the city, touching her fingers to her cheek. Caro thinks she looks like Brigid in that moment: nervous hands at her face, anxiety pulsing through her.

"That would be lovely," Caro says gently.

"I hope it's near the water."

She wants to tell Imogen, to confess and hear forgiveness. *I think I might love your father. It's awful, I know, but he sees a part of me that I haven't even seen before.* Caro tastes salt air and turns her head. Imogen touches her arm.

"Caro?"

Imogen looks back at her. Her huge blue eyes. Caro sinks lower with each moment Imogen looks at her. A full, rushing feeling comes through her. "Imo," she says. "Imo."

Imogen furrows her brow. The small, sudden wrinkle between her brows is Caro's undoing. The pucker of skin sitting like a bruise. A pulled hem. She takes Imogen's hand. Her fingers are cold from the wind, despite the summer sun at their backs. Imogen is always a surprise.

"Let's go, hen." Caro tugs at Imogen's hand. She lets the silence fill them in a way that her confession could not. They walk down from the Law with nothing between them but wind.

Wallis holds her hand out over the blank, blanched paper, a pen poised in her hand. She cannot bring herself to write the first word, to change the perfect whiteness of the page. The moment is too fraught.

I'm coming, Rosemary. I am finally coming.

She has purchased the stamps, the envelope, this new, elegant paper. She will remember this moment forever, when everything is still bright and possible and clear.

What will I tell John?

This is the one blot on her image of the future. She cannot be a coward and disappear wordlessly, as if she were a thief or a robber. She will have to watch his face fall, crumple, when she explains it all to him. She will remind him of the Hennesseys, fill in the hot-white gap of Paddy, and tell him that she is going to leave. That she can see her future with Paddy and Rosemary as clear as new jam jars. She will have to explain, in a low and morose tone, her own fraudulent relationship with him.

I never meant anything by it. I am sorry to have hurt you.

The words sound cruel, hollow, terrible. She cannot imagine looking at his face, so open and plain, when she says them.

She looks back at her blank paper, feels the grain against her fingertips. It should all be so much simpler. Just write one word. One word and then another, and then it will be finished. Only a few steps to the postbox. And then it will be done.

Wallis writes, *Dearest Rosemary,* and feels the life come back into her arm, feels her body turn liquid and electric. She watches her own hand writing a simple letter. She watches the ink sink into the paper, this sure, certain path, and makes no move to stop it.

~

The days stretch and merge, turn into weeks and then a month. A month and then a fortnight more. Caro always feels guilty, always feels sly within her new abandonment of everything expected. Swift and sneaky. Oliver does not understand this, instead concentrates mostly on the long column of her neck. Her pulse.

They lie on his bed in his small room. Speak to each other only when their mouths are not consumed with each other's lips. Below them people walk through the Green with their arms entwined, umbrellas held up above their heads. Imogen's hope floats about the room like a shrinking balloon: *a flat near the water*. After they make love, Caro can smell the ocean through the open window. Oliver puts his hand on her thigh.

"You have to tell her," she says.

His hand moves up to the cliff of her hip. Curls his fingers around it.

"You have to tell her." She does not know how many times she has spoken these words to him. It is as if he wills himself deaf and concentrates harder on her bones and the curves of her body. She is desperate for conversation and so finally says, "Wallis is in love with a ghost."

Oliver looks up at her.

"Do you remember Mrs. Hennessey, who put her head in the gas stove? Wallis is in love with one of her sons." He remembers the quick departure of the Hennesseys; there is no need to explain motive, circumstance, the possibility of sin.

"Since she was seven then?"

"I suppose so. Yes."

It is implausible to Caro, this strict definition of love. Had she loved Oliver, even as a child? Oliver in the sunlight of the Ferry, abandoning them for another woman. Even then, Caro was disappointed at the girl's plain, pinched face. Even then, she recognized her need for Oliver to pay special attention to her, praise her. She is unwilling to deny it at least.

Caro holds her hand to Oliver's window and looks out to the Green, feels the moisture climb through her skin and enter her body. She wishes they could walk in the rain. Wishes he could hold an umbrella above her head, guard her from nature, in front of strangers. Caro is tired of secrets, tired of scrubbing the scent of him from her body. She moves her hand down the glass to where it touches the sill—too fast—and feels the sharp stub of it travel through her.

⁓

A silver-blonde plait of her hair. A blue eye blinking. White-gloved hands. Pieces of Brigid float back to Imogen as if they have been travelling down the river all this time, seeking her out.

Today it's a cry. The sound of her mother's sobs; a snap and release of twine tightly wound. Her mouth a gaping cave when she'd found Oliver had gone. Imogen at the end of the bed, noticing the white sheet where, usually, Oliver would have lain. Creaseless, as if he was light as air. Or had never really been there.

To Morag she says, "Do you remember the day Oliver left?"

"Yes." Surprised.

"The bed was so big without him in it. There was so much white. As if it had snowed."

Morag looks at her. "You remember?"

"Yes." It is as if she has always remembered. Imogen remembers a little more every day; she lets herself be filled up without giving any thought to why these memories had been gone for so long.

"Tell me about it."

Morag looks at her. "About what?"

"You know. When you came to get me. When Brigid died."

Morag sighs.

"Tell me," Imogen pleads. She has tried to ask Morag for this so many times before, and every time it has remained the same: Imogen losing her nerve and Morag with her mouth shut, unwilling to let even the slimmest bit of the past into the room.

"It was a long time ago, Imo."

"I know. But I can't remember."

Morag closes her eyes and lets her head come back to rest against the sofa. She repeats, "It was a long time ago."

Imogen knows that Morag will not say any more. Imogen sits quietly in the room, thinking, *Ago, ago, ago.* A small, Oriental bloom, the edges lined in apricot. *Ago.*

When had she known what it meant? She tests the word in her mouth, "Ago."

"Imogen?"

She hadn't meant to say it out loud. Morag wrinkles her brow. Imogen smiles and pulls her mind away from the strangeness of the word. She tries to bring back the small pieces of Brigid that she has found. As if this is her cure; this might make her whole. Perfect gloved white hands. A blue eye half-closed, blinking. A silver-blonde plait of her hair.

The small green bottle rests in her hand. It is a luxurious moment when she tilts the bottle, holds it to her lips, expects the warmth in her throat. Associates the warmth, somehow, with Godfrey himself: the memory of his hands upon her throat capturing the same thick warmth.

Godfrey.

Since she last saw him, she has been unable to rid her mind of him. It seems anything—a door knocker, a white flap of laundry in the wind, small bottles in a cupboard—will bring him alive to her.

His dark hand on hers, his eyes so even, her throat so tight and stunned.

⁓

Brigid has left her mark on Oliver, a long, pale scar that runs down his left shoulder blade. Caro pushes away the thought of Brigid's nail, tearing at his skin every time Oliver touches her, but can't help but be reminded of Brigid: her white-gloved hands, her fragile body.

"What is it?"

Oliver's hand is on the curve of her stomach. His voice is a warm glow in her ear.

Caro is silent, staring at the ceiling. She wants to imagine birds, clouds, anything there but a rope threaded through a crossbeam. She closes her eyes. Puts her hands over her face to keep the darkness with her.

Oliver peels a hand back. The slight brush of air brings with it the chill in the room. Even in the summer, the ocean air is still cool.

"Tell me about India."

Oliver lies flat on his back. She watches his chest, the soft down of hair, the pale sheen. She tries not to see Brigid's hair falling there, trailing across him on an early Sunday morning. Caro is embarrassed by the thought.

"India. India." He runs his hand across her hair. "A lifetime ago."

"Then tell me about Brigid."

She is not sure why she says it. She does not want to talk about Brigid, nor hear him say her name. As if it might solidify this tension draped among the three of them.

Oliver rests his hand on her hair.

Caro says, "You left her."

"Yes. I left her." His voice is not apologetic, but weary. Caro thinks suddenly that Oliver must be disappointed with her question, with its slim shred of doubt.

"If you hadn't . . ." Caro cannot finish the sentence. She lets it hang, lets her breath escape with it. The words are too much to utter.

"Nothing would have changed."

Caro has never considered this. Caro looks at Oliver. He is staring at the ceiling, his hands in her hair, avoiding her eyes and the questions. She feels him pull one small footstep away.

Each morning, before the girls are awake and busy about the parlour, Morag lies on her cot and stares out the windows, watching the dawn unfold. Unfold and come down flat around her like a wilting bloom. She holds her hand to her throat. She hopes it will be clear, feel whole and smooth and normal. She touches her throat and climbs out of bed, reaches straight for the small bottle hidden beneath her clothes. She has kept it hidden from the girls; she insists that it is simply to protect them. She opens the bottle, drinks and chokes back the instinct to cough, to spatter the tonic back into her handkerchief. Wills it to work.

She taps the side of the bottle with her nail and cringes at the hollow reply. The tonic is almost gone. Only a fortnight and already only a few days' worth left. Already she has used the grocery money for the tonic, and the gas money too.

She returns to Godfrey's flat. The close, male scent inside, of sweat and hair cream and the tonics he keeps lined on the side table. A long line of dark bottles, clear bottles, bottles full of thick, green liquids. An apothecary. She listens sometimes as he moves the bottles, touching them lightly to one another, ringing like some kind of ancient wind chimes. Always surprising to Morag that his hands could be so gentle, as if they are cupping water.

Morag opens her change purse and counts the money.

Shuts her eyes. No more money for the tonic, certainly nothing for anything else. If only she hadn't woken.

Morag had been dreaming of her mother's eyes, the small round blue of them. As blue as the sea below, the sky above. Strange how earthly things are so rarely such a cerulean.

Caro mends his trousers, the grey ones that match his smart summer jacket. She pushes the needle in and through the material, noting the small, specific hole it leaves, and thinks, *Imogen should be doing this*. Imogen with her inherited gift to mend, sew, adorn. The mass of pricks on her thumbs when Brigid first taught her to sew. Caro pulls the thread through and watches as the hole tightens. As if there had never been a puncture at all.

She mends his clothes and stares out the window. A long blue sky. Morag sits in the chair next to her with her hands folded in her lap, still. There are so few times Caro can remember when her mother was still. Motionless, her head rests back against the chair. Morag brings a cigarette to her lips and sucks. Lets the smoke out into the already cloudy room.

Morag says, "What are you doing?"

"Mending a tear."

They are quiet together, unconcerned with the muted air of the room. Caro keeps mending. Suddenly she is aware that she is sitting next to Morag, mending Oliver's trousers. And all the while, Morag has said nothing. Caro folds the trousers and puts them aside. She has not expected this, to betray herself in such a thoughtless manner.

Morag exhales. "No. With him. What are you doing?"

"With who?"

Morag looks at her with lean eyes. "Do you think I have gone blind?"

Caro looks at her hands in her lap and realizes Morag knows they have touched Oliver, have held his head, his hands, his stomach. She closes her hands into fists.

"She will be devastated," Morag says with such sadness, such an overwhelming sense of fatigue, that Caro is profoundly shamed.

"I know."

"She's already so fragile."

"I know."

"It could break her."

"I know."

"Will you tell her?"

"Yes. No. I have no idea. Oliver doesn't know what to do." She feels like a fraud saying his name with such ease.

Morag sighs. "You will probably wake to find him gone one day."

Morag's words prick against her heart; Caro has never considered his love to be temporary. She says, "No. We have conversations. He listens to me. He loves me." She means it to be emphatic, but it comes out plaintive. Uncertain and washed away.

Morag takes a long drag on the cigarette. She looks at Caro. "I have seen this all before."

Caro closes her eyes. "No. He loves me."

"For now."

⌒

Imogen finds the photo one morning, and Wallis comes home to find her sitting in the tenement stairwell, holding it.

Imogen says, "Who is this?"

Wallis takes the photo from her and holds it in her hands. Paddy's wide, cheeky smile, his thick, dark hair. Wallis slides the photo into her purse. "You don't know him."

"Who is he?"

Wallis is cautious, nervous of Imogen's steady gaze, her propensity to tragedy and secrets. "Padraig Hennessey."

"The one whose mother put her head in the stove?"

The startling question brings back days after Mrs. Hennessey died: Rosemary's dull, detached air and Paddy's sullen, awful face. Paddy staring up at the sky with his hands stuffed in his trouser pockets, sure that his mother had bypassed limbo and gone straight to heaven despite the sin. Wallis says, "Yes. The same one."

"Why did she do it?"

This is a question Wallis has never been asked, a question she never allowed herself to consider. A thought she never allowed herself to have. Why did Mrs. Hennessey bend down on her knees and put her head in the stove? Some small gesture or crippling hurt. Mrs. Hennessey dirtying her knees on the kitchen floor, breathing in gas.

"I don't know."

Imogen nods, as if this is the expected answer, the reasonable one. Everything unknown and unknowable to her. She says, "Is he in Ireland?"

"I think so."

"You don't know?"

"Yes. I should have said yes."

"Do you write him?"

"I wouldn't know where to send it. I write to his sister." Wallis puts her hand in her purse to reassure herself that the photo is still there. She feels a corner and smiles. "How did you find it?"

Imogen shrugs. Puts her hands in her hair. "Are you in love with him?"

Wallis considers. She wants to share this with Imogen, but she finds herself holding back. Cautious with Imogen and her unreliable nature. Masked by such a face, so fair and sweet-looking. Wallis watches as Imogen raises an eyebrow. Impatient. She says again, "I don't know." Then, "It would be ridiculous to love him, wouldn't it?"

Imogen stubs her toes at the stair below her. Wallis finally sits beside her and stretches out her calf muscle. She is tired, weary from the day at the mill, and she leans her head against the cool wall. She puts her hand on Imogen's. "I'm so tired."

Imogen pats her hand. She says, "Maybe you should go to Ireland. Find Padraig."

Wallis sees Ireland shadowy in the distance. She surprises herself when she lets a bit of herself away and says, "Maybe I should."

They sit quietly together in the stairwell. Wallis has opened a door the slimmest crack and Imogen has walked straight in.

It's a clear day, a day full of yellow sun and summer and low-lying heat. Caro wanted to meet here, to stand on the street, where they might hear the clanging of church bells, fragments of other conversations. She is afraid to be alone with him, afraid she will lose her nerve. She stands in her blue taffeta dress on the corner letting the sun warm her.

"I can't do this." Caro is aware of the sun on the back of her neck: a hot, brilliant spot the size of a palm laid flat. All around her, summer is in vibrant bloom: dahlias, roses and day lilies mingle in a small plot at the side of the street. If she bent and touched the pollen, it would stain her fingertips. Red. Yellow. The palest purple. A rainbow would appear if she raked her fingers across Oliver's face. She's heard of tribes in colonies painting their faces this way. They must look lovely in the colours of summer blooms and fallen autumn leaves.

Oliver does not speak, instead watches as she moves her weight from one foot to another. She is uncomfortable with his gaze, so open and plain and honest. She turns her head and says again, "I'm leaving you."

"I heard you."

"We can't do this. Imogen . . ."

"She will be fine."

"She won't."

"Yes, she will."

"How can you be so sure? I'm not certain of anything any more."

He puts his hand on her cheek. "Caro."

She holds herself like stone for a moment, stiff in the

street in the sun in her taffeta dress, then she finds herself
leaning into his hand. She does not want to leave him but
cannot see any other way. She's felt her doubt about him
growing. What does she know of him, other than his aban-
donments? Books. Galleries. But Oliver is the only man who
has looked at her and seen more than her face, her body, the
coy tilt of her eyes, listened to her.

He puts his arms around her and rests his lips on her
forehead. She sinks against him, into the comfort and the
tenderness of his body on this street corner, the sun warm-
ing their bodies. There is nothing else for her to do. She
smells the warmth of skin at the base of his neck. She says,
"You have to tell her."

"Yes."

Her hands folded in her lap, Morag sits in the room on
Arbroath Road. She watches Godfrey at the table by the
open window, his shirt collar caught in the low wind. He
holds small glass bottles up to the light and they turn the
colour of sea-glass. Measuring. Pouring. Grinding. Carefully
mixing. Morag catches a sudden sharp odour, like pine.
Something starkly bitter. Godfrey's back curls as he pours
the two tonics together. His face lost to her; she watches his
back, his elbows, the darkness of his hair against the open
window. Morag waits patiently, accepting that Godfrey's
meticulousness is necessary. Essential. He is mixing a new
tonic for her. He says it came to him in the night. Woke him
from a deep sleep. A mixture of three promising ingredients.
Morag sits in the hard, high-backed chair and waits, careful
not to think, *Magic.*

This morning, she'd filled her purse with found coins and folded bills. Careful of the tinny music of the coins against one another. Money she should use for groceries, to pay the rent, pennies for the gas. She'd held the coins a moment longer than necessary, feeling their weight. She will not have enough to pay for the flat. It must be worth it. She will find a way, find the money somewhere. She imagines becoming one of the women who walk up and down Harbour Street, lingering when the jute ships come into harbour, full of hungry, mean men.

"There." Godfrey turns around from the window. He holds a bottle in his hand and his face is pulled tight by a smile. Morag thinks he looks hopeful, expectant as he moves toward her. "I think this is the one." Godfrey offers the bottle and their hands touch for a moment. His fingers are stained a pale purplish-blue and smell strongly of French lavender.

She says, "Thank you."

"It's French lavender to heal," he says. "It came to me. Healing."

Morag nods, watching the light come to his eyes as he speaks. She thinks he is as anxious as her for a cure. She imagines holding his hands to her face, breathing in the scent.

"Is it any better?"

Morag shrugs. She holds back the details: her dreams of her mother; her irrepressible cough; the blossoming bloodstains on handkerchiefs. She is tired, sleepless and weary.

She watches his hands as they come to her throat. His slim fingers find the tiny buttons at the collar of her blouse and begin to push them back through the holes. Silence escapes beneath his fragrant fingers. Morag breathes in quickly, uncertain. His eyes are fixed on his work. She is anxious, expectant; the quick possibility of her clothes falling away, her body exposed to the cool breeze coming through the window. Godfrey's deliberate hands learning the small crests of her breasts, the soft loose skin of her stomach. Years since any man had seen her that way, vulnerable and plain as daybreak. Morag wants the taste of his fingers in her mouth. A want so sudden and raw, she shuts her eyes.

Godfrey's fingers touch her neck, the pale skin now visible. A mole at the base, a purple-blue vein. His thumbs work their way down the column and then rest. He begins, slowly, to button her top three buttons. Morag opens her eyes.

He says, "There is still some swelling."

Morag does not want to say what she is thinking: *It's not working. None of it.*

"The new tonic should help." Godfrey sounds convinced, but Morag feels the flicker of doubt pulse through her. *It's not working.* But the doubt dissipates when she looks up to Godfrey's face and sees his dark eyes. She should never have doubted his abilities. She opens her purse and places the money on the side table. It feels rude, obvious. She puts her hands back in her lap.

Godfrey says, "Will I see you soon?"

Morag nods. "Yes, yes."

She stands and Godfrey moves with Morag to the door, places a dry kiss on her cheek. "Soon, then."

She grips the bottle in her hand as she moves down the steps and out into the glaring afternoon sunlight. Morag puts her hand to the spot where his lips have been. Thinks, *It will work. It must.* She looks up but sees nothing. Not even the shadow of him watching her.

Lost Letters

CARO HEARS ABOUT the drowned girl from the women in the post office. A girl who jumped from the new Tay Bridge. Fell like an overstuffed down pillow. Caro tries not to imagine the sound of her full body hitting the water.

"Poor wretched thing."

"Did they say who the man was?"

"Imagine her family." Mrs. Shea crosses herself. "It's a sin."

Caro is silent on her stool, biting at her lip. Another quick, swift death. Like Brigid and her fraying rope. Caro chews her lip.

"Horrid thing if the man wouldn't help her."

"I heard he wouldn't even speak with her. Just left her be."

"Maybe he didn't know."

"He knew," Caro says absently. The three women turn to look at her. "I mean, he must have. Don't they always?"

Ruth looks skeptically at Caro. Disbelief clings to the corners of her eyes. Caro looks away, busies herself with shuffling envelopes. Broughty Ferry. London. Glasgow. She wishes she were someone else, someone in one of those towns, waiting for her own mail. Not sitting in this warm room with windows smudged by fingers and the stale scent of bored women, with this burrowing nauseous feeling in her stomach.

That letter.

Her thick body, floating through the air. A kite caught on wind.

Perhaps he could have helped her. I could have saved her.

Caro has not expected this sudden rush of emotion. The memory of her hand carrying the envelope to the waste bin. Nor could she ever have expected the girl's throwing herself in the Tay.

Caro wanders through Murraygate and looks at the bridge before walking up Dens Road home. She does not bring the news of the girl home, but Imogen holds it out like a morbid gift when Caro arrives. Imogen brings all the news of death into the flat: Brigid, Elsie McRae and now Desmond's lover. Caro does not know how Imogen hears such gossip; it is a strange gift, this ability to collect news of other people's tragedies.

"She was one of the Kavanaghs. The youngest one, Alice. She was going on fifteen."

"Fifteen?" Morag says.

"Her mother has been given sleeping pills by Dr. Graham. She was wailing her head off."

"Couldn't she have been sent off somewhere, until after the baby was born?" Wallis asks.

"They have no money to send her away, and apparently the father wouldn't speak with her. Mrs. Kavanagh went to St. Mary's every day to pray for help."

Morag says, "You would think the parish could help them. Clepington would."

Imogen is trying to hold back a mischevious smile. Caro sinks onto the sofa, closes her eyes and hears Imogen. "Do you want to know who the father is?"

The flat is silent for a moment, but Caro is sure they can all hear the beating of her heart, thumping away at her chest until she is certain a bruise is flourishing across her breast. Summer peonies in a sad shade of purplish-black. She wishes she were standing in a field with drooping trees surrounding her, carrying a net for butterflies. She wishes she could sink to the ground and feel sunshine on her legs. She wishes Imogen's mouth could be sewn shut.

"Desmond Lindsay."

Like the slash of a knife through a kidney pie. Desmond has been changed from a philandering man to something worse, something between a child-lover and a child-killer. Either way, his hands have been stained. Indifference is close to blame.

Caro keeps her eyes closed for a long time, until she forgets she has closed them at all and drifts into a dreamless sleep.

In bed, Caro searches out Imogen's hand. Moonlight spills across Imo's face. "Imo," she whispers. "I saw that girl."

Imogen is still full of sleep. She stares at Caro in the dark.

"In the post office. I saw her and took a letter from her." Caro's voice is soft as a nighttime wish.

Imogen rubs Caro's hand in small circles.

"I took it from her," Caro says, meaning for Imogen to understand. Meaning to make a confession in the dark.

⌐

Hope is a private act.

Morag holds the bottle to her lips. Feels the liquid slip past and down her throat. Sting. The taste of flowers on her tongue.

Lavender to heal.

Flowers on her tongue. A song in her heart crying out to Godfrey. Slight as a wish. A prayer.

⌐

Warm brown eyes. That small gold cross about his neck. The sky behind him, a hard, startling blue against the white pavilion. One sigh. Her lips open—close again—open. She is suddenly struck dumb. She wonders where her voice has disappeared to.

"Wallis?"

He smiles at her. She feels her heart contract, nausea well over her. She will have to say the words. *I'm leaving. I'm sorry that you expected more of me.*

John puts his hand on her shoulder. Wallis closes her eyes to the blue sky, to this moment, to his face, gone soft and milky and calm.

"Wallis?"

She cannot manage the words. She stands staring up at him, wishing herself more courageous. One word. One simple sentence. Her lips are still while her head buzzes with words, carefully measured sentences prepared for this moment when she breaks the past from the present. When she forces the words from her mouth and moves one step closer to the future.

"What is it, Wallis?"

She opens her mouth, almost feels the words coming along her tongue, but only manages, "Nothing. It's nothing."

Imogen waits on the steps of the *Courier* building, waiting for Oliver and imagining how she might have stood here, waiting for him every day if he had never gone away. One moment, one decision, one door left open instead of slammed shut.

Is it all that simple? Can it all hinge on him?

"Hullo." Oliver appears beside her with a grin on his face. Imogen looks at his shoes and sees that they are in need of polish.

"I've been waiting for you."

"Well, here I am."

They walk together away from the *Courier,* past the Galleries and up onto Victoria Road. The streets are busy, crowded and bustling with people, and Imogen thinks of the sea. They are moving within a wave, being pulled by the swell of bodies. They walk down into Murraygate, where people are less rushed, less impatient. They slow a bit, so that they can move in the lazy manner of people done with their workday and gliding into the soft evening hours.

Oliver says, "Why were you waiting for me?"

A momentary crack of light in a darkened corridor. She says, "I want to know about Brigid."

Oliver looks at her. "Brigid?"

Imogen nods. She looks up at Oliver and waits. She wills

him to open his mouth and talk, draw in the blanks of Brigid swiftly and precisely.

He looks away and sighs. "What do you want to know?"

"Everything."

Oliver laughs. "Everything," he says. "You're not asking for much then, are you?"

Imogen smiles, softened and relaxed by Oliver's laughter. She says, "I want to know about when she died."

The moment the words leave Imogen's mouth, Oliver stiffens. He says, "I wasn't here."

The quick admission of abandonment almost stops her.

"I know. But you must know what happened."

"Imogen, why would you want to talk about that?"

"Because I don't remember. Why don't I remember?"

Oliver stops in the middle of Murraygate and looks at Imogen. He puts his hands in his pockets and leans back against the building behind him. He looks suddenly older and different. Not the father from years ago, Imogen thinks. She shuffles from one foot to the other.

He says, "Maybe you don't want to remember."

Could it be that easy?

"But I do." Her voice is more plaintive than she means for it to be.

"Come on," Oliver says as he moves away from the building. "Let's walk home. I'll even buy you a sweet."

Imogen follows quickly behind. "But I want to talk about Brigid."

Oliver stops, spins to face her and says angrily, "I don't want to talk about Brigid. Do you understand? I want to forget about it all."

Imogen is stilled, as if Oliver had reached out and struck her. She breathes in deeply, hoping to push the welling tears away. Oliver from years ago, angry with Brigid. She manages, "Oh."

Oliver softens and puts his arms around her. "I'm sorry, Imo, I shouldn't have yelled at you. Come on, we'll stop and get you a sweet."

As surely as if he had crumpled Brigid's photo, scratched the image of her face blank, Imogen knows that she will not speak again of Brigid to Oliver. She will not ask him to go back to those moments when he must have learned of her death. Instead, she takes his hand and lets him lead her through Murraygate in search of hard candy.

Caro walks to the harbour and stands on the shore. She wants to take off her shoes and stockings and feel the grit on her bare feet. She wishes she had a penny to throw into the Tay, though she is not certain what she would wish for. She feels childish ever to have wished for anything.

The men working on the harbour docks pull crates from the foreign boats in seamless motions. Their labour turns their limbs into taffy: stretching out, pulling back, stretching out again. She wonders if some of them saw the girl when she fell, noticed her nightgown billowing on the wind. They must have turned their heads for a moment in the cool morning sun, hoped for a slice of brilliance and instead saw her impossible wings. These men who would never get the sight from their minds, just as they would never remove the scent of the sea from their skin, despite lye soap and raw hands.

Caro turns away from the Tay.

I might have saved her.

Caro remembers the damp envelope slipping from her fingers into the wastebasket. The girl's forlorn scrawl.

She walked barefoot onto the bridge.

Caro cannot remember the face of the girl exactly. She remembers her wet hair, her thick fingers when she pushed the envelope across to Caro. When she trusted Caro with the small package with its lifeline to her future. Misplaced it. Caro knows what she would wish for now: to remember her face.

She must have closed her eyes when she jumped.

Another boat pulls into the harbour, bringing with it the low yells of the men and the deep creaking of wood suspended too long in water. Caro closes her eyes and hopes to breathe in a foreign country. She breathes, but only smells the Tay. Finds it strange when it comforts her.

"Are you planning to stow away?" Oliver has come up behind her while she is standing there with heavy, lazy eyes. She thinks for a moment, *Desmond.*

"Not quite."

He stands beside her and gazes out over the sea. Gulls fly close to the water, arc their bodies across the sky in some sort of unknown pursuit, land on pieces of driftwood. Rocks. Their sharp cries puncture the air. Caro looks down at her hands. She wrings them.

"I thought I would die on those boats," Oliver suddenly says. He does not look at her but faces the Tay. An inevitable listener. "You don't realize how much it rolls." He laughs. "I didn't realize."

Caro says, "Why did you come back?"

Oliver looks at her. Shrugs. "I'm not sure."

"Morag thinks you have left a woman behind. That you are abandoning someone."

"And what do you think?"

"You left Brigid."

Oliver turns to her. She has never seen his face like this: scoured of charm.

"I'm sorry," she says.

"I came back," he says. "I could have stayed away. But I came back."

"I didn't mean . . ."

"I know what you meant. I'm so tired of defending myself." Oliver pauses. "Come on, I'll walk you home."

Caro lets him turn her away from the harbour and up Hilltown. She lets him hold her elbow as they walk in silence, the only sounds between them the tapping of their shoes. Caro looks to him for his honest face, the soft one she sometimes witnesses, but it has disappeared. The memory of a night apparition.

⁓

In his small room in Magdalen Yard Green with its leather-bound books and prints that smell of saffron, Oliver pulls the pins out of Caro's hair, letting it fall. Caro loves the scratching feeling of his fingers there; skull down to neck. Up again.

Oliver says, "Tell me about him."

Caro looks at the ceiling; the tobacco and water stains make her consider the other bodies once in this room. "Oh, Oliver."

"Did you love him?"

"No. But I thought he might love me."

"Would that have made a difference?"

"I don't know. Maybe." Caro will not patronize Oliver. She will not lie.

Oliver says, "Did you want to save him?"

"No. I wanted him to save me." Caro stretches, long and languid as a cat, over Oliver's lap. She does not want to talk about Desmond. She wants to sink into the heat of his body and the weight of his hand resting on her head. "Does it matter?"

"No. But you are so mysterious about it all."

"I don't want to think about him."

"Did you know about the Kavanagh girl?"

Caro has not expected this. Alice Kavanagh. "Yes. Yes, I knew about her." Caro moves from Oliver's lap and stands at the table. She strikes a match and lights a candle. The quick scent of sulphur fills the room. She says carefully, "She came into the post office."

"Did you speak to her?"

"I took a letter from her."

Oliver looks at her across the room. She wishes she didn't have to reveal this slim part of her, the terrible act she wishes she could slice away. "I threw it away. It was a letter to Desmond and I threw it away."

Caro watches Oliver for the slightest glimmer of disappointment. His face does not change.

"You couldn't have known," he says.

"But I did. I opened it. She wanted his help, and I threw it away."

Oliver says nothing but lies still on the bed. After a moment, he crosses his arm over his eyes. Caro looks out to the sea far below, listens for the rumble of church bells but hears nothing. The slight crackle of the candle burning.

Caro says, "You think I'm horrible now, don't you?"

She thinks, This is it. This is when he will leave me.

Oliver says carefully, "No. You did a horrible thing, but it was a mistake. It was a mistake, wasn't it?"

"Yes. Yes, of course."

Oliver stands and crosses the room to put his arms around her.

Caro crumples against him and feels a sudden clarity. Oliver loves her. It is not clouded or complicated, but unbearably simple: he loves her despite her involvement with Desmond, her blind and baffling attempt to flee her family, her implication in the Kavanagh girl's death. It is not dependent on her beauty or her charm or her goodness. Oliver has managed, somehow, to love her unconditionally. She breathes in the scent of fresh laundry at his shoulder and lets herself be happy. She has Oliver's arms around her, the promise of a bright day tomorrow out the window. This is finally enough.

Morag has learned the route from her flat to Godfrey's so well that she could walk it in her sleep. Her sleep even full of him now. Her feet remember the uneven cobbles, the spot where there is a thick crack, which she avoids stepping on.

Morag holds her hand up to Godfrey's door, stops short of knocking. She smooths her hair, touches her cheek. A rush of vanity. She raises her hand again and raps on the door.

Godfrey opens the door and smiles at her. He places his hand on Morag's shoulder and she feels the warmth of his palm. He steers her toward the small settee and they sit. Morag says, "Don't you ever get tired of it all?"

Godfrey wrinkles his brow.

"Tired of helping everyone. Of the burden."

"It's not a burden. It's a gift."

Morag is quiet, considering. A gift. As if it is something to be given away. He must have nothing left for himself. Empathy—the smooth wash and tidal pull of it—consumes her. This new compassion suddenly coupled with desire. Her heart bends. She puts her hand out, lays it uncertainly on his thigh. It is her first, uncompromising gesture. Her hand lies heavily across the crisp pleat of his trousers. Godfrey does not move, does not say anything while Morag's heart speeds in her chest. A hard, thick thumping. She thinks, Do something. Say something. The clock ticks, and her breath comes out ragged. Morag waits for what seems like an eternity.

Finally, she lifts her hand from his leg and folds her hands in her lap. Keeps them quiet and still.

Godfrey says, "Well."

Morag stands and moves away from Godfrey and her hot embarrassment. She stands at the door, her face away from him, and says, "Good night then." Their hands briefly touch as they both reach for the doorknob. Morag pulls her hand back as he opens the door and leaves with her hands hidden deep in her pockets.

⌒

August 26, 1918

Dear Wallis,

I was so happy to get your last letter! You must tell me when you will come, so that we might meet you at the port. Of course, you will stay with Joseph and me—it will be just like when we were girls! As for Paddy—I have not told him yet, but will soon enough. I am sure he will be just as happy as we are. Oh, Wallis, imagine how fine everything will be . . .

⌒

Morag continues to dole out her wages to Godfrey. Tonics. Herbs. Copper healing bands. Morag watches the money disappear, biting at her lip and worrying her hands.

Wallis has paid for groceries, Caro has dropped pennies into the gas meter. Morag feels another surge of guilt with each coin's tinny drop. No one has asked about the money yet, though Morag has caught Wallis's worried, anxious eyes. Her youngest daughter and her worried eyes. What must they think Morag has done with all the money? What tales have they invented to explain her extravagance?

Wallis comes home with her arms full of groceries: carrots, soft peas, potatoes, a small portion of beef. With her back to Morag, she says, "What is it?"

Morag watches Wallis light the gas burner, then add a pot of water. Cut round, orange jewels of carrot. Peel back the skin of potatoes. Wallis wields the knife so efficiently in the small kitchen. The cords in her wrist. She chops and waits for Morag to answer.

Morag does not expect her own sudden tears.

"Mum?" Wallis turns and leaves her pot of water, the brief miracle of carrots against a blade. "What is it?" Wallis crouches beside Morag.

"I've been ridiculous," she finally manages. "I've wasted it all." Morag holds up the small green bottle. "This. All on this."

Wallis unscrews the bottle to smell it. "Perfume?"

"Lavender to heal."

"Heal?"

Morag's eyes are limpid, sorrowful. "I have the Fever. I've been seeing a healer."

"Oh?"

"His name is Godfrey. He's only been here a few months."

"Is it working?"

Morag says, "No." She does not have the words to explain him. Sudden shame at her desire for him, her unwavering belief in him. The scent of lavender comes over them again, a scent Wallis will forever associate with shame, with the foolish secrets of women.

Wallis knows now she will not cross the Irish Sea. Her body will continue to know nothing but hard labour, her wages now devoted to the running of their household. She will marry John. She will stay in Dundee. She will not see the spires of St. Patrick's Cathedral, she will not know the streets where Paddy has slunk through the night. She will not, really, know love at all.

The word *forsaken* comes to her mind like a ringing bell. A church bell and her mother's face, a funeral hymn.

⁓

Morag steps into Clepington in the early afternoon, after she is finished at the Works for the day. Her body aches; her lungs groan; her hands are stiff and sore. They all knew. Shortened workdays, a handkerchief full of blood. The other women in the Works spoke gently to Morag, their voices hushed. She spent the morning trying to hold back the used breath in her lungs, avoiding their huge, horrible eyes.

Unnoticed, Morag moves up the aisle with the ease of a ghost and sits in one of the polished pews. Its hardness reassures her; how many bodies have sat in this simple wooden pew, just as she does now, folding fingers and legs for prayer. Morag puts her hand on the back of the pew in front of her, steadies herself. How long has it been since she prayed for anything? She is not sure what she would want now, a cure or a quick death. A reprieve, that is what she wants. Instead of these days at the mill, nights alone in her cot, her mother's face. An afternoon at the shore, a fine silk scarf to wind about her neck, a silver pin at the lapel of her coat. Things that glitter. Brigid's face smiling up against the sun, Oliver's hand stretched out to her. That small portion of a day locked in her mind.

Morag opens her eyes to the kirk and the sunlight of the past disappears. There is the waxy, heavy scent of the kirk, the hardness of the pew against her thighs. The rattle of her lungs when she breathes. Morag can only hope for relief. She cannot dare to speak the word *death* so close to God.

⁓

Imogen does not follow Wallis any more. Wallis no longer goes for long, languid walks skirting the Howff, nor does she step into St. Mary's Lochee with the thin, limping man. Wallis has turned back into Wallis: dependable, predictable and ordinary.

Wallis hovers around Morag now. She watches her with careful eyes. Imogen always watching the watcher. Imogen watching Brigid through the night window. Imogen watching Oliver and Caro in the courtyard, framed by a slender willow tree. Caro with her hands in her pockets, Oliver reaching out almost to touch her. Almost. Stopping short so that his hand is still in the air. Imogen can almost feel the pulse in the air between them when she sees them from the window.

Imogen looks out across Camperdown Park and watches a wild rabbit cross the grass. Oliver, she thinks, has become smitten with Caro. Men always are. Imogen does not mind this, Oliver's innocent distraction with Caro. She is certain it is temporary, a reprieve from loneliness. Oliver, who has always found himself alone, first after Brigid's death and then, so many years later, after leaving India. This one act Imogen claims for herself: Oliver gave up happiness and love for her. To come back to her.

She has never seen a photo of the Indian woman, does not know necessarily that she exists. But Imogen imagines her fully constructed, a whole, lovely person. A woman standing at an open door, the heavy scent of spices—paprika, curry, saffron—behind her. A woman standing with the Ganges River ahead of her, its twisting and destructive nature so close. A beautiful brown woman with eyes dark as coal, slim, bangled arms and a mouth forever tempting a smile.

A brown woman waiting at a door. Nothing more, but Imogen likes this moment when the woman stands on the edge of everything—the rough lip of her doorstep, the river, her love for Oliver—considering.

The door shuts and the woman leaves Imogen's mind. Another door. Another lock.

With Oliver sitting on a bench in Baxter Park, Imogen says, "I'm sorry you had to leave her."

Oliver's hands turn still as stone on his knee. "You are?"

"Yes. You might have been happy."

"I might."

Imogen considers and agrees. "Or not." She watches the rabbit come out from the shrubbery and move across the grass. All that green, wet from last night's rainfall. "Are you happy now?"

"I am. Yes." Decisive. Without pause. Certain.

Imogen smiles and pats her father's hand as if he were a child. She is glad for his new joy, this late-summer afternoon in the park, the wild rabbit across the grass.

Just the flat landscape of a farmer's field, where green sinks into gold, then russet and back again. A small, primitive fence, sheep grazing. Morag is searching for the peacefulness of white against sky.

The tent has disappeared.

Earlier, she had been to his flat. She held her hand out, felt the cold doorknob and knew he had gone. Knew it without having to knock, without even the desire to do so.

Disappeared, vanished, as if he had never existed at all.

Heaven & Hell

IN COWGATE SITS A CORNER called Heaven & Hell. The John O'Groat's public house on the ground floor, full of men drunk on cheap, rough liquor who often fall out into the street, stumbling to the ground or erupting into brawls. Above the pub is the Wishart Church, where the famous Mary Slessor worshipped before she became a missionary in Nigeria. The clever juxtaposition is not lost on Caro.

She can see Oliver at one of the small tables under one of the front windows in John O'Groat's. Caro wishes she could step into the pub and sit beside him, but there would be nowhere for her to sit: it does not have a snug for women. She imagines Oliver has a full pint on the small, nicked table and the *Dundee Advertiser* open to an article from Joseph Gray, the "fighter-writer." Oliver is always reading newspaper articles, though he claims he does not want to see the news of the War, does not want to hear about the trenches or the gas.

Caro thinks about the last time they made love. He had run his hand down the knobs of her spine to the small of her back where sweat had gathered. He'd said it reminded him of India, that small pool.

"Tell me about it," she said.

Oliver ran his hand down her cheek. "Ah, you don't want to know about all that."

Caro trapped his hand firmly in hers. She said, "But I do. I want to know about her."

Oliver had thrown his arm across his eyes. "Caro."

"Tell me. I want to know."

It had been a slow, cautious extraction; Caro a woman in a desert, digging to find the bones. She had listened to him speak, to the details of India and the anonymous woman, and turned it searingly alive in her own mind.

There had been an afternoon in India when he watched the woman sleep, her back to him so that her body formed a rise and fall of low mountains, where her ribs turned into her waist, then again to her hip. There had been a few drops of sweat, still, at the base of her spine. He said the heat was unbearable, impossible to explain. Imagine the heat from the gas burner on your wrist; now imagine that heat like a cloak around you, always. In this impossible heat, Oliver bent to lick the sweat from her back. She did not wake; she was used to the feel of his tongue on her bare skin.

It's those small moments—Caro's damp back as he pushed into her from behind—that remind him of those years away. Years that he said he wished he could forget, wipe from his memory with the back of his hand.

The last time he saw her—the morning he left India, tucking himself onto one of the jute ships destined for Dundee—she stood on the veranda in the shade. Early morning and already the sun was unrelenting, spiralling heat up from the dirt roads. The smell of cardamom clung to the house, mixing with the scents of the previous night's cooking.

She stood in the shade, her skin dark against the white sheet wrapped around her body. Gold bangles on her arm elicit music on the close morning air. She pushes her hand through her hair, letting the dark strands fall through her fingers. Midnight rainfall. She says, "Oliver."

Oliver is standing away from the house, away from her in the white bedsheet he had lain on the night before, in the early sun. He can feel the heat on the top of his head, burrowing through his hair. He wishes he had a hat, or could move into the shade.

She says, "Oliver. Please." In her accent, this plea becomes a song. He wants to forget the sound of her voice.

"You'll be all right," Oliver says. "He'll be back soon enough and you can forget all of this."

"I won't forget you."

"You'll have to." He knows she will lock the memory of him away, just as she had put away the image of her husband while he was gone. Oliver was not even sure where he had been; all she would say was business, business, and wave her hand. The music of her bangles. Two months of business, and only one letter. A letter she tucked into the folds of her green sari. Oliver watched her hands for days, but never saw her unfold the letter. He imagined she must have woken in the middle of the night, crept from the bed they'd shared, and read the letter by moonlight. To Oliver, her husband is a faceless man. He could pass him in the street without notice.

She does not deny it, just leans against the porch column. The bedsheet slips and exposes the side of her breast.

She catches Oliver staring at her and moves forward, still in the shadows, until her toes touch sunlight. Slowly, she unwinds the bedsheet and lets it fall away from her body. The dark shadows of her breasts, the brown-black nipples, the curve of her abdomen, the dark patch of her pubic hair nestled between her soft thighs. That spot where thighs meet torso, where Oliver's lips had travelled and rested. Breathed in her unwashed skin, the soft down there.

She holds his gaze. Dares him to step forward, back into the shadow of her husband's house, the comforts of her body.

Oliver moves to her, collects the sheet from her feet and wraps it around her. He says, "It's not enough." He touches the side of her face, lets his hand graze the heavy curtain of her hair. Then he turns and leaves, already trying to push the image of her naked body from his mind.

He had walked into town, to the port where the jute ships waited, and then left the country behind.

Oliver had turned to Caro and said, "India feels like years ago, not months. A different life, a life belonging to someone else."

Caro turns from John O'Groats and begins her walk home. Tonight she will stand at the corner of Thistle and Mains Road and wait for Oliver to appear in the dusk. His feet on the stone, coming more quickly when he sees her.

In the flat, there is a door that is always closed. Her small hands push against it, but it does not give. Her small hand around the knob. The striking chill there.

To her left is the window where she watched Oliver leave. Beyond that, the sea. Always the sea.

The blue ribbon in her hair has come undone. The edge of it trails along her face. She pushes it away as she stands at the door. A tendril of hair now in her mouth. Her hand at the door. The blue ribbon. The cold metal knob, the roll of it in her palm. Push. Push.

This is where Imogen's memory stops. Stunned as a bird that has flown into a window. That dull, detached sound of feathers to glass.

She sits across from Oliver in his room and says, "Did you come back when Mum died?"

"Imogen."

She has promised herself not to ask him again but cannot help herself.

"Did you come back?"

Oliver sighs. "I was already on a boat to India. I didn't find out until months later."

"Did you know how it happened?"

He looks at her. She avoids his eyes, but is aware of him in her periphery. He says, "Yes. Morag told me."

She is afraid to ask him any more. She wants him to fill in this blank, colour it with all the vibrancy of Brigid, but knows he is reluctant.

He says, "You still don't remember, do you?"

Imogen looks at him, feeling sudden shame in this admission. She says, "I dream about her. About the bedroom door."

"What do you dream?"

"My hand is on the knob. I have a blue ribbon in my hair."

Imogen waits for Oliver to respond. She cannot read his face. She wonders if Oliver misses Brigid as acutely as she does. She says, "Do you miss her?"

"I did, once."

They sit together, quietly, in the stillness of the room. Oliver's bed tucked into the corner, clothes stacked on a chair, small candles set at the window. Oliver's life reduced to this small room in Magdalen Yard Green; a small life in a small room. She touches the newspaper clippings that clutter a small side table. Oliver's name in stark black ink. She says, "Did you ever write about her?"

"No. That's not what I write about."

"Did you write about India?"

"Sometimes."

Imogen turns to Oliver and searches his hands, the greyness of his temples. *India.* There is nothing in his face to let her into his life. He might be sitting next to her, but she realizes he is as unknown to her as when he was away.

With the girls full of sleep and moonlight on the parlour floor, Morag knows when she closes her eyes that she will not open them again in the morning. She settles into this new knowledge not with fear or anxiety but with a strange new calm. Her aching lungs. The weariness pressing down on her like a giant thumb. The strain of opening her eyes to another bloodstained handkerchief.

Caught somewhere between sleep and consciousness, Morag sees the gentle face of her mother. The slight smile. The memory of her hand on Morag's as they walked down Broughty Ferry's pier.

Mother.

Morag opens her eyes to the flat, silent in the night. The wedding photo on the mantel. Had she ever really been that young? She does not even recognize her own face any more. The delicate teapot, the chipped cups to match. The porcelain figures lining the windowsill. She has stood at that window for two decades and watched the neighbourhood below. Children laughing in the close. Women across the tenements waving to her.

Morag wants to get up and watch her daughters sleep. Something she has not done in years, watch the rise and fall of their chests. The flicker of their eyelids, holding back dreams. She wants to see their faces, the slack and innocence of sleep. She remembers their childhood smiles. The smell of their hair. All this softness, this sheltered love around her. Morag wants to look at her daughters, but cannot find the energy even to brush back the alcove curtain.

She lets herself sink and settle into the bed. Feels her body relax as she thinks about her daughters, her sister, her father, her niece. Sees her mother's face again. The past forty years come to her in a gentle haze: profiles of faces; long rows of trees and farmers' fields; boats coming into harbours; children's hands held in hers; sunlight and rain and spring blooms.

Come.

That soft whisper. It could be the wind, but Morag knows it is not.

Come.

For the first time in months, Morag breathes without pain. Can imagine sleeping deeply enough to dream of summer skies above Arbroath, perhaps of a parasol on Broughty Ferry's pier. She has missed dreaming.

Come.

Morag closes her eyes and is covered in darkness.

Wallis comes into the sitting room and feels the chill of the new day. She is comforted by the scent of the kitchen—gas, heavy margarine, steeped tea—and then looks to Morag in the alcove.

Stillness. Not even the labour of a single breath.

Wallis knows what she will find before she puts her hand on the heavy blanket that covers Morag. Knows she will never forget this moment, when the room is still and quiet and hers completely; before she will have to wake Caro and Imogen and begin the laborious process of grieving. Dresses of black and sombre faces. Wallis imagines a photo of the three of them, their pale faces shocked and still with sorrow. A gap where Morag once would have stood.

The songs of autumn birds will always remind Caro of awakening this startling bright morning in September 1918. Wallis sitting still in the paisley chair with her hands together. Closed. Peaceful. Wallis staring ahead as if there were something to see besides Caro. The moment before Caro knew of Morag's death, when the day was still full of possibility and normalcy. The gift of morning sunlight.

Wallis is afraid to tell Imogen about Morag's death. She tells Caro that she is afraid Imogen will be reminded of Brigid's death, that it will be something like a dam let open. "It will be too much for her," Wallis says.

Caro says nothing. She imagines Imogen made elastic, stretched and tugged and pulled back again, finally snapped. The two strange ends of something that was so recently whole. She is still too stunned to know that Morag is truly gone to speak.

"I'll have to be gentle," Wallis says. She has expected to be the one to console Imogen, to take on the role of protector and provider.

Caro says, "I think I should tell her."

"Oh—of course."

Oliver, Brigid, Morag. Caro will be the one to shatter Imogen's life again. Wallis will make funeral arrangements while Caro will be the one, again, to break their cousin into splinters.

Later, Wallis sits on the hill overlooking the long stretch of farmland just outside Dundee, the patchwork of green and gold and brown. This is where she has come to be alone, silent and solitary as a tree in the wind.

Ahead and to the right there is the rapeseed field in all its golden, furious glory. It is hard against her eyes. Cows moving lazily in the calm green of the pasture to the left, coming across the field to her. Wallis thinks, *Comfort,* and closes her eyes. The scents of green and the sea mingle together to form something predictable, reassuring, solid.

She watches as the farmers cross the fields, pausing only to lay their hands on the cows' gentle hides. Wallis imagines their warmth, the thick, soft hides. There is a simplicity here, where the sky dips down into this breath of a valley, where farmers still know their herds by the shape of their ribs.

Wallis rubs the rosary in her hand. Here, her own private cathedral. This long, open plain of countryside. Where green stretches up to meet blue, where yellow leaks into the surrounding earth and makes a golden glow. The closest she will come, now, to the greenness and cathedrals of Ireland.

Once, Caro asked Wallis if she still prayed as they had as children. Wallis had been too ashamed to admit it, that she found relief and comfort in a small conversation at night. Her lips moving, her eyes sealed tight. Her hands worrying the rosary in her hands. Wallis prayed for everything and nothing at once.

Now, Wallis holds the rosary and thinks of her mother. Morag. There is an ache and she feels her fresh tears before she realizes she is crying.

A line of ambling cows move across the field. They pause every so often to put their mouths to the ground and bite off slender blades of grass. They move slowly, certainly, contained by the low, rickety fences. It seems absurd that such squat wooden borders could hold these animals in.

Whispered Hymns

IN THE DAYS after Morag's death, they move about the flat, unsure of how to behave with one another. They move cups, place them two inches to the left, move them back. They do not speak of her death, do not acknowledge the new plains of grief. Instead, the three of them stand together at the sink and wash the same knife three times over. Miss when lighting a match. Miss again until finally the room smells of smoke.

They lie together in the same small room, Morag's alcove hidden behind its curtain. Imogen holds her hand to the window. Caro twirls her hair. Wallis stares blindly at the ceiling. They do not speak but breathe in synchronization. This continues for days before Caro says, "How long will this go on?" She has become terrified of the silence of the flat; she craves anything obvious: raucous laughter. Terrible grief. Joy. She wants to break glass after glass on the floor, just for the sound. "I can't stand this much longer."

They discuss the plans to make, a headstone, a service. Caro says, "What should it say? *Mother? Wife?*"

Wallis says, "Not *wife*. She hasn't been a wife in years."

Caro says, "*Mother*, then."

"It's terrible, isn't it?" Wallis asks. "She wasn't anything else. She wasn't much at all, in the end."

Caro balks; the words are like a cold stone wall, too thick for Caro to step over. The sheer breadth of it against her palm, the shock.

Imogen says, "Maybe there should be an angel."

Caro looks at her, her head tilted to one side, her hand at her mouth, her mind somewhere beyond the confines of the flat.

Wallis says, "No." Unflinching.

Caro listens to the rise and fall of their voices. There has been a definitive shift, a sloughing away of their old lives.

Imogen with her hand in the air, feeling the wind. A sharp, chilling breeze comes off the water, the kind that only those who live by ocean shores ever know. The mix of salt and wind whipping into her, burrowing to settle. Imogen has only ever known this wind. At night, she feels it churning within her, never letting her be.

Now, Imogen stands in the wind as she stares over the harbour and out to the bridge. A heavy monument. Her grandmother present as if she were a part of the structure: a leg, a cross rail. She is not part of Imogen's memory, but just as real. Another borrowed memory that has become her own. Like Brigid's face. If she closes her eyes, a flash of Brigid from a photo: her face still and stiff, posed. Brigid's stark white gloves against her dark coat.

The water slides up to the harbour and eases its way into slices in the sturdy wood of the dock, fitting into the absences there.

She squeezes her eyes shut and wills herself to remember Brigid, but finds that all she can recall is Morag's face. Her grey eyes, the way her hair came loose at the temples after a long day at the mill.

But Brigid.

Imogen moves her hand in the air and feels the salt deposit on her skin, the stain that is left there. She tastes the skin on the back of her hand. Something she had done as a child, a day walking down Main Street to Isla, early Sunday, with the spire of Clepington in view. Imogen's hand cleaved to Oliver's as Brigid trails behind. The sounds of her shoes on the stones. Her whimpering at Oliver's back.

Imogen can remember the walk, the rub of her stocking inside her shoe. The sound of shoes on stone. But not the actual argument, her mother's anger earlier. Just her presence behind Imogen, the quiet of her plaintive voice. She remembers the feel of Oliver's hand in hers, the darkness of his good suit. Later, she searched her hands for any ink that might have migrated from his fingers to hers.

⁓

There is no funeral hymn, no lengthy service, no gasping and weeping. That kind of grief would be too gaudy, too extravagant. It is not what Morag would have wanted, so they are still and silent.

Caro, Wallis, Imogen, Oliver, Bessie Lyon and a few other women from the tenements and Reverend McWilliam stand about Morag's gravesite dripping in the rain. No one from Bowbridge, where she had spent so much of her life.

The minister has thought to bring an umbrella and holds it up now over his head. There is the sound of the rain hitting the umbrella, the wet thwack of it. Rainfall and the quiet trills of birds high up in the trees. They watch the funeral from their branches, interested perhaps in the glint of the silver brooch on Caro's lapel. They watch the brief funeral, interested not in the muffled sounds coming through the rain but in the woman leaning in closer to the tall man. Wallis touching her eyes with a handkerchief. Oliver holding Caro's arm gently. Imogen tugging at the edge of Oliver's coat. The strict triangle of their bodies with Oliver at the centre, even in the Eastern Cemetery on a rainy afternoon. Rain coming down their bodies, turning the ground below them to mud.

When Wallis looks up to the sky now, something has shifted: she will work in the mill without believing that, one day, she might know something other than the carding machines, the din of the tight rooms, the inevitable injuries. Just this morning, she had stepped onto the mill grounds and paused under the glint of the hanging camel and thought of Morag. The camel ever looking down upon their hesitant steps and surrendering spines. No more imagining Paddy as a grown man, sitting across from her at a warm hearth. Now, when Wallis looks up she sees only ordinary clouds in a blue sky.

She does not have to lie to others about meeting John after a Union meeting but finds herself still uttering an excuse when she leaves the flat. She says, "It'll be a long meeting tonight. I'll be late."

Wallis and John walk down Ancrum Road, toward the park. She worries that he might notice something unhinged in her, but, if he does, surely he assumes it is grief. He does not suspect that she had been so close to choosing another life, to leaving him suddenly and silently. She looks up at him and smiles, a smile born out of guilt and a softening for his kindness. John smiles back at her and glances at his pocket watch. "A walk through the park then?"

They move silently up toward the park and Wallis thinks that, surely, John must hear the buzz in her head, must feel the heat coming from her. She glances at him, his gentle smile and the vulnerability of his limp on the grass, and feels a sudden burst of pleasure at walking with him. She smiles at him and believes, in this moment, that this could be her future.

They round the edge of the footpath and come across the pavilion. Wallis says, "Let's sit and look at the stars. It's nice out tonight."

Wallis is full of contradictory thoughts and the consistent hum of her body in the night. She looks at the stars, at her own hands and, finally, at John.

Paddy's eyes.

She lets herself believe it, fall into the heavy well of a mimicry of hope, and the split is swift and certain. She is gazing up into Paddy's eyes, sitting beside Paddy on a dark bench in a park. She leans toward him, presses her body up against his side. She sighs and lays her head on his shoulder. He opens his mouth to speak, and she leans in farther, angling her head so that he is silent, gazing back at her. His mouth is warm, wet, reminiscent of dark rooms scented with incense or roses in the damp. She arches into him, pushing her breasts against his chest.

The scent of green, the sensual nature of a park. Hands against her hips, travelling up to her breasts, searching her out beneath her coat and her blouse. The fabric gives, wavers, beneath his hands. His hand, finally, reaches skin and cups her breast. Wallis sighs against his mouth, encouraging the exploration of her body. She reaches out and feels the quick sting of cool metal against her fingertips; she undoes his buckle and reaches her hand down into the fabric of his trousers.

She is light-headed, her body and mind buzzing with the nearness of his body. She is tingling as he leans her back on the bench and turns her breathless with the bulk of his body.

He presses against her as he kisses her eyelids, the softest spot on a face, the tenderness of eyelids. His lips are light, sublime, as they travel down to her neck. He has swiftly, easily, managed to pull her skirts up to her thighs, and his hand now searches out the edge of her underpants. A tug, a quick twist of his wrist, and she feels the fabric come down against her thigh. His large hands, her pliant thighs, the tension between skin and hidden cotton. He moans against her.

She opens her eyes and at first sees only the depths of the creamy wooden underside of the pavilion. The trees in the distance. The weight against her chest, the sudden unreliability of breath. And then, his eyes. Eyelids, only, as he kisses her neck. Eyelids and then his hairline, the red of his hair.

John.

She is sorry, mostly, for the strained look that comes across his face as he positions himself between her legs. It is a tight, uncomfortable look, nothing like the hazy romantic gaze she imagined would appear on Paddy's face when she lay beneath him. His brows tighten in concentration as he pushes himself into her and she looks away.

There is a hot sear of pain and then a spreading ache. John keeps pushing against her, and Wallis keeps staring out at the darkness of the park. She watches the snaky limb of a tree, the shiver of a tulip in the breeze. John moves faster, his breathing quick and hot in her ear. She listens to him breathe, wonders if this was all there ever would be: his breath on her face, his weight pressing against her until she feels she could collapse. She wonders if this numbness is all she is supposed to feel.

When John rolls off her, Wallis tugs at her clothes, trying to reclaim her modesty. She covers her exposed breast and shrugs her coat around her. She says, "I need to get home."

He blinks as he does up his belt. "Of course."

Wallis is shamed, blanched. He is good, honest, understanding. She recoils and feels her stomach drop and heave. She stands from the bench and feels her legs quiver.

There is no possibility of Paddy any more.

At night, the harbour turns into something else entirely: an inky memory of work, of hands skinning a walrus, the heavy scent of oil. In moonlight, the sea turns a cool white as it rolls and eases between the docks. Only a few abandoned boats remain, tethered securely, set lightly on the water. The masts whisper against the wind, shivering in the Scottish night. Decks used to a more gentle climate, perhaps, the raw heat of foreign ports.

Oliver tips the whisky bottle to his lips and says, "Let's go away."

"Away?"

"Anywhere. Just us."

"What about Imogen?"

"She doesn't need me, Caro."

"But I do?"

"I'd hope so." He tilts the bottle again. The scent of whisky comes to Caro. A heavy, syrupy scent that makes her lick her lips. He passes her the bottle. She takes a long, deep sip and lets the whisky burrow down her throat and into her stomach.

She says, "No."

Oliver turns to her, his face half in shadow. Caro notices the grey at his temples, turning silver in the moonlight. She puts her hand up to feel the air.

"We can't go away."

Oliver sighs. He puts his head in his hands and says, "I know."

She touches her hand to his temple, moving from hair to skin. He catches her hand in his, tilts his head into the warmth of her fingers. Caro sinks into this gentle moment, seeing herself clearly, as if reflected in a pool of water. She moves into his arms and smells him, tobacco and soap and wool.

—

As they move deeper into the throes of fall, news of the War comes quickly and cruelly. Deaths, victories, injuries all mingle into one story that appears in the *Courier* or the *Advertiser.* By October, there is word that the War is coming to a close. Victory is within reach. The evildoers will be stopped. Victory is added to church sermons and prayers. There is a crackle of excitement running through Dundee. Men smile sheepishly and greet each other cautiously in the street. Women begin to make congratulatory quilts. No one wants to read the casualties reports that still appear in the papers; they all begin to believe again that this war might end.

Oliver says into his room of women, "It's not over yet. We thought it would only last a few months and it's been four years."

"We?" Wallis repeats.

"We," he says definitively.

"You were in India," she says. "You weren't here to see them all go."

"No, I wasn't."

Wallis says, "Why didn't you go?"

This question is fraught with implication: cowardice, fear, disloyalty. These three women face Oliver in the small flat. They've lit the glass lamps and opened the curtains to let in the slim light offered by the end of the day. Outside is dreary, unchanging.

"I wouldn't have been admitted."

"Why?"

Caro rubs her thumb and forefinger together, uncomfortable. Imogen looks away—out to the soft night—but her eyes are quickly drawn back to Oliver.

"My eyes." He smiles a genuine, honest smile despite Wallis's pointed question. He pulls a pair of spectacles from his pocket, slides them onto his nose. Pulls a face for Imogen.

"I don't remember you with spectacles."

"Vanity," he says, and removes them. Imogen holds her hand out and places the glasses on her nose. Crosses her eyes, sticks out her tongue.

"Isn't vanity a sin?" she asks.

Oliver says, "Oh yes, but we've all got our sins, don't we?" Wallis deflates a little and Imogen goes back to pulling faces.

Caro is suddenly tired of this tableau: the four of them pretending to be a family. A patchwork left over from the War. She suddenly thinks Oliver a fool for ever coming back.

On Sunday, Wallis tells Caro and Imogen that she will not be going to church with them. She stands before them straight and motionless in her coat and hat.

"Are you ill?" Caro's eyes are watchful, careful in their narrowing of Wallis.

"No."

"What then?"

"I'm going to St. Mary's Lochee."

The room is quiet. The tick of the clock, the muffled sound of a voice in the hallway, shoes on the floor. Wallis touches her hat.

"St. Mary's?"

"Yes," Wallis says. "I used to go with a friend. I'd like to go again."

Wallis smooths the front of her dark dress. There is nothing else to be said.

Finally, Imogen asks, "Did you go with Padraig?"

Wallis looks at her, surprised. "No," she says. "It was someone else." She turns and moves across the flat, knowing that if she gets to the door, if she crosses the threshold there, it will all be done. She puts her hand on the knob and pulls.

Caro says, "Will you meet us at Franchi's for tea?"

"Yes," she breathes, pleased, as she steps into the hall. "Yes, I will meet you there."

Her steps are light, quick, past Hilltown and toward Lochee. She will meet John, sit next to him in a pew, unconcerned with all that it implies. She is giddy, unencumbered— she is walking to the church on a Sunday morning, unashamed. She does not search the crowd for familiar faces, does not fear being found out.

She steps past the storefronts, and the buildings at the edge of Lochee come into sight. She moves with a smile on her face, her eyes toward the church, and walks right into Oliver. She says, "Oh," before she realizes who it is. "Oliver."

"Wallis. Lovely morning," he makes a grand, gallant effort and sweeps his hand out with a flourish. "Where are you off to?"

Wallis straightens her shoulders. For some reason, it is more difficult to admit this to Oliver than it had been to tell Caro and Imogen. She breathes in deeply and says, "To St. Mary's."

Oliver leans his head to the side, considers her. He says, "Ah, I see. In preparation for all the churches in Ireland."

Wallis flushes. Her whole life sits plain and unadorned. And Oliver has been witness to it all, unnoticed. She looks at her shoes, at the scuff marks there. "Well, that doesn't matter any more. I'm not going."

"Why?"

"I can't. There's Caro and Imogen. Someone has to pay the rent, the gas meter, the groceries." Wallis does not say, And now there is John.

Oliver smiles at her. "And you are the one to do that?"

"Yes."

"What if someone else wanted to do that? What if it wasn't your burden?"

Wallis regards Oliver coolly. She can't be sure of what he is saying. He left Brigid and Imogen. She looks at his dark hair, his handsome face and terrible, lovely smile, and thinks, *He is not a man to be trusted.* She says, "But it is."

"Wallis." Oliver reaches into his pocket and pulls out an envelope. He takes her hand in his and presses the envelope into it. "There is enough there for the boat passage and more."

Wallis looks down at the envelope. She can see the impression of bills beneath. She feels herself swoon then steady. "I can't take this."

"I want you to have it. I want you to go and be happy."

"Why?"

Oliver sighs. "I know a little about these things. You need to go."

Wallis stammers, "There's Caro and Imogen. There's the flat. There's—"

"You've already taken care of them. It's not your concern any more."

"I don't understand."

"Wallis. The rent money. The gas meter. You've done enough." Oliver smiles at her, but it is a different smile; he is not meaning to charm, to persuade or please. He means for her to understand that he will take over this role, he will care for Imogen and stay with Caro. He will give Wallis money, give her this lifeline back to Ireland and Paddy, give her the future she has so carefully planned out. Despite everything, she has, somehow, been granted all she needs: to be the woman standing on the deck of a boat, drifting toward a new life. She squeezes the envelope tighter in her hand.

Oliver says, "The service will be starting soon."

Wallis nods, smiles at Oliver. He has saved her. She is not prepared for this: one stretched hand, a small white envelope.

She says softly, "Thank you." She reaches out and touches Oliver's arm, briefly.

Oliver smiles. He turns from her and walks away, leaving her standing at the border of Lochee, leaving her amazed and surprised at this gift in her hand, leaving her watching as his figure becomes smaller.

She turns back toward Hilltown and the spires of St. Mary's Forebank.

The Eastern Necropolis, also called the Eastern Cemetery, sits cold and gated among the long stretches of farmland outside Dundee. Green everywhere Caro turns, as if the burgeoning of autumnal greenery itself is a monument to death. Soon there will be winter blooms, fields dotted with fallen leaves. Yellow. Orange. Something close to burnt. Then, it will truly seem like a cemetery.

Morag's headstone is simple, similar to the many others around hers. Stone, the colour of the coldest North Sea. Her name and dates carved in until they are lighter, the palest grey-white possible. Just deep enough to fit the tip of Caro's finger.

Next to Morag's grave stands a crumbling headstone detailing the brief lives of small children. Seven years. Five months. Two years. Eighteen months. Ten years. Caro thinks their own lives could be worse, could be summed up so simply on a headstone.

She acknowledges Morag's death in a formal manner. Imogen wanders away as Caro places her bluebells on the grave, sits and stares at the headstone. At home, everything has changed; they are caught up and tangled in one another. There is nothing to keep them solitary and separate. Now it is Wallis lighting the burner, heating water for potatoes. Wallis coming home from the mill, exhausted by two looms, by the din and roar of the warehouses, by the new weight of responsibility. Soon enough, Caro thinks, Imogen will know about her and Oliver. There is no way around it.

"Come with me to Brigid's." Imogen is impatient with her hands full of fresh wild roses. Her hands heavy with the petals, mindful of the thorns.

They move over to Brigid. Brigid's small headstone is misplaced here, clouded by the slightest whisper of sin. Caro looks at Imogen for any trace of knowledge, wants to say, *Don't you remember, her shoe was off?* One shoe on the floor. Macabre details Caro has stored away, as important as the careful, good memories. Brigid's one shoe and Oliver's lips on her navel. She watches Imogen lay the roses on her mother's grave. A flourish of orange melting into pink and back.

Wallis's hand rests on the spiked gate of the Eastern Cemetery. Her other hand is hidden in her coat pocket, rubbing the smooth rosary beads. She counts the beads against her palm. She gets to nine before she steps past the gate and into the cemetery grounds. She has never liked cemeteries, never liked the elaborate tombstones with tiny lambs, skulls and crossbones, miniature crosses. She finds them ghastly. She moves across the cemetery grounds slowly toward Morag's grave. She has not brought flowers, not even a handful of the wildflowers that grow at the side of Arbroath Road. She keeps her hand in her pocket.

She stands slightly back from the headstone, mindful of the imagined trajectory of Morag's grave beneath the grass. Her feet are tight together. She is standing quietly in the damp afternoon air. Wallis knows why she is here alone, why she has hidden away a small portion of her pay for all these months and years. She steps forward, carefully, and puts her hand on the cold gravestone. A morning downfall has left the cemetery grounds wet. Her feet sink slightly into the earth.

"I meant to tell you. I always meant to tell you," Wallis says. "I've been going to St. Mary's Lochee with a man I met. A Catholic man from Lochee." The words come out suddenly. It is a small confession, but necessary to Wallis. "And I'm going to Ireland. I've loved Paddy Hennessey since I was a child."

Wallis feels a rise in her chest. Morag, now, the last person to know. Wallis wishes she had thought to bring the photo; she might have been comforted by the presence of his small, young face.

Wallis takes out the rosary from her pocket and says a quick, silent prayer for her mother and leaves the grounds.

Such a long journey. So few steps.

A Dropped Shoe

ON SATURDAY, the Greenmarket fair is set up at the foot of town. There are open-air stalls, carnivals during holidays, steam-organ music, shooting galleries, the hiss of machinery powering gondolas and hobby horses. The air is thick with the scent of oranges, open bottles of sarsaparilla. The men behind the carts wear greasy aprons and slick smiles. Small children suck on pieces of horehound, beg their parents for a Boston cream. This is where industry and poverty meet, drawn to the necessities of life.

Imogen walks slightly behind Caro and Oliver, who have stopped at a booth promising "The Human Skeleton." Imogen has never liked the sideshows much; she would rather have a bag of whelks and sit on one of the wooden benches. Watch the mothers tug at their children's hands. See the spinsters slide into the psychic booth: Will I ever marry? Imogen watches all of Dundee move past her, strolling toward carts of fresh haddock, others piled high with red grapes. Caro and Oliver wander between the booths; Imogen knows that by the end of the day, Caro will have her arms full. Tonight they will have fried fish, perhaps the thrill of a sliced mango.

Imogen sees the woman through a part in the crowd. Two men in turbans frame her, one with a thick beard, the other clean-shaven. The man with the beard speaks to the woman, touches her elbow. Imogen sees her pull away a fraction; nerves in the woman. She bends her head and steps back from the two men. She is lovely with dark hair smoothed up and back, shining like wet tar in the sunlight. Bangles hang from her wrists, golden chains about her neck, earrings glittering from each ear. She is swathed in pink and gold silk, brilliant in the sun. Only her thin wrists, neck and face show. Imogen leans forward to lean on her knees, looking at her. She is instantly certain that the woman across Greenmarket is Oliver's Indian lover. The woman from India who gave him the delicate handkerchief. She is suddenly sure of it. She opens her mouth to call out to the woman but does not know her name. Has never heard Oliver utter it. She watches the woman run her hand over her hair, then touch her dark neck. Imogen imagines scent there, a slight, coy perfume that could only be smelled when you leaned in close. She watches the woman's hand as it drops from her neck to hang passively at her side.

The woman moves through the crowded glee of Greenmarket between the two men. She seems lost, overwhelmed amongst the stands of this Saturday-afternoon market, a stranger on this island. From the tilt of her shoulders, her eyes darting from one stall to the next, one face to another, Imogen believes she has never before left India. Perhaps she has come with her husband and brother. Perhaps she has come in search of Oliver.

Imogen watches as the woman intersects with Oliver and Caro. There is no flicker of recognition, no acknowledgment of their bodies, close as they move past stacked cabbage. The woman reaches to touch the purple filigreed edges.

Imogen moves across the crowd to stand beside Caro. "Cabbage," Imogen says to her.

Caro looks at her.

"I want some cabbage."

"You don't even like it."

Imogen does not answer, but selects a head—the head she believes she saw the woman touch from across the crowd and waits for Caro to pay. She bends to smell the leaves.

Wallis walks the edges of the Howff, a quiet square of earth in the midst of the city, passing headstones with Gothic messages. A skull and crossbones to keep evil spirits away. An anchor to remind that the buried man was, once, a fisherman. The gravel and grass are loose beneath her feet. Willow trees sigh and bend where a bone would break.

She thinks of John, and remembers him on top of her in Lochee Park with revulsion. She feels ill every time she thinks of his knee pressing between her thighs, the searing pain of his body pushing into hers. In that one moment she gave something away she could not take back; she had let John into her life, into the slim slices that had been meant for Paddy. *It should not have happened. I should never have gone with him to the park.*

She reads the names on gravestones and finds herself wondering what these people might have once looked like, what they did, how they died. This one perhaps a fisherman, casting nets into the dark grey sea. Another perhaps giving way to scarlet fever. Diphtheria. Names that move in her mouth like something beautiful. And now the Spanish flu. If the Howff hadn't already been closed, it would be overflowing by now. Every day, another death. Another tiny casket brought home by a grieving father, whose eyes are red from grief or drink. Men whose hands will always remember the weight of a child's coffin.

Only a few days ago, Mr. Grant from the second floor had carried a plain pine coffin up the tenement stairs. Wallis listened to the sounds of his footsteps on the stairs with her eyes shut. She did not want to let in the sorrow of his face. From the window, she saw people line the street when Mr. Grant carried the coffin out. Mrs. Grant followed, held up by neighbours. She pressed her hand to her mouth as if that might hold back her wailing. She pushed her teeth down, bit hard on her hand.

When John appears—heralded by his many keys—Wallis does not know what to do. He smiles when he sees her, an honest, unencumbered expression. He quickens his pace, eager to be near to her, pulling his stiff leg along. His smile—the trust and happiness Wallis sees there—makes her falter just a little.

It should never have happened. How could I have let it happen?

She does not try to gently lead into it. Her own shame will consume her if she does not open her mouth to speak. "I can't see you any more."

John's face is struck still. Stunned. Wallis swallows thickly. She is horrible. She is cruel and shameful and full of regret she will never be able to expel. *If only* . . . "I just can't, John."

John grasps the top of her arm, his fingers hard with his lack of understanding. "Wallis?"

She pulls her arm free. Words seem to fail her. All are inadequate, fences blown over in winter winds.

Later, Wallis will recall John's face, the confusion and sadness and betrayal. The small wrinkle that deepened between his brows. The sunlight low and hazy orange behind him.

Wallis only explains herself briefly. She remembers the words *Paddy, Ireland* and *passage for boarding*. Since Morag's death and since Oliver's generosity, her life has become clear: she will step onto the boat. She will move away from this life and into another one; not only the one she will share with Paddy, but the one she has imagined for herself away from Dundee. Wallis acknowledges this without thought or fear. She does not apologize or cry, as she feared she might. Instead, she touches his arm briefly, leaves John standing in the long shadows from the late-afternoon sun and walks back up Victoria Road feeling suddenly lighter than before.

A cold silver knob. A blue ribbon. An abandoned shoe. Small pieces to a puzzle. Imogen squeezes her eyes shut and tries to see her more clearly. Imogen leans into Oliver to smell him. He says, "What are you doing?"

"Trying to remember her."

"Imo."

"She had your smell."

They sit in Oliver's room. A strange room, anonymous save for his few sparse items.

"She smelled more like spring," Oliver says.

Imogen leans her head back to consider. Spring. White blooms. Brigid's white gloves. Wonders suddenly where her gloves had gone.

Oliver is speaking—she can see his lips moving—but Imogen can only hear her own loud thoughts reverberate. She looks out to Magdalen Yard Green. She tries to imagine Brigid putting her small foot on the grass. Brigid walking there, light against the grass and the dark sea beyond.

"Imo?" Oliver says.

Imogen looks back to him. Oliver is smiling. His face is young, kind. Imogen smiles back at him and her heart tilts.

He says, "You understand then?"

Imogen keeps smiling, unsure of what else to do. Oliver leans over to kiss her forehead. What has she missed? She seems to always be missing something. She looks out to the Green again, letting the warmth of the room surround her. There is something new in the air, something new in Oliver's admission that she has missed.

A purple spine of a book catches her eye. One slim book in the stack he has collected. She moves to the table and touches the book with one finger. She says, "This reminds me of Brigid."

"She didn't like Wilde."

"This colour."

Her finger traces the book. Up and down. Up again. Each time she is with Oliver, another fragment of Brigid appears. Tangible in this purple book spine.

He says quietly, "You know it had nothing to do with you. Brigid's passing."

Imogen moves away from the book, from the doom she suddenly associates with purple: the colour of dying blooms, of water so cold it's moved past blue, of bruises.

⌒

November 11, 1918. The War ends. The world rejoices.

Hilltown comes alive, a sea of bodies flowing between storefronts, flats, the middle of the street. Pipers, singers, fiddlers have all joined the celebration. People make their way down to Victoria Road and the city centre to the strains of music. *We made it. We have survived.*

Imogen twirls in her pale dress down Hilltown. The clock has struck the wrong hour once, twice, three times by now. She has a huge, honest grin on her face when Caro looks at her: Imogen being twirled by Oliver, the edges of her skirt moving faster and faster, a thrilling and dizzying speed. Caro thinks that Imogen will soon collapse, or be sick.

It seems unreal: Imogen and Oliver's gleeful dance in the street, Wallis's brilliant smile. They move past the butcher's, the shoemaker's, the dentistry shop. Caro feels for a moment as if she is in a nursery rhyme—*the butcher's, the shoemaker's, the dentistry shop*—whose characters are spilling over with unfathomable joy.

It's over. Can it be over?

They continue down Hilltown steadily, until they are even with Ann Street and the glint of St. Mary's Forebank just behind. Caro realizes that this day, this eruption of joy, will never end. It will move into nightfall, into the next day, and they will all still languish.

The pride of victory apparent on an average street. Music in her ears.

Oliver has turned to Caro. His hair has fallen across his eyes, giving him the boyish look she loves. She lets him take her hand and is engulfed into the movement of the street. It pulses and hums around her.

The War is over. The world will return to normal. Caro is danced down the street with Oliver's hand tight on her back.

⁓

Wallis opens the letter slowly, cautiously. She is aware that the whole of her future hinges on this moment. She runs her fingers across the ink. Her own name. 96 Caldrum Street. She smells the envelope and believes this is what travel smells like, what lies beyond the borders of this town. Rosemary has written to her again, after hearing of Wallis's plans, after promising to speak with Paddy.

November 20, 1918

Dear Wallis,

I've spoken to Paddy, and he is anxious to move out of
Dublin, to the country somewhere, but I have managed
to talk him out of it. I told him that you would be here
soon, and that Joseph and I need him here. He is so very
serious about his politics now . . .

Wallis reads the letter quickly, greedily, and then reads it over again. The sight of his name on the page enough to convince her that she is doing the right thing. Her stomach clenches.

Wallis has spent hours staring at Ireland on a map. Such a tiny island. Dublin is smaller even than the tip of her smallest finger. Dublin. Wallis lets the name stumble on her lips. It is time for her to go now, before they do as Paddy wants and move out of the city. Then they would be lost to her.

Wallis surprises herself by thinking that she might be brave. She hasn't meant to be.

Fall in eastern Scotland means heather, autumn joy, thistle; the thick scent of the sea mingling with the fresh, wet smell of the new season. Imogen loves autumn—the changing leaves, the crackle and crunch beneath her feet. The sudden chill in the air makes her slip on a cardigan beneath her coat. She walks through Nethergate, passing the old remnants of the city wall, and on toward Magdalen Yard Green. She sees the grey cast of the sea beyond the vibrant green of the yard. The pavilion with its creamy top poking up into the sky. The houses that line the street that belong to either widows like Mrs. March or wealthy families who wear silken blouses and fur-collared coats. She looks up to Mrs. March's house, to the window where she hopes she'll see Oliver's face, and sees only a darkened window staring back at her. Black eyes. She smells the ocean and the damp grass. Another fall day, years ago, when Brigid stood in the rain, holding a newspaper in her gloved hand over her head. A smile on her face, knowing she would open the *Courier* to see Oliver's name. Imogen thinks that, perhaps, it was the absence of his name in smudged ink that shattered Brigid. Opening a paper to see someone else's name where Oliver's used to be.

Imogen moves across the Green. Did that ever happen, Brigid's weeping over a newspaper? She can't be sure. *The cold doorknob, the blue ribbon, the dropped shoe.* She looks down at her own shoes, damp from the dew. She wiggles her toes.

Imogen cannot yet bring herself to admit what she has remembered.

She woke this morning as if the memory had always been with her. Turning the knob and pushing the door open. The cool air of the room rushing over her. The window must be open; there is a breeze. Imogen steps into the room, feeling her ribbon flicker against her cheek. It is blue to match her dress, the blue one with white trim, the dress Oliver bought her last Easter. She wore it to church, felt it bundle and crease beneath her knees.

Imogen sees the dropped shoe first, beside the small wooden table that is usually beside the bed. Why has Brigid moved the table? The shoe is dark against the floor, dark against all the light and breeze coming into the room. Her eyes move up from the shoe to the table, but are stopped before they reach the open window: Brigid's feet, one covered by her shoe, one vulnerable in its stocking, hang in mid-air. The slight sway of those feet.

Imogen must have known what to expect, what two hanging feet would mean, because she cannot remember feeling surprise. She looked up to see Brigid's limp body, her twisted broken neck hanging from the rope, tied through exposed crossbeams. Brigid's face already tainted with a blue pallor, a colour until then that Imogen had always associated with the sky, water, surfaces so cold they burned her bare hands. Blood vessels have broken in Brigid's face, and under her eyes. Like a small map. Puffed and bloated until her lovely face was almost unrecognizable. And a thick, purple bruise peeking out from around the rope. Imogen stood still in the cool, breezy room and gazed up at her mother hanging from a rope.

Imogen has come now to speak to Oliver, needing him to reaffirm this new memory. Memory is a trick of light. The hummed chorus of a forgotten song. It's so difficult to tell what is real memory and what is not. She looks up to the dark window of Mrs. March's house again. Sits on a small bench. Stares down at her dark shoes in the grass. Wiggles her toes.

Winter

THEY WALK DOWN HILLTOWN, through Murraygate and on to the Firth of Tay. It is early December; the sky hangs steely, cold and hard above them. They shiver slightly before they settle together on a small bench. Their elbows touch. Their knees bump through stockings and woollen dresses and long coats. They are comfortable together, the three of them sitting on a low bench, watching the sea. Caro pushes a stray piece of hair from her face. Imogen leans forward on her knees. Wallis settles and sighs. Caro can see the steamy exhalation of Wallis's breath.

Finally, Wallis says, "I'm going away for a while."

Caro has expected this. She says, "Does he know you are coming?"

"Yes."

They are quiet again. Imogen warms her hands on her knees.

"But I'll go to Rosemary and Joseph's when I get there."

Caro nods and looks out to the Tay Bridge. Wallis will have to cross the bridge, will have to come face to face with the ghost of their grandmother, to get to the port in Troon.

The slow clack of the train across the tracks. Wallis's face in the train window.

Imogen says, "What will we do?"

Wallis says, "You both will be grand."

Caro is silent.

Imogen says absently, "Maybe we'll live somewhere near the water."

Wallis relaxes, satisfied with this answer. Caro does not know how else to answer. She is not certain if there is another answer. She knows her life with Oliver will continue, gracefully aging into something acceptable. A two-room flat with Imogen sharing a bedroom wall.

"Will you write?" Imogen says.

It has not occurred to Caro that Wallis will stay away. Caro is more prepared for Wallis's teary return with a broken heart and no more mooning over Paddy Hennessey. Now she must consider Wallis permanently across the water, surrounded by nuns and saints and martyrs.

Caro looks out to the Tay. Large whaling boats are coming in, slowly bobbing on the water as they steer toward the harbour. Soon Wallis will be like these men coming in from foreign countries; Wallis will see this harbour, this small low bench, as something foreign. *Home* is a changeable word. Her home will be with Rosemary and Paddy, with their Latin masses and clutched rosary beads. Caro feels suddenly that she has already lost her sister. She turns to Wallis and sees for the first time that Wallis has settled into her face, into the roundness of her cheeks, the almond of her eyes. Caro has lived with Wallis all her life and has never noticed her sister is beautiful.

Caro takes Wallis's hand, squeezes it conspiratorially. She hopes that Wallis can understand the complexity in this small movement: apology and love entangled.

Imogen says, "It's cold."

They walk back the way they had come, slower than usual past the flats and shops of their youth. Caro thinks that they might all be aware of the finality of the moment, that this might be the last time they walk up Hilltown. They listen to the chime of the Hilltown clock together, standing still on the corner at Main Street. Caro has not let go of Wallis's hand yet.

⁓

The shop window displays bolts of Irish linen, crisp cottons, fine silks. Imogen stands on Hilltown for a moment, staring at the fabrics, shifting her weight from one foot to the next. She cannot decide between the velvet—Caro would love the dark red—and the Irish linen. So simple, yet so intricate in its simplicity. That's the trick of it. She looks from the crush of the velvet to the starched linen. She tries to imagine which Caro would love more, but finds herself only able to imagine the pink and golden sari material that covered the Indian woman's body at Greenmarket. She pushes open the shop door and steps into the warmth of the store.

Imogen's love for Caro faltered when she realized Oliver was in love with her. A small skip, something like falling in love but with a heavy feeling in the pit of her stomach, like she might be sick. But she found she could not blame Oliver;

she has loved Caro her entire life. Yet, she is surprised; Caro is so different from Brigid.

But he left her.

Oliver's heart has surely been torn into even smaller bits now; small sections for Brigid, Imogen, Caro. Brigid's portion shrinks—close now to forgotten—while Caro's flourishes. Imogen imagines sewing her father's heart whole.

She trails her fingers over the fabrics—stiff taffeta, thick cotton, fluid chiffon–as she moves around the shop. Imogen breathes in the clean scent, wood polish and women's perfume. She looks from one bolt to the next and finally says to the woman behind the small cash desk, "Can I have some of the Irish linen, please?"

She watches as the woman cuts the length of fabric Imogen requests, her hand steady and sure, the scissors smooth through the linen. Imogen closes her eyes and remembers a day when she stood in a fabric shop with Brigid, watching her feel the edges of lovely fabrics: silks and satins, their shimmering nature like oceans in Brigid's hands.

Imogen looks at loops of cording and sees only the rope with which Brigid hanged herself. Purple bruises, a golden rope hanging from the beams.

Brigid left me alone.

"Dear?" The woman behind the counter holds the fabric out to Imogen. Imogen pulls coins from her purse and lays them on the counter.

She says, "Thank you."

Imogen turns the linen into a beautiful handkerchief, edged in delicate lace much like the Indian one Oliver keeps.

She sews quickly, efficiently. Small pinpricks, the bumping up of ancient scars to new punctures. She embroiders Caro's initials on it, and then starches it until it is hard as wood.

That's the trick of it.

She gives it to Caro one night after Oliver has left the flat. The room complicated with just the two of them.

"What is this for?"

Imogen shrugs, unable to put her intention into words, something to do with her knowing that Oliver still carries the Indian woman's handkerchief in his pocket. She knows that Oliver loves Caro. She can see it every time they are in the same room, when his body lengthens and his face brightens at the sight of her. Imogen wishes that she had the same effect on Oliver, but she understands this is impossible. She adores him and yet loves Caro almost as much. The three of them always bumping uncertainly up to one another. She has loved Caro all her life, but how can she love her still? She looks at Caro's milky profile. *He chose her.* Finally, she puts her hand on Caro's.

"It's beautiful," Caro says.

"Brigid taught me to sew. That's all she really left me with, you know." This is not what she meant to say, but these are the words that come out. *All she really left me with.* She begins to cry. Caro puts her arms around her, coming off the chair and onto her knees on the floor. Imogen cannot stop the tears, does not know where they come from, cannot explain what she is crying for. It is a deep, dark feeling, something unspeakable. Unbearable. This is what Imogen grieves: her mother's selfishness, her one act that eclipsed any possibility of kindness or love for her daughter. She sobs against Caro's shoulder, holding on to her protruding shoulder blades.

Caro wakes in Oliver's bed. She stretches, unused to the solitary chill of his room. The sheet is creased from the heat of their bodies. She breathes in his pillow and realizes that Brigid must have once done this: rolled into the spot in the bed, still warm from her husband's body, and smelled the last traces of him. Caro wonders how long it took for his scent to fade, how long it took for Brigid to realize he was not coming back. She sits up and the cool air greets her bare breasts as she looks out the window at the bright December morning. There is frost on the grounds of Magdalen Yard. Winter is upon them. The War is over. Morag is dead. Wallis will soon be gone. The world is strange and new, suddenly bereft of anything that comforts Caro. She moves around the room naked, not wanting anything to come between her body and Oliver's possessions. She picks up a purple leather-bound book, holds it to her chest as she looks out the window.

Caro puts her hand to the window. The quick shock and the frost there, the tight grasp of ice coming back to touch her. She squints to see if she can see her fingerprint on the pane, but instead sees the fog of her breath. Wipes it clean and, in doing so, believes she wipes away a trace of Brigid.

Caro will sit with him at this window, mend his trousers, let him love her at night. Love him back with equal ferocity, her teeth marks on his shoulder, his side, as if they had wandered across his body like an explorer and marked the territory.

She wipes again, determined now. She wipes and wipes at the smudged pane, turning it clean and clear so that it might be free to let the light in, to let December come into the room with its clarity, the crisp winter smell of a new year coming.

⌒

In the rain, Wallis stands on the corner of Methven Street. She holds an umbrella above her head. Moves from one foot to the other. Is dreaming about a boat and the morning when she might awake in Ireland.

They come down Bright Street, each of the children holding one of his hands. Anne wears a red coat, her small feet brilliant in their new white shoes. Stephen trails slightly behind his father, looking behind, as if there is something following him. They move in a solemn manner; they are a cohesive whole, their bodies in sync.

Wallis needs this moment, needs to stand in the rain and stare at this family that was almost hers. She watches them move past her, oblivious to her, and up the front steps of St. Mary's Lochee. She tightens her grip on the umbrella and inadvertently drops it to the side. Water comes down and onto her face, leaving her cheek wet. She wipes it away as John and his children disappear into the church.

Saoirse

WALLIS WATCHES as Troon slips away from her. For an anxious moment she thinks about leaping off the boat and into the rumbling sea. Trying to swim back to shore, knowing she would not make it. Another short life drowned. She turns away from Scotland and looks to Ireland. Imagines the distant suggestion of buildings, smoke, a town. Wishes to see spires or hear church bells.

Wallis has one small steamer trunk containing her green dress, her grey skirt, three blouses, a photo of Caro laughing at Broughty Ferry, a Bible, four silver spoons, three embroidered handkerchiefs, one of Morag's china teacups and a packet of folded pounds. She has Rosemary Hennessey's rosary pinned to her brassiere, beneath her camisole, her blouse and her coat. She has a pin on her lapel, and she has coiled her hair up. Wallis stands on the deck of the boat and is rolled toward Ireland.

The blue-grey sea churns below, cresting with white. She holds her hand out to see the stark white outline of her fingers, her palm. The length of her fingers disappears into the waves. This water, this hard expanse stretching out and beyond. Everywhere she turns there is nothing but the blue. Sky leaking into the sea. Sea spraying back into the sky.

She smiles at a man who stands next to her. He tips his hat. She knows he is going home, can tell by the soft look in his eyes, a well full of expectation and comfort. Home. Wallis has not arrived yet, but she knows home is no longer the flat on Caldrum. She has a sudden, physical ache for it: for the smell, for the sight of Caro lazing on the bed they shared, for Imogen's laughter, for Morag's hand reaching out to pass her tea. Wallis feels tears spring to her eyes. She wishes for one more moment with them all, one impossible moment when they might all sit together, sharing a pot of tea. Wallis looks out to the sea, closes her eyes momentarily, and listens to the cresting of the sea to the boat. When she opens her eyes, there is a calm; in her mind is her last moment with Caro and Imogen and Oliver. The three of them standing on the platform of the train station, waving as she pulled away. The yellow light of the morning, the serenity she saw there. She keeps the picture in mind, and lets everything else fall away from her silently.

On this morning there is nothing but Wallis's face in sea mist, the creaking of the boat against the sea and the wakeful nature of the blue. From her pocket she takes out a sprig of broom. It is hard, dried from its bloom earlier that year, pricking the softness of her palm. The sight of it—dusty yellow against all the blue—startles her. She holds the sprig out, over the edge of the boat, and lets it fall. Watches as it is caught on a grey-blue crest, tucked under the curl of the water, and comes up again, floating on the Irish Sea.

Acknowledgements

Thank you to my wonderful family in Scotland: Valeen (Blacklaw) Lyons for lodgings, tea and tour guide services while in Dundee; Walter and Betty Blacklaw for memories, history and photos; Elaine and Stewart Craig for chats and transportation information.

To my parents, Bob and Lesley MacPherson, and my grandparents, Tom Rowbottom and Gertrude MacPherson, for continued support and enthusiasm. Thank you for first giving me a pencil and encouraging me to use it.

Thank you to Sara Gittens, Kristine Waddell and Amy Rusk for making the first tentative steps into the history of Dundee with me. To Chris Labonté for being a trusted first reader. To Jane Hamilton for much needed distraction and discussions of peonies. To Carolyn Swayze for her unwavering belief and subsequent championing. To the entire team at Random House, especially Craig Pyette for his passion and kind insights into shaping the novel. To Heather Sangster for her fine copyediting and Barbara Czarnecki for astute proofreading.

Research was essential to the authenticity of the novel, and two books, in particular, were of great help: TM Devine's

The Scottish Nation 1700–2000 (Penguin Books, 2000) and AW Brotchie and J J Herd's *Getting Around Old Dundee* (NB Traction, 1984).

Great thanks to Leah Harper from Discovery Point and Caroline Brown from the University of Dundee for information on the mills of Dundee; Gordon Campbell from Clepington Church for his help with the history of the church and its ministers; Iain Flett and Richard Cullen from Dundee City Archives; Deacon Arthur Grant from St. Matthews; Dr. Martin Melaugh of the University of Ulster, Magee Campus; Elizabeth Harford of the National Library of Ireland; McManus Galleries (Dundee) for their fabulous exhibit of turn-of-the-century Dundee.

To Stephen Donnery for laughter and love.

And to my late grandmother, May Rowbottom, who was the inspiration for the novel.